# Eyes of Devilla

Len Rayne hails from the charming town of Arbroath in Scotland but currently calls Dunblane home. Married to Elizabeth and proud father of two grown-up boys, Len's journey has been intertwined with words from his professional days.

However, it was during his sons' formative years that Len's creative flair began to flourish. Regular woodland walks with his boys heard Len making up tales of talking trees and mystical creatures to captivate their imaginations.

In "Eyes of Devilla," Len invites readers into a world of imagination, nurtured during these woodland escapades with his young sons. The Eyes of Devilla promises to offer you a glimpse into a world where magic and reality intertwine in the most unexpected ways.

# Eyes
# of
# Devilla

*A Bonnie Banks Adventure Story*

## Len Rayne

*For Elizabeth, Matthew, and Lewis.*

# Prologue

**1970**

Not once did the sun hit the cottage sitting in the middle of the forest. No matter how brightly it shone, the building stayed in the shade.

Inside the cottage sat an old woman called Florence Parker. She would sit in her living room for hours every day thinking about times gone by. These were never happy thoughts. The only memories she had were bitter ones. Bitter memories, and a lifelong desire for revenge.

Florence was dressed from head to toe in black. Almost every item of clothing she wore was black. In her wardrobe, there were a few white tops with frilly collars. But, even for many years ago, they were old-fashioned. When these tops were worn, they would always be covered by other black garments and the white was almost impossible to see.

Florence was old in years, although not as old as she looked. The years of bitterness had aged her. Keeping hatred inside ages you from within – but she just couldn't let it go. Her face was withered and old. Wrinkles had appeared long before their time. A head that had once held a mop of black hair was now grey from the roots to the tips. Her fingers were long and thin. Nails were discoloured and brittle. They were long and sharp, like they belonged to some kind of mythical creature. Even her teeth were black – at least those remaining were. The old woman would occasionally venture from one room to another. On good days, time would be spent in the garden. But she would never venture any further during daylight hours. Only after dark would she forage for edible plants and berries from the forest. She found it difficult being a witch.

Alongside foraging, meat would be brought to her door with a simple spell. 'Anhopyoor rabbit,' was said out loud, three times, then repeated six times more, in groups of three. That evening, the nearest bunny would arrive at the cottage. Despite her withered fingers, she would grip the rabbit tightly as she prepared it for the pot.

In the previous ten years there had been two visitors to the cottage. Her younger brother Brandon came to tell her their mother had passed. Not that Florence cared. She had no time for her mother – or her brother. There had also been a visit from her twin sister Davina with the gift of a book. *Twins?* she'd thought. *We're the furthest things from twins.* Davina had been blessed with a happy spirit and a joyful smile. All Florence had ever felt was hatred. This wasn't uncommon in the Parker family. If you were given the evil streak, there wasn't much you could do about it. As for the gift of a book – what was that supposed to do? She hadn't even opened it. Her twin was supposed to know her, to be there for her. But all she could do was bring silly gifts and that smug, happy smile of hers. Florence hated Davina. And the hatred she felt for everything burned through to her very soul. Everything, with one exception. Her black cat, Dionadair, was always there for her. He knew her power, and he protected others from her. He also protected Florence from herself.

If Florence's arrival on this earth had been two hundred years earlier, they would have tried to burn her as a witch. Even by looks alone, there would have been a guilty verdict. Not that they would ever have got to her. Her spells were too powerful. But growing up in the time she did, witches were less feared. They had become nothing more than a subject for scary stories and folklore. Before the start of the Second World War, Florence had moved to the cottage in the forest, which had taken her away from her mother, brother and twin sister. She shunned all human contact.

And that's how her life was lived. Bitterness and hatred, with hardly a soul to talk to. Florence passed a few short years later, leaving nothing but the old cottage and a black cat.

# Chapter 1

# Watched

**Present Day**

Bonnie Banks was lost in the forest. She wasn't afraid. Yet. This was her local forest, and she knew it well. But, through a lack of attention, she found herself in a less familiar part. Her walk had taken her much deeper into the trees than usual. It wasn't long before it would start to get dark, and inside the forest it had already become gloomy. And it had started to rain. Bonnie wished she'd brought her head torch – for comfort, if nothing else.

She loved the peace and quiet of the forest, and spent many hours walking, sitting and observing. But today, Bonnie was on her own, lost and missing David, her dog with the human name. Her schoolmate Rachel Parker was *not* on her list of people she was missing. She would be the last person to go on the list. Bonnie was thinking of lots of ways to hurt Rachel. Make her feel pain and humiliation. Bonnie knew she wouldn't actually do anything. That wasn't her way. But dreaming about it made her feel better.

She could hear Rachel's voice in her head. It said, 'I know hundreds of people. And I know even more on social. And out of them all, you're the ugliest.'

When Rachel had spoken these words, earlier on in the day, it was through gritted teeth. *I wish I could get David to bite her*, thought Bonnie. *And then pretend it was an accident. But no. I couldn't ask him to do that.*

Bonnie was even more annoyed because, when she thought about it, it hadn't even been the cleverest of insults.

'And out of them all, you're the ugliest,' she mimicked, in a slow, sarcastic manner, wiggling her shoulders and tightening her chin as she said it. She could have coped with the insult alone. But *everybody* had laughed. Even Molly – her best friend. Not that Molly wasn't on her side. The truth was, everyone was afraid of Rachel. And Molly wouldn't say or do anything to single her out for Rachel's attention.

Bonnie knew standing up to Rachel was the right thing to do, but it hadn't worked out as planned. Her responses to just such an event had been rehearsed in her head so many times. What she would say and do. And what was the best reply on the day? The reply that would humiliate Rachel? The reply that would make everyone laugh and turn Bonnie into an instant hero?

'Shut up.'

That was it: 'Shut up'. And she hadn't prepared herself for the almighty push Rachel had dished out, a split second after saying, 'Who are *you* telling to shut up?' Bonnie had landed on her backside. It wasn't a big shove, and Bonnie was bigger, stronger and older than Rachel, but it had caught her off guard and caused her to fall over, hurting more ego and pride than anything else. But it had smashed the screen on her phone. As she looked at her reflection on the cracked screen, Bonnie was devastated. And this wasn't helped by the laughter from those around her. Bonnie hated Rachel. She *really* hated her.

At least I don't have to look at her horrible comments on my phone, thought Bonnie, alone and lost in the woods. Her attention was brought back to her current situation by an almighty flash. The whole sky and forest lit up for the briefest of moments, then a few seconds passed before there was a loud rumble of thunder. Fear wasn't far away now. Bonnie knew it was time to find her way onto a familiar path and get home. Lost in the forest overnight, or explaining to her mum about the broken phone? She wasn't sure which would be worse.

Bonnie kept on walking, hoping she was heading in the right direction. Her mind drifted off again as she marched along the unfamiliar path. She thought about her birthday and becoming a teenager – although it was still a few months away yet. Her age frustrated her. She wanted to be older and wiser.

As the rain got heavier, she pulled up her hood and zipped her coat. Bonnie wasn't one for the latest fashionable clothes. She preferred outdoor wear to designer names. Her Berghaus jacket was hard-wearing and practical, and she loved it. It gave her a sense of invincibility, being out in all weathers but staying warm and dry.

Her pace quickened. The exertion in her legs became more difficult to bear as they carried her faster. Not running … but getting close to a jog. It made her think of school sports – which was not her favourite class. In her view, there was no sense in running as fast as you could or jumping the height of yourself. Bonnie liked walking. A good, brisk walk every day – just her and David.

*Is that a familiar clearing ahead?* she wondered. Her pace quickened again. Now she *was* jogging. Bonnie wished her mum was here right now. Or David. Not that he would be much use. He wouldn't exactly show her the way home. But he would be company and he would make her feel more at ease. It was becoming darker by the minute. Her thoughts moved on to her relationship with her mum. Anything, other than thinking about being lost – she didn't want to start panicking. Bonnie got along OK with her mum, but they didn't communicate well. Something wasn't right. But, whatever it was, they didn't talk about it. Probably something to do with her dad, Bonnie guessed. But whatever was behind their lack of communication, she wished again that her mum was with her right now.

Her pace quickened again. It had now become a fast jog. The heat was building uncomfortably inside her jacket. And now there was another thing. An uneasy feeling. It felt like something out there was watching every move she made.

# Chapter 2

## Lost

The forest had a varied landscape dominated by tall Scots pine trees. There were lots of other trees around, but this was mainly a pine forest. There were lochs – but no monsters that Bonnie knew of. The paths around and through the forest were wide enough for a tractor or forestry truck to drive along. These were the easiest paths to walk, but there were also the 'well-trodden' paths. These had been worn into the landscape by thousands of pairs of feet over hundreds of years. There were mountain bike trails, too, which had begun to appear over the past few years.

The path Bonnie found herself on was a barely visible one. Only those with a bit of familiarity with the forest would take these paths. They were great for exploring in the better, drier weather. But the needles of the pine trees covered everything in a dull beige carpet. The less worn paths had become more difficult to see, particularly as the day drew darker.

As Bonnie walked along the path, it opened out into a clearing. Forests are funny like that, she thought. One minute it's dark and gloomy, a tiny narrow path through the trees. Then, the next minute, a clearing. Daylight and a feeling of safety. Bonnie knew the rain wasn't far away. There had been another couple of lightning flashes but it took her a little longer to hear the thunder rolls each time. Hopefully the worst of the weather would pass before she found her way home.

Walking past the puddles of muddy water, Bonnie kept a brisk jogging pace. She wasn't running flat out, but she definitely wasn't taking her time. The wild grass and ferns at the side of the path had died off for winter. The forest had lost its autumnal beauty of a few weeks ago.

Bonnie stopped to try and get her bearings, knowing she had to get back onto a familiar path. It was mid-afternoon, in January, and it would be dark soon. There was no sound – in fact, it was deathly quiet, the way it gets before the heavens open. There was no movement. Not even the trees were swaying. But Bonnie knew she was being watched. She could sense it.

Her eyes darted all around. Nothing. She thought of the scary movies – the ones a group of them watched at Molly's house – where the evil red eyes watch you from the darkness. She was not one to scare easily, but her heart rate had quickened. She shook off the thought that Rachel could be hiding in the trees like an evil witch. Bonnie found herself thinking, *that's exactly what she is. An evil witch.* A gentle smile appeared in response to her own joke.

It was at that point that the eyes appeared. Large and piercing. Staring and silent. But, somehow, not threatening. Comforting? She moved a fraction towards them, and they blinked. They were too close together and too big to be human. Then wings flapped, as the owl sensed her discomfort and aimed to put her a little more at ease.

*Why am I so spooked?* Bonnie wondered. The path led towards the owl, and she was drawn towards it. Now only ten meters away, then eight, then five. But the owl flew away again, settling just close enough for Bonnie to see it. She followed and the owl flew on again. This was repeated a few times and, each time, Bonnie instinctively followed, still on the same path. After a few minutes, her distance from the owl became so small that she was almost underneath it. The forest was as dense as she had ever known it. Time was marching on, and the darkness had started to eat into the last light of the day. There was a little bit of fear starting to creep in. Bonnie looked at the owl and wished again that her mum or David was with her. Then, she looked at the tree in front of her. It seemed to have a face.

Bonnie closed her eyes for a second and shook her head. When she reopened them, the 'tree face' was even more pronounced. It was like the tree was staring at her. Not in a scary, threatening, 'Rachel' kind of way, more of

a 'Mrs Bell' kind of way. Mrs Bell was her English teacher
– firm, friendly, but a little bit scary. Bonnie's legs felt
heavy, like she was walking through a big bowl of syrup.
She stared and felt drawn towards the tree. Small steps,
getting closer. The tree held her gaze. This was an
almighty Scots pine tree. Not the tallest, but one with an
odd kind of presence. It had an aura which dominated
the surrounding trees.

Bonnie figured it was an old tree, perhaps hundreds
of years old. Raising her right hand slowly, she reached
towards the tree as the owl watched on. But something
strange was happening – this wasn't Bonnie choosing to
move forwards and reach out. She couldn't help it and
had no control over her movements. Her hands touched
the tree on what she imagined was its face. The stumpy
eyes – which felt nothing like eyes. The wonky nose. Her
hand touched what she saw as the tree's toothless mouth.
What was happening? Then, suddenly, and as nimbly as a
pickpocket, the tree's lower branch grabbed her by the
hand.

Bonnie got such a fright; it all happened so fast. Her
hand was now trapped – but she was not in pain. She was
afraid … yet calm. She looked up and saw the owl, which
continued to watch. Did it wink at her?

I'm going totally mad now, she thought.

As she calmed a bit more, there was the sound of a
voice. Weak, distant, but … yes. A voice. Was it coming
from the tree?

'What are you saying?' she asked the tree. She looked at the owl, who was praying Bonnie would understand what was happening. The faintest of voices could be heard inside her head. The voice said, 'Help. Help us, Bonnie.' There were no two ways about it. The tree was speaking to her. It was asking *Bonnie* for help.

Bonnie looked into what she saw as the tree's eyes. Her hand was gripped firmly by the branch of the tree. Bonnie repeated the word: 'Help'. And, in that split second, the tree released her. She stepped back and the face had gone.

Bonnie had received a message. She knew something was wrong and she knew the tree had asked her for help. The owl opened its great wings and flew further down the path. It sat watching her from a short distance away. Bonnie followed and, within five minutes, she was back on a path she knew. Her legs carried her home as quickly as they could.

Her heart was racing when she arrived home, still trying to process everything. It was now dark outside. Bonnie breezed past her mum and felt glad to be back home, in the safety of her room. It was when she was shutting the curtains that she saw another pair of eyes outside. The dark creature stared at her for a few moments before disappearing into the darkness.

# Chapter 3

# Dìonadair

A cat with the shiniest, blackest of fur sat attentively. Its eyes glowed like two burning candles as it absorbed knowledge from its latest class. 'Spell advancement' was the topic, and the cat was enjoying every word spoken by the teacher. But this was no ordinary school. This was a sorcery teaching centre which had been in operation for hundreds of years. It was found on Oilthigh Island, a tiny area of land only accessible by boat ... or magic. The island was a very nondescript little place on the surface, with only a handful of trees and a scattering of wild gorse bushes. But if you knew the spell to access the secret door on the island, you would enter a world of magic. There were 183 steps to descend on the spiral staircase before you arrived in the reception. A sign in large golden letters was the first thing that caught your attention. It said, 'Welcome to the WWW Learning & Development Centre for Modern Magic.'

In this instance, 'WWW' stood for 'Witch, Wizard & Warlock'. Over the years, the students had come to refer to it by its nickname – the much more manageable '3WiLD Centre'.

The learning centre had been recently transformed into a bright modern building. It was deep underground, but with an air of freshness and space. Gone were the dark and musty smelling classrooms of old. These had been replaced with modern learning areas using the latest teaching technology. Everywhere you went, from reception to canteen to classroom, there was a sense of magic. As you stepped into the facility, there was much to take in. But more striking than anything else were the bright magical scenes. They were on every floor, wall and ceiling. They looked as though they had been created by artificial intelligence. The soft, delicate images were so realistic and too perfect to be true.

Of course, these images were created by a spell. This was something quite fascinating to watch. As the spell was cast, the imagery would slowly start to appear from the floor, up the walls and onto the ceiling. Few were lucky enough to be able to watch the spell work its magic. But, if you did, you would see the grass growing before your very eyes. Trees would grow in the background. Hills, streams and mountain ranges. Flocks of birds, changing weather patterns from sunshine to snow, it was all there. There were scenes depicted that would take thousands of years to form in nature but, here, would grow before your eyes in only a matter of days. People, animals, buildings, plants would all come to life on the walls. Over many weeks, the spell worked its way across every inch of the building.

But these images were not still. They were like giant TV screens showing an ever-changing view. Skies would appear and change from bright blue to cloudy. Dark clouds and thunderclouds would form. The grass you walked over would create a warm and dry sensation on your feet or, if the spell decided, cold and wet. The leaves on the trees would change with the seasons. The 3WiLD Centre reflected the outdoor world.

Every room was different, with some rooms showing historical scenery. There were windmills and watermills in the distance and the air would smell clean and crisp. Other rooms were parks with play areas and ponds, the noise of traffic in the background and the smell of the city. The Council in charge of running the 3WiLD Centre were very proud of their building. They were proud of its history, its students and all the teachers.

The school had changed a lot over the years, as witching and wizardry had become more mainstream. In years gone by, there had been a sense that wizards were the 'good guys' of magic. Witches and warlocks were seen as evil and dangerous. But like everything, it changed over time. In modern-day magic, your ability to cast spells tended to decide whether you were a witch or a wizard. In simple terms, witches had the ability to make people do things. Wizards were more magical – they could make things appear or disappear. As for warlocks … well, you'll hear a little bit about *them* later.

At the 3WiLD Centre, the students learned about changes to witching and wizardry. They learned that modern sorcerers now fell into four different groups. They were categorised as good, hidden, bad or evil. If you were a sorcerer who was bad or evil, the 3WiLD Centre would do its best to encourage you to change your ways. If you refused, or cheated the system by pretending to be good, you would be expelled. The most senior lecturer at the school would also cast a spell on you. This would leave you unable to speak and so unable to cast your own spells. But, like anything else, over the years there had always been one or two exceptions. Sorcerers with too much power sometimes couldn't be contained.

For the experienced lecturers, it was easy enough for them to work out what kind of sorcerer a student was. All you had to do was watch them and, over time, it would become obvious. There was also a little rhyme which was well known throughout the school. This reminded everyone about the different types of sorcerers:

*A modern sorcerer uses their power for good,*
*A hidden sorcerer is shy, and knows that they should,*
*A sorcerer that's bad gets their own way by harming,*
*A sorcerer that's evil so often seems charming.*

In addition to departments for witching and wizardry, there was a department for warlocks. In modern-day sorcery, warlocks are harmless. They have a little magical power but can't get it to work properly. They tend to be quite hapless individuals but with plenty of confidence. The school did it's best to put this right, but many warlocks would graduate with very little ability. Most of them ended up as politicians.

But there was yet another department in the school. This was the biggest department and it specialised in teaching familiars. Now, familiars are typically animals – most often, cats. They are there to help and aid witches and wizards that have good or hidden power. But, as with anything, there are always exceptions. A bad or evil sorcerer with a like-minded familiar is a dangerous combination.

The school's main job was, of course, to encourage good sorcery. In charge of the Familiars department was a large, wise old cat. Her name was Beatrice Múinteoir. Not only was she clever, but she was strict. Firm, but fair. And, if you have ever tried to get a cat to do something, you'll know it's almost impossible – unless the cat *wants* to do it. But Beatrice had a unique way about her. She knew what to do and the other animals, including the cats, treated her with the utmost respect.

The black cat with the candle-like eyes was called Dìonadair. His role was as a witch familiar. While he was paying attention and enjoying his class, he felt a little bit grumpy. He had two hundred years of familiar experience, and still he had to go back to school. But times had changed, and he had to learn more about modern day sorcerers. An old-fashioned familiar would be no use to any student graduating from today's 3WiLD Centre.

His teacher Beatrice was 'old school', which was why Dìonadair got on well with her. Despite her age, her black fur was silky smooth. Her eyes could pierce right through you, like an arrow through cotton. When Beatrice entered the classroom, the pupils fell silent in an instant. Her presence commanded their attention.

There were lots of different animals in the classroom. The days of familiars only being a black cat were long gone. There were dogs, crows, foxes and even a couple of horses. It made an interesting mix in the classroom. Dìonadair was always a bit wary of the dogs. They could be serious one minute, then chasing you around the room the next, although never when the teacher was in the room. The magically painted walls held pictures of famous familiars. There was Larry the Cat, a corgi called Port and a border terrier named Angus. All were charged with keeping their owners on the straight and narrow. And some were more successful than others.

There were six black cats in Dìonadair's class, all with the same black fur and intense orange eyes. In total, there were thirty-nine creatures in the room. Even in magical schools, they had a problem with class sizes.

Dìonadair was by far the oldest familiar in the room. He had served with lots of different witches over the years. Each of the familiars would be assigned a witch or wizard to look after. And, like with any other job, there were some familiars who were good at what they did, and some who weren't. Dìonadair considered himself to be rather good at his work – and he had evidence to back this up. In all his time, he had never once had a bad review from the Witches High Command.

Dìonadair was the most knowledgeable of the pupils and was held in the highest regard. Other familiars would speak to him for advice if they needed help with a tough assignment. But even familiars with as much experience as Dìonadair had dreams. And his was to secure the biggest job in witching – looking after the country's most powerful witch.

He had been a witch's cat for over two hundred years and would continue to be for two hundred more. As a familiar, he had learned the spells and potions that prolonged his life. His last job had been to look after a woman called Florence, who had passed many years ago. He had found this a dull assignment. She was a witch that had shunned any kindness with other humans and had spent all her days being bitter. But she was from a line of powerful witches that seemed to get more powerful with each generation. He was glad he had kept her from causing harm, but it had been an uneventful existence. Even the daily affection that most humans show to their animals had been lacking. Being assigned a new witch after many years of waiting would be exciting.

It used to be a popular misconception that all witches were bad. Witches were feared, years ago, so they often hid themselves within society. Being exposed as a witch almost always led to an untimely and unpleasant death. Now the modern-day witching population are harder to spot. Unless, of course, you are an experienced familiar. Fortunately, there are more good witches than bad these days. Witching power can be used for many positive things. The role of a good familiar is to help them do this. In the classrooms for witches, they are taught to focus their power away from the path of evil. Every class focuses on using their power for a lifetime of good. But that isn't always as easy as it sounds.

Today was the day that Dìonadair would finally find out the name of his new witch or wizard. He hoped it would be a witch, as his skills were better suited to this area. He had listened attentively to every lesson. Each test had been studied for and passed with ease.

Dìonadair learned that his assignment would be to protect a young witch by the name of Rachel Parker. He would be her familiar and would protect her throughout her life. She was actually shaping up to be an evil witch – but didn't know it yet. All she knew was that she hated most people, and it gave her great amusement to emotionally hurt them. Rachel wouldn't receive the calling to go to the witch's school for a few years yet.

This would need to wait until her non-magical education was complete. The Witches High Command had decided, many years ago, that young witches and wizards should remain with their parents until adulthood. But they were all aware Rachel's mother, Kimberly, was a problem. An evil witch with great power and a greed for financial riches. There was little chance of her ever changing her ways. They hoped this trait could be changed in her daughter … and if anyone could do this, it was Dìonadair.

He had dreamed of an appointment like this. A young and powerful witch with a nature that could be shaped towards good. When the time was right, he would need to steer the child onto the right path. Only time would tell if the daughter had the ability for good, or if she would be like her mother – evil to her very core. This would be no easy task, and there was no guarantee of a positive outcome. But he knew he would do all he could to make it happen. He had to. Rachel Parker would grow up to become the most powerful witch ever known.

Dìonadair learned about Kimberly, the mother of his witch. All the records kept over the past four hundred years suggested that she had, so far, the potential to be the most powerful at the witching craft. He would need to try and control this, but it would not be easy. There were two things that would help him. Number one: Kimberly Parker had not yet learned that she had witching powers. Yes, she could sense she was a bit different, but she was unaware of her ability to cast spells. Number two: at her young age, Kimberly's daughter could be taught to use her powers for good. This would be important, as he would need Rachel to help protect him from her mother's power.

He also knew that Rachel, his witch, would need a true friend. Someone who would form a lifelong bond with her and help her on the path to good. There were a few options out there – humans that he had scratched a few years previously. If this scratch was passed on to their unborn child, it would mean the child would have the protector's scar. This scar would give them powers to resist a spell. And it would release powers to allow them to harness the might of the animals. He would need to find these children who would, by now, be around the same age as Rachel. And, once Kimberly Parker discovered her true power, he would need all the help he could get.

Dìonadair graduated from the 3WiLD Centre with distinction. This was expected, with his experience. And he was now fully trained in the practices of the modern sorcerer. But there had been another little change. The research and development team at the 3WiLD Centre had invented a familiar's shield. And Dìonadair would be the first ever familiar to receive one. It was a bit like James Bond getting a special new gadget from Q.

The shield was tiny, about the size of a button, but taking a shield-like shape. It would go around his neck with a silky tie, making him look like a well-pampered pet. Dìonadair would need to learn all the powers the shield gave him but, for now, he only felt a compulsion to sit and stare at it.

As he looked at his own tiny reflection in the shield, he started to see other images appear. It was like gazing into a crystal ball. He could see a young, happily married Jack Banks besotted with his baby daughter, Bonnie. But he could also see Kimberly Parker in Jack's life. Despite the fact that she was unaware of her witching power, Dìonadair could see that she had cast some kind of spell over him. This meant Jack found Kimberly occupying his thoughts more and more. There was very little he liked about Kimberly. But, for some reason, he couldn't stay away from her.

He had then started to see the young Misty Mullins, the soon-to-be Mrs Misty Banks. She was blissfully happy with her partner Jack and dreamed of having her first child. Her hopes were for a little girl she would call Bonnie.

Dìonadair could see the young family together: Jack, Misty and their baby daughter. He could see in the images a perfect little baby. And, despite the tiny screen, he could make out an odd little scratch mark on the back of her hand. A scratch identical to the one on Misty's hand. He could see himself in the image, luring a very young Misty closer to him as a harmless and affectionate cat. She had been taken by the bright orange eyes and jet-black fur. As she went to stroke him, he had lashed out at her, scratching the back of her hand. The deep scar had never faded – and now, it had been passed on to her daughter.

In his shield, Dìonadair could see that Jack's family were everything to him. But he also saw his handwritten note left in the family home. It said he was sorry, but he was leaving for good and would never be back. It had happened out of the blue and destroyed Misty.

The images faded, only to reappear with the face of a laughing Kimberly Parker. He could sense a woman who dreamt of nothing more than wealth, success and winning at any cost. He could see her plans for an empire of hotels and holiday resorts. He saw a woman taking satisfaction, more than that, joy, in breaking another woman's heart.

As the images of Kimberly started to fade, he saw her terrifying and charming people in equal measure. She would do anything to get her way. He saw Kimberly's father, Brandon. He was speaking to a very young girl Dìonadair assumed was also Kimberly. 'You have the witch's streak in you, young lady,' Brandon said.

The young Kimberly had liked the idea of having some kind of witching power, although it had never crossed her mind that it may be a reality. As the last image faded, Dìonadair felt a sensation in his body that he wasn't used to. The sensation was fear.

# Chapter 4

## Alone

Bonnie was still a little bit shaken from her experience in the forest, as she came down from her room into the kitchen.

'How come you're late?' asked Misty.

'I took the longer way home.'

'I tried to phone you, but your mobile went to voicemail. What's the point in having a mobile phone if you don't answer it?' Misty would always get angry if she called Bonnie and there was no reply.

Bonnie wasn't ready for this now. She knew she would have to tell her mum about the phone. And the bullying. *It won't be much of a conversation*, thought Bonnie. It would be a one-way, fifty-thousand-word sentence rant about everything she should have done. And what her mum was going to do about it which would only make things worse.

'My battery was flat,' said Bonnie, continuing with the little lies. 'I forgot to charge my phone last night.'

Her mum was about to say something else when David saved the day. He came bounding down the hall and exploded into the kitchen. He was travelling at top speed, unable to stop, and crashed into Bonnie. David was so excited; his tail was going like windscreen wipers on double speed. He was jumping around like he hadn't seen Bonnie in years. Bonnie wasn't just pleased to see him. She was delighted. He had saved her from any more of a telling-off.

Bonnie wished her mum had named the dog something other than David. It was her sense of humour: 'David the Dog'. So, David it was.

And with these thoughts, Bonnie headed to her room, with David following at her heel. 'I've got loads to tell you, David,' she said, closing her bedroom door.

Her relationship with animals was why she had got David as a present. He arrived as surprise present - a little bundle of fur with a collar and name tag. Misty was always commenting that Bonnie had a way with animals. Every day, they would get a visit from the cat next door. Fritzy was one of those fluffy white cats that did exactly what it wanted. It knew it would get some tasty treats, a nice sleep and a change of scenery. Misty and the woman next door joked about who owned the cat.

'You're a right little Dr Dolittle,' Misty would say to Bonnie. 'You should be a vet when you leave school.'

David sat next to Bonnie. He put his head on her lap, and she patted and stroked it. 'Guess what, David? I was in the woods today. I went there after that horrible girl Rachel was super-bad to me at school and made me break my phone. I got a bit lost. I was in a part of the forest I didn't know, and it was getting dark. Then, the strangest thing happened. I got my hand gripped by a tree. Are you listening to me, David?'

David's eyes met Bonnie's, and it was almost as if he nodded and said, 'Of course I am.'

'Then there was this owl, and it seemed to be directing me out of the forest – like it knew I was lost. Then I came up to this weird-looking tree – it had a face. Do you think I'm going crazy, David?' David kept her gaze, and Bonnie continued, 'The tree drew me towards it. It had some kind of presence. Like it was alive. I touched the tree – its eyes, its face. And then, do you know what happened, David, can you guess?'

As if to say, 'Yes, of course I know what happened,' David moved his head from her lap. He broke her gaze, then gently squeezed her hand with his mouth. To say Bonnie was surprised at this would be a massive understatement. 'Yes, yes, David! That's exactly what it did. And I heard it say 'Help.' At that moment, as Bonnie said the word 'Help,' she heard it repeated in her head. It was the same experience she had had earlier with the tree – she shivered and looked at her dog. 'Are you talking to me, David?' David was now on all four legs, looking at her and wagging his tail. 'You are, aren't you? I can sense it.' Bonnie felt a warm glow inside as the word 'Help' shone as brightly as a neon sign in her mind. Her eyes closed and she could see giant machines flattening a forest. Animals were standing watching, terrified.

As the warm glow left her body, David had returned to normal, if you could use such a word to describe him. He started to have one of his 'mad half-hours', or an attack of the 'zoomies', as they were known. He would run around, jump on the chairs, bark, chase his shadow – anything other than be calm. He was great fun when he did this, and he did it a lot. And he *did* appear happy about something.

Bonnie tried to get some thinking time to herself, to attempt to work out what had happened. It had been an eventful day. From the exchange at school, to the walk in the woods and now David seemingly being able to 'talk' to her. But she couldn't concentrate with him running around like the biggest, daftest dog ever. Bonnie's mum then walked into her room. She didn't knock, never had, despite Bonnie asking her over and over again. 'What's wrong with David?' asked Misty. 'He's over-excited.'

Before Bonnie could answer, Misty spotted Bonnie's phone – it was sitting on her bed. The subject under discussion changed.

'You've broken your phone.' Well, she didn't simply *say* it. It was more of a statement of simmering fury.

'Mum – don't overreact. I dropped my phone at school. It was an accident. And it still works fine.'

Bonnie's mum could fly off the handle at the slightest thing, sometimes. She never used to be like that, according to Bonnie's gran, but she was now. And then she would go quiet for a few days, until her mood settled back to normal. Bonnie didn't need this right now. She needed to get her head together. But all she had was a broken phone, a crazy dog and a furious mum. *Perfect*, she thought. *Just perfect.*

Bonnie figured honesty was the best strategy and she should tell her mum about the incident with Rachel at school. If she said nothing now, then it would all start again. 'Look, Mum, please don't go off on one. Rachel was being horrible to me at school. Everyone was laughing at me. I told her to shut up, and she pushed me. I fell on my phone and broke it, OK? And before you threaten to do this, say that, write to the head teacher or whatever else … just don't. It will only make things worse. Will you please, please, for once, just let me be? I'll sort it out myself.'

Both of them stood still for a moment, then David – now calm – walked past Misty. He put half of his body weight against her leg and brushed past her, showing his affection. Walking around Bonnie, he made a half circle around her legs, never losing contact. He then sat at Bonnie's left-hand side, leaning into her. He stared at Misty with his puppy dog eyes.

'You know how to take the sting out of cross words, don't you, David?' said Misty.

Mother and daughter looked at one another. Bonnie had been unusually outspoken, which hadn't gone unnoticed. She couldn't hold her emotions together any longer and felt her eyes welling up. And she had no idea why, but her mum was also close to tears.

Misty had never been 'huggy', but at that moment, she took hold of her daughter and held her close. Bonnie was as tall as her mum, despite being only twelve or, as she preferred to say, 'nearly thirteen'. They held one another for a good couple of minutes. David kept close contact with them both.

'I'm sorry I can be difficult at times,' said Misty. Bonnie thought she was hearing things. An apology from her mother? Surely not. 'I don't know why I'm telling you this now. I always like to put a brave face on things. Like you are doing now with Rachel. But I miss your dad. I miss your dad and I hate being alone. I know I have you and Granny, but sometimes it's hard 'adulting' on your own. Sometimes I hate hearing myself moaning and shouting all the time. And, even though it was twelve years ago, I still miss your father. And I've been angry at him for not being here for you. Angry, and missing him at the same time. For twelve years.'

Bonnie had wanted to find out more about her father. Who he was, what he looked like and everything about him. She had seen old photos of him, but her mother would never talk about it. Now, it would seem, she was ready to speak.

Misty spoke for over an hour, without interruption. She spoke about the good times and how everything was so perfect, then how it all suddenly changed. 'It was like being hit by a train.'

Bonnie didn't know her mum had been trying to come to terms with it all these years. But of all the words she spoke, the hardest one to speak had been the word 'sorry', as the old song goes. But she did say it, there and then.

'I'm sorry I've not been the best mum. And sorry I've sometimes kept you at arm's length. I promise I'm going to change for the better. And I promise to rant less. Well, a little bit less, at least.'

Bonnie had lots of questions about her dad, but they could wait. For now, her mum needed her, and she needed her mum. The tales of what happened in the woods today could wait for now. Mum and daughter held one another and provided comfort. And then Bonnie made tea and slices of toast so hot the butter melted through it. There were, of course, some doggie treats for David as well.

Misty felt a certain calm. It was like the weight of the world had been lifted off her shoulders. Why she hadn't opened up to her daughter before now she would never know. Misty gazed, lost in her thoughts, out of the window into the darkness.

Bonnie had disappeared off to her room. The scar on the back of her hand that had been there since she was born was irritating her. As she looked at it, the shape had changed from a simple straight scar. It was now a line with what looked like a square on its side in the middle, and four little lines coming out of each corner. *Probably just some scratches or an allergy from the tree*, she thought.

# Chapter 5

## Superpowers

If you were able to talk to David the dog, he would have lots to tell you. The first thing on his mind would be his name. He would tell you he doesn't like it. His preference would have been Max, or Rover, or something like that. And he hates the 'puppy talk'.

'Awwww, come to Mummy, precious little David,' they say. But he would tell you he is three years old, and not a puppy. David is a Labsky. His mum was a Labrador and his dad was part Siberian Husky. He's proud of that – being part Siberian, although he looked much more like a Labrador than Husky.

David is a handsome dog. His well-groomed black coat and his dad's 'melt your heart' piercing blue eye. He does have *two* eyes of course, but only one of them is blue. The other is brown and from his mum's side of the family. David is a smart dog. He knows all the human words and gets frustrated when the humans don't understand his bark.

David spends most of his time with Bonnie. They are best friends, one girl and her dog. David would say Bonnie understands him better than any other human does – she seems to 'get' him. When Bonnie and David go on long adventure walks together, other dog walkers often compliment him on what a good-looking dog he is. As soon as you mention 'part Siberian Husky', some people wonder if he may be a bit scary. But he's the furthest thing from it. Never try to hurt Bonnie though. He would protect her with his life.

David is an ambitious dog. One of his goals is to pee on every tree in the forest, and there must be about five thousand of them. He even has a system, with various landmarks around the forest. He would proudly tell you he is already halfway there, and he'll have the job finished in the next couple of years.

The other thing about David is that he is perceptive of danger. He can sense something is not right with the forest, but he doesn't know what yet. There is a woman he has seen visiting a few times, and he can sense she is evil. The animals and trees in the forest can sense it too. They haven't worked out what the danger is, yet. But they will.

As well as perception of danger, David has other skills – some would even call them superpowers. Now, so far in his life, he hasn't had to use them for anything other than a bit of fun. But they are *real* superpowers, and he is ready to use them whenever the need arises. There are three of them.

**Superpower #1:** He can talk to the trees and all the animals in the forest. Now, this won't sound like a normal conversation to you, but they *do* talk. It's like understanding another language. And their conversations are filled with the same stuff as us humans. General chat, forest gossip, things they are looking forward to … and some worries. In his conversations with the forest inhabitants, he has learned that the birds are smart, as are the trees. The rabbits gibber on endlessly and get easily confused. It may surprise you to learn the mice are geniuses, as are the dragonflies and the squirrels. David gets on well with the crows but finds them a bit rude. And then there are the owls. Everyone thinks owls are smart, and they are. But they are also very sarcastic.

**Superpower #2:** David's second superpower is his ability to get anyone to do as he wants. He does this in two ways. First of all, there's his stealth movement. You can be minding your own business then, suddenly, he's there. All innocent and charming, catching your attention unexpectedly. The other thing involved in this two-stage process is the eyes. Blessed with beautiful, hypnotic eyes – one blue and the other brown – he can grasp hold of someone's gaze. As Bonnie says, he 'applies the eyes' and people are defenceless against his hypnotic charm. He can then decide what he wants them to do: beat their chest like a gorilla, dance like a ballet dancer or sing like a vicar at a wedding. Once he has applied the eyes, he can get them to do almost anything he dreams of. It's quite a skill.

**Superpower #3:** And, finally, his third superpower. He can clear a room of humans in under forty seconds. Yes, David's a bit of a windy dog. Now, admittedly, this takes him a bit of preparation. It needs a rich diet, or even some old roadkill that's been at the side of the road for a week or two. But David knows what to eat, and his perception of danger tells him when to eat it. Of course, there are other times he'll use superpower #3 for fun. Like when he had been on a family visit a few weeks previously.

Misty had taken Bonnie to see her grandparents – Jack's mum and dad. David could never figure out why they would visit them, after all, their son Jack had left Misty a few years earlier. But Misty wanted Bonnie to have a relationship with her grandparents and would visit from time to time. They were a rude couple, often questioning her, or telling Bonnie she had to work harder at school. This annoyed David, and he could see it upset Bonnie and Misty.

But, this time, he was prepared for the visit. An unfortunate mix of food had been consumed about two hours before everyone set off in the car. A mixture of leftover, on-the-turn Chinese food and some old fruit. His timing had to be perfect. Eating it too early would have been dangerous in the enclosed space of the car.

And if consumed too late, then superpower #3 would be unusable when needed.

Misty and Bonnie had been there for an hour. It had all been civilised, up until then. Tea and biscuits, chats about work, school and the weather. And then the rudeness started. Bonnie, not for the first time, was getting it.

'Your grades should be higher, you need to work harder.' And Misty got it too. 'Why are you not paying more attention to her schoolwork?' 'That dress doesn't suit you.' And on and on it went.

David released superpower #3. Dogs call it kerflumptulation. There was no noise. Just a silent, deadly smell.

**Superpower #3 deployment +6 seconds.** It was at this point noses had started twitching, each person in the room sizing up the other, looking for a culprit. But, after a moment or two, they had realised this was no ordinary smell. This must have come from the dog. A dog belonging to the Devil himself.

**Deployment +10 seconds.** The air in the house had taken on a life of its own. It felt almost sticky – like it would be difficult to walk through it and you would need to wade. Eyes were closed and hands were held to faces, as if this would make it more bearable.

At **deployment +15 seconds**, vision had become hazy and retching noises could be heard from each of the occupants.

The grandparents had been unable to stand it any more and had started to wail.

'Oh my God, get that dog out of here. That's disgusting. I'm going to be sick,' said the granny.

The grandfather got to his feet and forgot to put his slippers on. With his hand over his mouth, he staggered towards the window. He misjudged where he was going as his eyes were streaming with tears and he was shouting, 'It's like mustard gas!' He caught his pinkie toe on the wooden foot of the couch. Crack. 'Aaaaargh. Ya little git, I've broken my toe,' he shouted. But the pain caused him to take a deep breath which made him light-headed. At **+20 seconds**, he made it to the window. His wife had already gone through the door in the opposite direction. His mouth and nose were covered by his hand and sleeve, but by now panic had set in. He was disorientated and his eyes were streaming. He couldn't remember how to open the window. Handle up? Down? Push? Pull?

At **+24 seconds**, he shot across the room following Bonnie and Misty, who had also headed out the door. Still shouting in pain over his broken toe, he limped across the living room at high speed. He held his breath as best he could, shouting 'That dog absolutely stinks!'

**+28 seconds** and the room was empty. David was proud of his achievement. It was a unique superpower, but you never know when it could come in handy.

David was a dog who was lucky enough to be in a loving home with Bonnie and Misty. But he felt he was a bit different from other dogs. A bit more, well, human. And he suspected he had these superpowers for a reason. Was it to protect his humans, or was there another reason?

# Chapter 6

## Cat

Kimberly Parker was not liked by anyone. And, equally, there were few people in this world that *she* liked. A ruthless woman, she would stop at nothing to get what she wanted. She sat in her office in an expensive one-piece trouser suit and matching shoes. On her head sat one of a dozen-or-so pairs of designer glasses that she owned. One pair would never be enough for Kimberly. She had stayed single; earlier partners hadn't stayed long once they experienced her bad temper. The slightest thing could set her off on a tirade of insults, reducing anyone to a shivering wreck. Kimberly hated almost everyone.

The thing was, she was clever. Clever enough to know better than most about almost anything. At school, she had been one of those pupils who could get high grades with little or no effort. And by the time Kimberly was in her final year at school, she had held most of the sporting records. Fastest, strongest, highest and longest –

all the records were hers. As long as they were individual events, of course. Team efforts were not her thing.

By the time Kimberly was twenty-four, she had thousands of pounds in savings and three businesses. A woman of ambition; power was what she wanted. To hell with what anyone thought of her. If she was their boss, people would need to do it her way. Orders would be taken from no-one. At twenty-eight, Kimberly had owned three hotels. By the time she was thirty-three, this had risen to nine: all part of The Parker Hotel Group.

Her employees were well paid, and the hotel reviews were excellent. The only thing no-one liked was a visit from her. Anything that wasn't right would be spotted. The hotel manager would then understand exactly where they had gone wrong. No-one was happy after one of her classic reprimands.

At university, Kimberly had had a long-term boyfriend called Alan Smith. A few years later, she had dated a young man called Jack Banks, who had left his wife for her after only being married for a few months. On Kimberly's part, it was more a test of how much she could control him. Within a few weeks of Jack leaving his wife, Kimberly had finished the relationship with him. She had proved to herself she could have anything she wanted. Now it was time to move on. Success was more important.

Alan was different. He had broken her heart. Kimberly had thought she would never forgive him, until they met on a night out not long after she had finished with Jack. After an evening of what felt like a rekindled romance, Alan had disappeared again. And Kimberly had discovered she was pregnant. Nine months later, Rachel had arrived in Kimberly's life. As she held her daughter in her arms for the first time, she had said, 'I will look after you, Rachel Parker. And as sure as you will grow to be beautiful and clever, I will have my revenge on your father for leaving me.'

But as one door opens, another often closes. A few months after Rachel's arrival, Kimberly's father passed. Brandon Parker was a horrible man who ruled with a ferocious discipline. His daughter had inherited his furious temper and nature for revenge. His funeral was a strange affair, with few people there. The minister had found it difficult to find comforting words about a man so universally disliked.

As the ceremony was ending, Kimberly had watched her father being laid to rest. It was an odd moment to notice a black cat watching the burial. It had been sitting there with bright orange eyes, staring at the funeral. She soon forgot about it as the coffin was lowered into the ground. And still, no-one had shed a tear – not even Kimberly. Returning home later that day she had sat alone. A strange sensation began to run through her entire body. It was like pins and needles, running from her head to her toes. This had happened to her before, and it usually meant something. Quite why Kimberly had felt she needed to go back to her father's grave she had no idea. But that was the only thing that had occupied her mind. She had known she had to return. And soon.

That evening, Kimberly had put her daughter into the car and driven back to the cemetery. It was dark now, but this held no fear for her. If she was honest, Kimberly preferred the dark – always had. And by the side of her father's grave, it was peaceful. Her daughter was in her arms, wrapped up against the cold.

Kimberly had said nothing and had felt no emotion. Her only action had been to stare at the grave, the fresh earth covering her father's coffin. Then something had caught her attention. The cat was still there, sitting, staring. She had spoken to the cat, 'Hello. What brings you here, cat? You like the graveyard, do you?'

Kimberly had stepped forward towards the cat. She gave a terrifying hiss to scare it away. She had surprised herself. This hiss had been almost demonic. But Kimberly had been, for once, face to face with something that didn't fear her. The cat had stood its ground and stared back.

'Blasted cat,' she'd thought. 'You had better not mess up my father's grave or I'll come back here, catch you and cook you.' Now it had been the cat's turn to hiss back. And this was no ordinary hiss. The cat had crouched on its front paws, its hair standing on end. An almighty hiss had come from its mouth, which was more like an alien monster's scream than a cat's hiss.

Kimberly had also remained unafraid. She'd stepped forward and hissed back at the cat, a more human-like hiss this time. Her baby daughter was peaceful and still in her arms, unfazed by any of this. The cat had sat still. Kimberly had spoken *at* it, not *to* it, her words slow and menacing: 'I hope your stumpy tail falls off.'

But that hadn't quite been the end of it. Kimberly had a funny little way with certain things and activities. Like locking doors – she would check they were locked three times. And she would repeat this process three times. Nine checks in all. It was an obsessive habit she was aware of but couldn't control. It was the same with insults or wishes of misfortune. Whatever it was would be repeated three times, in blocks of three. And that's what she did with the cat.

I hope your stumpy tail falls off.
I hope your stumpy tail falls off.
I hope your stumpy tail falls off.
I hope your stumpy tail falls off.
I hope your stumpy tail falls off.
I hope your stumpy tail falls off.
I hope your stumpy tail falls off.
I hope your stumpy tail falls off.
I hope your stumpy tail falls off.

This process usually helped to calm her – but not tonight. Looking at her daughter, she had then spoken, in a voice still full of simmering hatred. 'And I hope your father never, ever sees you, little one. You are *my* child, and no-one else will be part of your life.' And she repeated it three times, three times.

I hope your father never sees you.
I hope your father never sees you.
I hope your father never sees you.
I hope your father never sees you.
I hope your father never sees you.
I hope your father never sees you.
I hope your father never sees you.
I hope your father never sees you.
I hope your father never sees you.

The following day, a former boyfriend of Kimberly's was sitting in a doctor's surgery. Out of the blue, Alan Smith had lost his sight. Nothing was visible to him any more. None of the medical experts could work out what had happened to him; it was a complete mystery. Understandably, he was upset. He had a young daughter to a woman in Scotland. He had hoped one day he would be able to see her.

Kimberly had spent lots of time researching her business ideas. She had looked at everything, from an outdoor theme park to a water-bottling plant. They were all good ideas, but they didn't have the ability to earn the amount of money she was looking for. She had kept researching and soon her idea of All Star Lodges was born. They would offer a holiday home for every budget. And the holiday park wouldn't be big. It would be enormous.

She had started to explore and plan where such a dream would be built. At home or abroad? Scotland or England? After hours of research, one place had turned out to be exactly right for her plan. And it was on her doorstep: Devilla Forest.

Devilla is in central Scotland and close to the big cities, making it easy to get to. Kimberly had driven to the woodland and parked at the entrance to the forest. A sign offered four different walks around the woods. It told of 'easy to spot' red squirrels. Dragonflies and otters could be seen, along with lots of other wildlife.

Walking around the forest, there were lots of birds and relics of past times. Many of these were hidden away among the trees. There was a stone monument marking a thousand-year-old battle and a 'witch's cemetery' with old gravestones, all worn by the passage of time. As she stood in the spot next to the graves, something had caught her eye. There was movement in the trees ahead of her. Kimberly shook her head, putting it down to a breeze through the long grass.

This area had history long before the forest was planted. It had originally been moorland, with tales of witches and suchlike. *Absolute nonsense*, Kimberly had thought. *An ancient excuse to torture some poor soul based on no evidence whatsoever.*

Her walk had been a long one. Sometimes at a pace, sometimes ambling to think and plan. Her first idea had been to bulldoze and rebuild. Improve the natural area with some manufactured restructuring. Having seen the beauty of the area, she had changed her mind. It gave her a strange sensation of feeling at home. And then that warm, pins-and-needles-like feeling hit her again. But there had been no instinctive message this time. There was only a feeling of comfort, making her all the more convinced she had found the right spot. Never before had she felt so at home.

It was not going to be easy to secure this land. She would need to think creatively and produce a plan like no other. And the pockets of a few important people would need to be lined along the way. But the location was perfect. She had decided there and then this was where she would build All Star Lodges. This was going to earn her serious money.

She knew she could get investors. Kimberly could always get money. The problem would be planning approval and local agreement. The residents would see a significant lift in people travelling to the area. In fact, 'significant' would be an understatement.

As she walked back towards the car park, she had been excited about her plans. And then, there it was. Sitting on the path ahead of her. The black cat. It had moved to its familiar position of hair on end and crouched low at the front. Looking her directly in the eye, it had given another of its ferocious hisses. *Could this be the same cat?* she had wondered. *No, clearly not – it's got half of its tail missing.* Before Kimberly could react, it had disappeared into the long grass and was gone.

# Chapter 7

## Wishes

Kimberly Parker worked best on her own. Discussions with colleagues and employees were kept as short as possible. She knew she worked best like this, as other people annoyed her. Her task for the day was to work out how she would win over the various councils and authorities to agree to her plans. This would not be easy, but Kimberly knew a little 'incentive' would always help.

Her other task was to practice her presentation. Without this, she wouldn't win over any of the various investors and politicians to get the money she needed. Kimberly stood in her living room. It was a big room, with ceiling-to-floor doors looking out onto unrestricted views of the hills. Her eyes caught her own reflection in the glass doors. The mirror image she saw made her do a double-take – for a split second she saw her reflection as someone without a soul. With thin lips and leathery skin. And her eyes, showing a deep, malevolent glare. A blink, and she was back to her normal reflection. She dismissed this as a trick of the light and returned her focus to her preparations. In her mind was a room with a mixture of investors, residents and politicians. The media were there.

And then she was distracted again. Beyond her reflection in the glass, was that a pair of orange eyes looking back at her? Kimberly shook her head and rubbed her eyes, then crossed to the window for a closer look. There was nothing there. 'Hmmmm. Why do I keep thinking I see that manky cat? And weird reflections of myself?' she said, half-whispering to herself.

Her presentation practice began. 'Ladies and gentlemen, thank you for joining me today. For the next thirty minutes, I'm going to share with you a vision …' Kimberly spoke clearly and concisely to no-one. Her ambitions were outlined, and she imagined the audience applauding her every word. She then went on to explain about the park itself.

'I'm going to tell you four things today. Number one – The Journey. You will be worried about excess traffic. I'll tell you how that won't be a problem. Number two: All Star Lodges. My short video will build the park before your eyes and let you see the future. Number three: The Environment. The squirrels, the trees, the otters. I will tell you there will be *more* trees, *more* wildlife, *more* diversity. And, finally, number four: The Benefits to you and Scotland. I'll show you how it will be done, and the benefits it will bring to the area. So, if I may, allow me now to take you on this journey …'

Her rehearsed speech was perfect. There was even imagined applause. Of course, only part of what she said was true. Yes, there would be a giant park and ride to move people to the lodges with electric buses. But what she didn't say was that the buildings would be built entirely of new, non-recycled plastic, moulded into log shapes. Kimberly also knew the workforce used to make the lodges were mostly children from a far and distant country. But that all helped with lowering the costs. And lower costs were a good thing. Nor would she mention that the destruction of the forest would be relentless and unforgiving. To hell with any wildlife caught in the way.

Plenty of money would be needed to get her plans approved. Authorities were not cheap to bribe. Especially Councillor Malcolm, pompous old fool that he was. Everything she had produced so far had been criticised by him. Kimberly knew: of all the people needed to support her plans, he was crucial. The trouble was, he didn't listen to a word she said. It was all about him and *his* thoughts. The image of him filled her head and started to make her angry. 'If only he would listen,' she spat in a half whisper, while shaking her head.

Kimberly continued to voice her thoughts out loud. 'Idiot of a man. Thinks he knows it all. You have two ears and one mouth, and you should use them in that proportion. But no, no. Not you, Councillor Malcom.

You know better, don't you? Always poking your nose into things. If you would only shut up and listen for five minutes you would get on much better. I hope your cheap whisky turns your nose a Rudolf shade of red. That way we'll all get a warning when you are poking it in somewhere. I hope it glows like a traffic light. And, while we're at it, I hope your ears double in size so you can start to listen to what people are saying. You pompous old fool.' She had worked herself up into a temper and used her little technique to calm herself down.

I hope your nose turns Rudolf red. And your ears as big as your head.

I hope your nose turns Rudolf red. And your ears as big as your head.

I hope your nose turns Rudolf red. And your ears as big as your head.

As always, she repeated this twice more.

Her mood settling, attention was refocused back onto her presentation. It was true that her park would create lots of jobs, and she was happy about that. They were mostly minimum wage jobs, but jobs nonetheless. Her research showed the park would bring thousands of people to the area every week. And her enclosed restaurants would cater for all of them.

There was another thing Kimberly missed out from her sales pitch. To make this development happen, money would change hands behind the scenes. It was funny, she thought. You could get the hardest-nosed politician, environmentalist or planner. But a little 'incentive' could always persuade them to look the other way. Approvals would be granted for something that wasn't in the best interests.

But while she was an expert at these negotiations, she hated it. Slobbery politicians, full of their own self-importance. Particularly Councillor Malcom. And environmentalists that think they can save the world single-handed. Having to listen to their small talk. Boring her half to death with tales of how clever they were. And listening to them chew. She *hated* listening to them chew.

Over on the other side of Firthshire, Councillor Malcom was finishing his lunch. His colleagues were now bored half to death with long stories about how great he was. He had been a local councillor for many years but, the way he spoke, you would have thought he was president of the world. In his head, he was an expert on everything. There was nothing he didn't have an opinion on. His latest tale was an exaggerated story told many times before. It was made worse by him slurping whisky and talking with his mouth full. His suit and tie proudly displayed the remnants of many earlier lunches.

He was finishing his slice of chocolate cake when he felt a strange burning sensation in his nose. This then spread across his face into his ears. It was the most unpleasant of feelings. He finished his whisky with one final slurp, excused himself and made his way over to the bathroom. By the time he stood in front of the restroom mirror, he was struggling to see. The pain in his nose was making his eyes water. He ran the cold water tap and splashed his face to try and ease the pain. After a while this started to make a difference. He took a discoloured and crumpled handkerchief from his pocket and dabbed his eyes. The pain was easing as he wiped away the last of the cold water.

Councillor Malcom stood motionless in front of the mirror and looked at his reflection. He had always thought of himself as a handsome character, although few would have agreed. But the reflection looking back at him was far from good-looking. What he saw reflected back was an enormous red nose, and even larger ears. *What caused this?* he thought. *Good Lord, what do I look like? My nose is glowing like a beacon. It's horrendous. I must have taken an allergic reaction or something.* Then, he started to hear noises in his ears. Lots of noises. He could hear everyone in the restaurant talking. Nothing made any sense, though, there was too much noise. He heard the birds outside chirping. He could hear the waiter punching the buttons on the restaurant till. He heard everything, all merging into one giant noise.

Then he saw the reflection of his ears. He looked like Mickcy Mouse. *I'm a mixture of Rudolph the Red-Nosed Reindeer and a Disney character*, he thought. Then he heard all the noise again. It was becoming unbearable. He held his hands against his ears and cried out in anguish. 'What's happening to me?'

Len Rayne

# Chapter 8

## Trees

Trees can talk. Not like us humans do, but they can communicate with one another. There's a large pine tree in Devilla forest who goes by the name of Sylvester Pine. He's the tree in charge of all the others, and he's a character.

'It's true, you know. Us trees – we can talk to one another. We have our own 'forest internet' we use to communicate.' He was speaking to a young robin who had landed on one of his branches for the first time. He explained to the robin that, over the years, the trees have used the forest internet to warn one another of any invading bugs or disease. He continued, 'Our roots are all interconnected, you see. So you can get a message from one side of the forest to the other quickly. We call it our 'wood wide web'. Or 'www' for short. Oh, and for the record, it was us that invented it first. We can also talk to all the animals – not just you, little robin.'

The robin knew the trees could speak, and of course he had already had conversations with some of the other animals. But this was the first time he had spoken to Sylvester. The tree went on to explain further.

'We're quite different, trees and animals. What interests me is not of much interest to a squirrel. But when something important – or even something worrying – happens, we all talk. Sometimes you animals will even stop trying to eat one another for five minutes while we work out a plan.' The little robin laughed at this.

'Now, here I am, chatting away to you and I haven't introduced myself. My name is Sylvester Pine. I'm a Scots pine tree, and a rather mighty one at that, if I may say so myself. This is my forest, and it's been here for hundreds of years. Although some of us have been here for much longer. Me? I've been here for over two hundred years. When I was a sapling, there were no cars on the roads. In fact, there were few roads. And the only thing flying in the sky were little birds like you. Humans thought flight would be impossible for them, all those years ago.'

Sylvester loved to tell these stories to new animals in the forest. 'Over the past few thousand years, we've got on well – humans and trees. We grow, and yes, they chop us down to make things. But that's OK. We're working together. If we get to grow for a few years to do our tree things, we can then serve a new purpose. We love being made into useful things – like fences, boats or furniture. It makes us feel useful. But we hate getting cut down for no reason. And we don't like being chopped down just for firewood or to make way for horrible new buildings. We *really* don't like that.'

The little robin sat on his branch, enjoying the story. 'I suppose you could call me the boss of the forest. I don't tell the other trees what to do – we don't work like that. But the other trees talk to me. They tell me what is happening and if there is anything we should worry about. We stick together. If you see a tree on its own, it could be lonely. And it would love a visit from you, little robin. We do like company, you know.

'One of my best friends is Chaff. Chaff is small, and she has an olive-brown colour, and boy, can she fly! She flirts through the trees and branches at great speed, wagging her little tail as she goes. We all love Chaff, although she can chatter a bit. In fact, she chatters a *lot*. Not everyone understands her, but we do all know if she's excited or worried. Yesterday, she landed on one of my littlest branches. There were all sorts of chirping noises, and she was squeezing my branches with her little feet. I could sense there was something wrong.

'I may as well share this with you now, young robin. We have some big worries. The trees at the edge of the forest have heard negative talk from a human. Several humans, in fact. They are talking about cutting into this great forest. We are meant to be protected, but money is changing hands. And the more money involved, the more you can get humans to do.

'One of our other senior trees lives close to the entrance to the forest. Dr Roburt Oak is the largest tree we have. While we are a pine forest, there are a few oaks too. As well as being the biggest and oldest, Roburt is by far the wisest. He's been there a long, long time. He has sensed the first ever steam engine, the first ever motor car and the first ever aeroplane. He remembers a time when the air was clear and pure. He will tell stories to anyone willing to listen. And if you are a nearby tree, you don't have much choice,' laughed Sylvester. 'You'll hear all about days gone by and what his roots have sensed. His roots connect him right across the forest, you see, and he can talk to other trees far away. That's our rule for becoming a doctor – you must have long roots. Oh, and, for the record, some people call him 'Robert', and he gets tetchy about it. His name is Ro*burt*.'

While Sylvester was chatting away, it was through the roots he mentioned that Dr Roburt Oak could sense danger. And, right now, his roots were warning him danger wasn't far away.

# Chapter 9

## Plans

A few weeks earlier, four humans had gathered in the forest. They had much to discuss. This is not unusual, and the trees hear many things discussed by visitors to the forest. None of which make them fearful, usually, but these visitors were different. They had talked about removing large parts of the forest. They spoke about creating space for buildings and new paths and roadways all over the forest. Hundreds of trees would be cut down. They would build long plastic tunnels to let visitors stay dry as they moved around the area. Boats and jet skis would be allowed onto the lochs – which had got the fish into a real panic. Roburt is right in the way of this work, and he would be one of the first to be cut down. They had spoken about all this while standing in his shade, and he had heard every word.

Trees don't hear every word like humans do. They hear the sounds and expressions. They sense what is being said, and they've learned to understand it. And what they heard was not good. The humans had said more space would be created for a car park and welcome reception. Paths would be widened to allow vehicles access to each of the lodges. And they would build the lodges using plastic – which trees hate. It stays on the ground and in the forest forever. Roburt had heard them say they would build the lodges in a foreign factory, then ship them over to Scotland. It was cheaper to do it this way. The trees they removed would be used for fencing and suchlike. But most of it would be used for a great stock of firewood for the log-burning stoves in the poshest of the lodges.

The developers were planning to do this at the utmost speed. Bulldozers and log-clearing heavy plant would clear the space. They would dig large parts of the forest to put in electricity, drainage and water supplies. The main gathering area would be covered over with some kind of giant canopy. This would be made from new plastic material. Nothing would be recycled because it was cheaper to buy it new.

Roburt had heard the humans laughing about this. He had also heard them say, 'We have a supplier in East Asia that will make these for us. The workforce they use are young and poor, but they make good products.'

The woman in charge had been heard saying, 'I can get everything manufactured overseas and shipped across. When it arrives here, we'll only need to assemble it. And all for half the cost of making it here. They even give green manufacturing certification. Although that's not worth the paper it's written on – everything's made of plastic.' She'd laughed at this.

Roburt had continued to listen. He'd learned that the humans called the woman 'Ms Parker'. He could tell the people with her were also powerful. But she was the one that was firmly in charge. Large sums of money would be paid so the others would agree to her plans. Roburt was, of course, worried for his own future. But he was more worried about everyone else. As the woman had continued to speak, one of the others asked about the wildlife. She had looked at each of them in turn. Her face had been like thunder and her brows were furrowed. The earlier laughter was long gone. Speaking with her teeth clenched and the rest of her face screwed up, she had said, 'I'll say whatever needs to be said, and sign whatever needs to be signed. But let's be clear here. This development will happen quickly and to Hell with anything that tries to stop it. The forest is only full of rodents and vermin. I'm not going easy with the heavy machinery because of some squirrels and a few birds.'

Word had spread around the forest like a viral post on *TikTok*. Roburt is a great authority in the forest, and the trees and wildlife all respect him. But even he was afraid. The holly trees can be emotional, and they were devastated. The chattiest of them is called Jabs. She's an amazing tree and is aware of everything. Bad weather and storms coming in? Jabs is first to warn the forest. Wild campers starting a fire? She keeps nature on its toes.

Jabs and her best pal Sorbus, one of the rowan trees, lead the communication across the forest. They joke about Sorbus being the 'magic' tree. Many years ago, she was planted because the forest had a problem with witches. She would offer some kind of protection against their magic. But she offers no protection against bulldozers.

With all this news, Sylvester arranged a meeting of the forest elders. He was joined by his second-in-command, Krab. Roburt and Stoor were there to represent the oak trees and Jabs and Rebery were the senior holly trees. From the rowan trees were Sorbus and Cupar. Now, this didn't happen like any meetings you would recognise. The trees are far away from one another. But they use the forest internet to communicate, so everyone can hear what is being said. There are no secrets in a forest.

Roburt told the story again. He repeated everything he had heard. Jabs and Rebery also had more to share. At the edge of the forest, more trees would be cleared to make way for fencing and an off-road safari trail. Children would drive little buggies around all day to spot fake wildlife embedded in the trees. There would also be an outer road around the forest to give access to the lodges. Anything in the way of the fence or road would be cut down or bulldozed. At the far side of the forest, the most northerly point, hundreds more trees would be removed. Mostly pine, but they would also need to rip out some of the rowan and holly trees.

Some trees had overheard talk of a 'central hub.' This would be for restaurants and a giant leisure area and would be like a giant retail park, covered over with a plastic canopy. This would cover part of the main loch as well – so there was year-round access to water. Hundreds more trees would die for this part of the development alone. And many of these would be young trees, not due for felling for many years yet. This was all shared with the meeting, with some of the trees hearing it for the first time. One of the oak trees near one of the lochs told of plans for a giant underwater tunnel. This would let the humans walk along under the surface of the loch. There were many other tales of changes, buildings, bulldozers and the like. And they all involved the destruction of the forest.

Roburt had an idea. He explained, 'If we are to stop this, we need to find a way to get help. And the only ones we can get help from to stop the humans destroying the forest, are … humans. We know lots of people visit us every day. Hundreds. And we know most of them enjoy our forest. They leave it as they found it. And we know of a few humans that stray off the paths and explore a bit deeper. The ones that sit amongst us. The ones that like to be as close as they can to nature. We all know there are a few humans out there that want to protect us.'

The forest fell into an anxious silence. Sylvester asked Roburt to explain his idea. 'The oldest amongst us will have heard tales from our ancestors about the ancient ritual of Quoji.'

The birds did not tweet. The squirrels sat stationary. The breeze settled and there was complete calm. Roburt continued. 'For anyone that hasn't heard of Quoji, it was practised by our ancestors many thousands of years ago. It was where all of nature joined together. Human, animal and plant. We talked and communicated with one another. Not all of us, of course, but those chosen to speak for the species. Now, this ability died out many years ago and only a few of us have an idea of how it works.'

Roburt explained his plan. He spoke with authority and in detail, with all the trees in the forest listening to his every word. Stoor, his second in command believed he could carry out the art of Quoji with a little help.

'We have found a young human,' Roburt said, 'with a positive and intelligent mind. One that loves being in our presence and believes in us. She has a close connection with and love for animals. And, most importantly, this human carries the protector's scar on her hand. It is this scar that allows the Quoji process to work. The power they gain from this will allow them to talk to all the animals. We've already had a trial contact with a girl called Bonnie Banks. She understood we were asking for help. We now need to go a bit deeper and give her the ability to talk with the animals. We need to put her through the full Quoji experience.'

The plan was agreed and put into place. Bonnie Banks would be drawn into the centre of the forest. The owls would help. Once she returned, the full process of Quoji would begin.

While all this was going on, Bonnie was sitting in her class. It was difficult to concentrate that day. She had the oddest of feelings she was being talked about. And an anxious sense that something bad was happening.

# Chapter 10

## Path

Bonnie had decided not to tell her mum about what had happened in the forest a couple of days earlier. At least, not for the time being. If she was honest with herself, doubt was beginning to creep in. A talking tree? Whoever heard the like? In fairy tales or films, perhaps, but this was a little village in the centre of Scotland. It wasn't Hollywood. Since they happened, Bonnie had thought about the events in the forest every day. She'd had the incident with Rachel and was upset and angry. The weather had been cold and wet. There was thunder and lightning. It was getting dark. And of course, she'd been a bit lost. All these things would have played with her mind. The more she thought about it, the more it felt likely that it had only happened in her imagination.

Yet, her mind was not at ease. She had to be sure. Bonnie decided to venture into the forest again and try to find the same spot. The tree that took her hand should be easy to find. It was only a few days ago and so not too difficult to remember.

Saturday morning came around, and Bonnie was up early. Hot tea and toast with butter was her breakfast, consumed a little too fast for her mum's liking. On went the outdoor gear. Her favourite Berghaus jacket, walking trousers and her outdoor boots. No hat or gloves today, it was a pleasant morning for the time of year.

David was being a complete pain in the neck. Every time she turned round, he was under her feet. He knew he was going for a walk. As soon as Bonnie put her jacket and boots on, David got excited. Whenever this happened, he would run from one room to another at top speed. Nine times out of ten, he would forget to stop in time. The result was a high-speed slide across the floor and a crash into whatever was in his way. He would then recover and head off at top speed in the opposite direction and do exactly the same again. Next, he would run around at Bonnie's feet and get in her way, tail wagging at 'level four'. This was a bit of a family joke, and they would try to figure out David's mood by the speed at which his tail was wagging. If it was on level nine or ten, then the whole house was a nightmare with his antics. So, level four wasn't too bad, Bonnie reckoned.

'Have you got your water, Bonnie?' shouted Misty.

'Yeeas, Mum', Bonnie replied, with a little bit of attitude in her voice. Her mum could be heard drawing breath to fire out some more questions. This was her 'rapid-fire question' mode, as Bonnie called it. Before her mum asked the next question, Bonnie got ahead of the game. 'And I've got on my boots, walking trousers and jacket. And I've packed a snack for me and David in my rucksack. And my phone's in my pocket. It's charged and still working fine. And I won't stray off the paths. And I won't talk to strangers.'

Misty ignored the sarcasm in her daughter's voice and said, 'Good. You're learning.'

Checklist completed, Bonnie and David got on their way. Bonnie and her mum stayed in Copsehead, close to the banks of the River Firth. They had a small house on Fraser Terrace. This was on one of the local housing estates near Knoll Castle. Bonnie could walk to the back of her estate and through a large steel farmer's gate. From there, it was a walk along the side of the forest before joining one of the main paths. Bonnie loved this part of the walk. She would step out along the road two or three times a day and never tire of the view. It was nothing spectacular in comparison with the forest views. But it meant that nature was on her doorstep, and that made her happy.

Bonnie and David made their way along the pavement. Within a few yards of their house, they went through the gate and along one of the less trodden paths. David had no lead on and was obediently following by Bonnie's side. To be frank, David could have done with increasing the pace a little. He had some serious tree-peeing duties to perform. Today was going to be a tricky one, as the trees he needed to attend to were on the right-hand side of the road. And he liked to lift his left leg to do his business. So, his options were either to turn around every time or to lift his right leg. The thoughts and challenges of a three-year-old dog …

Bonnie noticed David was even more impatient than normal. And he was walking a bit funny. *Daft dog*, she thought. *What's he up to today?* They walked along the side of the woods, on Bonnie's mission to find the path from a few days back. It was a lovely day, the warmth of the summer months now long gone, but the sun still supplied warmth on their backs. *The jacket will need to go in the rucksack if it continues like this*, thought Bonnie, looking around. *Was that some movement high in the trees?* She concluded it was probably just some pigeons flying around.'

They were heading in the direction of Redmoor Loch – the largest loch in the forest. Their route took them along one of the paths that ran alongside the trees. Bonnie's memory from the other day was a turning off the main path. This led into the denser part of the forest. A brighter day meant it was easier to see – and a lot less creepy. Bonnie was enjoying the peace and quiet. David was preoccupied and definitely hell-bent on peeing on every single tree. She noticed he would toddle up to them, spin round, and cock his leg. He would then have the world's fastest pee before repeating the process on the next tree, and the next, and the next. *What goes through that dog's head, no-one will ever figure*, thought Bonnie. 'David, come on! We'll be out all day if you carry on like that.'

While the path was not an 'official' route into the forest, it was well used by local dog walkers. Ramblers and those familiar with the area would use the path when they were out for a walk. It was one of these narrow paths, no wider than your feet; if there were two of you, you would need to walk in single file. There were bushes and long grass on one side, and trees on the other. Lots of twigs were on the ground, and there were occasional dips in the path. Water would gather here when it rained. Today, however, the path was dry. Bonnie found herself irritated by litter left by others using the paths. And even more annoying were the occasional dog poo bags hanging from tree branches.

After about twenty minutes of walking, the peace of the forest had fully descended. That moment when you no longer hear man-made noises of cars, or of people generally being busy. That moment when you hear nothing. And no noise can be beautiful, at times. As she always did around this moment, Bonnie stopped and listened to nature. It was so calming and peaceful. There was bird song, although she could never work out which bird sang which song. Every so often, a pigeon would drone in with their usual call: 'Hoo hoo hoo … hoo … hoo hoo.' Bonnie often thought that they could vary this, even a little. But no. They all said the same thing, over and over again.

David continued to be the happiest dog in Scotland. He had made his usual trip to one of the little burns and drunk as much water as he could. It was like he was topping up so he could continue to pee on every flaming tree, thought Bonnie. And there was that noise in the trees again. It was definitely bigger than a pigeon or a crow. But she couldn't see for sure. Bonnie and David carried on along the track until they joined one of the main paths. This was better constructed and was a good path to walk on. She walked past the burn and headed towards the water. Bonnie knew that there was a turning by the loch that she was sure would take her to the tree from the other day. The forest was almost all pine trees. But her memory from the other day was of a different variety of tree in this part of the forest. Another noise came from the trees. Bonnie still had this feeling of being watched, but she felt safe enough. David was with her and there were others nearby using the paths. But, nonetheless, a little discomfort had entered her thoughts.

After walking for another fifteen minutes, Bonnie came to a turning and stopped. Was this the route? It looked familiar, but she wasn't certain. Movement. A feeling of being watched again. Eye contact. It was an owl. Could that be the same owl from the other day? It was further along the path so, instinctively, Bonnie walked towards it. David continued to pee on every single tree he went past. 'Daft mutt,' she said, out loud. Bonnie didn't have to walk far until she came across another path, leading deeper into the forest. Now, *this* was familiar. This was the path. The fear of the previous day was gone, and Bonnie felt safe; if only David would keep up and stop peeing on every … single … tree!

And then, sure enough, visible in the distance was the owl. The events of a few days previously were repeated as the owl guided Bonnie deeper and deeper into the forest.

# Chapter 11

## Quoji

efore long, there Bonnie was, back in the same spot. Her surroundings were familiar, and the sunlight filtered through the trees. The sunshine made the area much less intimidating than before. She stared at the tree – the one with the 'face'. On one of its largest branches sat the owl. Bonnie touched the tree. Almost instantly, but not in a frightening way, the tree once again grabbed her hand, holding on to it with its smallest, finger-like branches. This time, though, the message was less clear. The word she heard sounded like 'Quoji'. It was spoken repeatedly. 'Quoji. Quoji. Quoji.' It wasn't a chant, as such – there was no rhythm to the words as they were spoken. Bonnie stood and let it happen.

After about fifteen or twenty seconds, the tree released her. She stepped back and looked at it. 'What's that all about then?' Bonnie asked, under her breath. She half expected the tree to answer. What she *didn't* expect was to hear the owl speak to her.

'Can you hear me?' said the owl. Bonnie stared, unsure if the bird was where the voice was coming from. The owl spoke again. 'Are you going to answer me, or gawp like a goldfish?'

'Are you talking to me?' said Bonnie, looking into the owl's eyes.

'No, I'm talking to myself,' said the owl. 'Of course I'm talking to you.'

Bonnie was a bit taken aback, as you might expect. Not only was she talking to an owl, it was a sarcastic one at that. Ignoring the sarcasm, she tried again with the first question that came to mind. 'Do you have a name?'

'No, they call me Owl,' it replied. 'Of course I have a name! Do you think we're *all* called Owl?'

'OK' said Bonnie. 'No need to be so sarcastic – I've never spoken to an owl before. In fact, I've never spoken to *any* animal before, at least not one that speaks back! So, tell me your name, *please*.' Bonnie spoke the word 'please' with plenty of attitude. The size of her new ability hadn't yet hit home.

'My name is Iccuat,' said the owl, this time with no trace of any sarcasm.

'And why, may I ask, am I talking to an owl?' Bonnie continued, keeping with her attitude. 'And, before you answer, there's no need to be rude or sarcastic. I wasn't expecting to be chatting with an owl today, or any other day. So, please explain to me what's happened. And then I'm sure we'll get along.'

Bonnie surprised herself with how assertive she was. *Perhaps it's easier to be assertive with an owl*, she thought, in a self-mocking kind of way.

Iccuat spoke, in the poshest of voices, a bit like an old-fashioned head teacher.

'We all know you in the forest, Bonnie. And we know you like us. And, yes, I know I can be a bit sarcastic. I'm sorry – it's an owl thing. It's true what they say about us though, we *are* wise. But being wise brings alongside it an impatience with stupid questions. Anyway, the forest needs your help, Bonnie. What you have experienced is an ancient art called 'Quoji'. It's the forest's way of being able to talk to a friendly human, and it's not been performed for hundreds of years. But *you* have been chosen to help us, Bonnie.'

The owl continued to stare at her. Well, with those enormous eyes, it was difficult for the bird to look at anything in any way other than staring.

'There are a team of people, and they are going to build homes. Holiday homes, I think. And they are going to build them here, in the forest. They say that we will be left pretty much alone, and they won't destroy the woodland, but we know that's a lie. We've heard them speak about what they plan to do. One of our oak trees, Roburt, lives at the entrance to the forest. He has heard the conversations. And he knows that these people are paying money to get their plans approved. Important people with power that can allow things to happen have been paid, Bonnie. It's only a matter of time before everything is approved and they start to cut us doon.'

Iccuat sounded a little less posh on that last word, thought Bonnie. She was about to ask him a question when she heard another voice.

'Since when did you become all posh, Iccuat?'

It was David that was speaking. Bonnie realised her jaw had dropped open. *I can hear David talking*, she thought. *Although his mouth isn't moving?* Come to think of it, the owl's mouth wasn't moving either. A crow flew past and shouted, 'dogs stink,' then laughed as it disappeared into the distance. Bonnie was struggling to process all this. She blinked her eyes a couple of times and rubbed her face.

In the next few moments that passed, Bonnie tried to get her head around what was happening. Then, Iccuat replied to David, 'I can be posh when I want to, as well you know, dog. I may have a bit of an accent, but at least I don't spend my entire life peeing on trees.'

'Well, it's better than sitting on branches scaring people with your big stare-y eyes.'

Iccuat was about to reply but only managed to say, 'That's …' before Bonnie interrupted them both.

'Will you two please shut up for a second and let me work this out? I'm talking to an owl. And I'm talking to my dog. And my dog and the owl are having an argument. And a rude crow has flown past and insulted my dog. And someone is going to destroy the forest. This needs a bit of processing.' Bonnie drew a breath, slowed her speech and raised her voice a little. 'So would you please both shut up for a moment while I think about this?'

Bonnie then heard David speak. As usual, he was excited, and it was as if he had been able to speak to Bonnie since he was a puppy.

'Bonnie! Bonnie! The tree is speaking. Unless you are connected to them, you can't hear the trees or plants, but I can. You stand and think: 'I'm listening to the tree.'

Bonnie's whole body drooped as she took on board this latest information. Her head shook slowly as she spoke, ignoring the instruction to be quiet. 'David is talking to the tree. Well, I've heard it all now. I suppose you are on first name terms with the tree as well?'

'He's called Stoor,' said David. 'He says hello. He hopes you can help. He says the forest doesn't want to be cut in half, with cars and plastic houses everywhere. Some of the younger trees are crying, not as you would notice, but in a tree-like way. He says he needs our help.'

Bonnie struggled to regain her composure. 'OK, so let me get this right. Hang on, what's the tree's name again?'

'Stoor.'

'So, Stoor the tree is talking on behalf of the forest. David, you understand him, and you and I can now both talk to the forest animals. And the forest needs help urgently. Is that it?'

'Well, I've always been able to talk to other animals. And I seemed to have a connection with a couple of trees. They told me not to pee on them,' David said, with a smirk. 'And, yes, now you can too, Bonnie. At least the animals, anyway.'

Bonnie stood silent for a moment. The little scar on her hand had started to itch, adding to all the thoughts going through her head. 'What does he want us to do?' she said, to no-one in particular. Stoor and David 'spoke' in silence. After no more than a minute, a less-excited David sat and spoke to Bonnie.

'The woman behind the development is called Kimberly Parker. The trees had worked that out while overhearing conversations. They know there is some kind of meeting soon. They keep talking about 'pushing a button' in the early spring, although no-one is sure what this means. They think it's some kind of meeting date which will approve their plans. The ownership and management of the forest will change. It will move from 'Devilla Woodland Council' to 'The Parker Hotel Group'. All the important people have been given money, so they don't expect anyone to say no. The forest wants us to expose that the plans are lies, or half of it will be cut down. The Parker Hotel Group doesn't care about the forest.'

'But what do we do? How do we stop this?' said Bonnie. There was more discussion between dog and tree. David was on all fours again, tail wagging at level ten.

'All they know is what they've heard. They're relying on us to fix it, Bonnie.' Tail now reduced to level six.

Bonnie looked at Stoor, not sure if she could see a face in the tree or if it was her mind playing tricks. 'I've a lot to think about. This meeting sounds at least a few days away yet, so we have time. I'll come back here tomorrow and let you know what I'm going to do.'

David's tail was now back to level ten, and he was barking. Bonnie was pleased to hear him bark, and almost wished things could go back to just that. Nice, simple barking. *Talking to animals? What's happening to me?* she thought.

The walk home was the oddest one ever. The conversation with David was non-stop, with Bonnie asking him what it was like to be a dog. David asked her what she did all day at school, and why it was important. He wanted to know why humans needed clothes, gadgets, phones, foods wrapped in plastic, presents and money. He couldn't figure out what money was all about.

'So, they cut down trees to make paper, which they turn into money and people can buy things made of trees. Is that right?' asked David.

Bonnie struggled to explain the concept to him. It turned out he was more curious about her than she was about him. But he was still David. And still over-excited about almost everything.

David answered her questions as well, like why a walk was the most exciting thing in the world. Three times a day, every day. 'You get the chance to run around in the fresh air. There's total freedom, seeing nature in all its beauty, taking in all the smells. And the forest is soooo rich in smells. It's brilliant!'

David was a bit unsure about his compulsion to pee on trees, though. He couldn't explain that. Other than to say it let other dogs know he had been there, and that this was his patch. And it happened so often to the trees, they didn't say anything about it … with one or two exceptions.

This was the most unusual of days. Bonnie and David were both content in their newfound ability to communicate. In some ways, being able to talk confirmed what they both already knew: they were the best of friends.

Bonnie could now see her house. Neither she nor David noticed the black cat watching their every move. It was as though it was watching to see exactly which house the girl and her dog lived in.

# Chapter 12

## Cottage

Kimberly Parker was in the forest. She was on her own, walking around and familiarising herself with the woodland. While walking along a path surrounded by trees, she had an odd feeling of being watched. The paths were narrow, causing her to walk carefully. Something in the distance caught her eye. It was a building that wasn't easy to see through the trees, but she could make it out in the distance. Always curious, Kimberly headed towards the building.

She was well kitted out for her walk, her outfit including walking trousers, sturdy boots and a Barbour jacket. Gloves and a warm woolly hat completed the outfit. It was a cold day, and her breath was visible in the air. The strange feeling of being watched continued. But Kimberly was not one to frighten easily. The building came more clearly into view as she navigated her way through the bushes and overgrown grass. It was an old, abandoned cottage.

The cottage was situated behind the trees. It must have been at least a hundred years old, Kimberly estimated. It was tucked away behind the trees and almost hidden from view. As she got closer, she noticed the birds sitting in the trees.

Kimberly got closer to the cottage, still feeling someone or something was following her every step. The cottage was an old-fashioned building. The walls were of red brick, and the cement between the bricks had mostly fallen out. The windows were boarded, and the cottage had been vandalised. Vandals had written, 'Witches live here,' and all sorts of other graffiti, with spray paint. Most of it was on the boarding, but some was on the outside walls.

Kimberly went in through what was once a gate. She stood and looked at the cottage, imagining its beauty from many years ago. Her imagination painted a picture of a family sitting in a once-beautiful garden. Walking to the front door, Kimberly gave it a push. It moved a little. She pushed the door more firmly with her shoulder and felt it give slightly more. One final push, with all her weight this time.

The door moved enough for her to squeeze through. The cottage was eerie. On the walls were the remains of old-fashioned floral flock wallpaper. Lots of the paper had been torn away. Damp had made its way into the walls, through the plaster and had stained the old wallpaper. *It must have been decorated in the 1950s*, Kimberly thought.

As she walked into what was once the living room, a nervous tingling sensation travelled down her spine. Kimberly was not comfortable, but she would not allow herself to feel afraid. On the back of the door into the living room was a jacket, hanging there on a wire coat hanger. The jacket must have been there for years, and she could smell the dampness clinging to its fibres.

Kimberly noticed the fireplace. It was beautiful but dated, with a cast-iron front and wooden surround. There were metal rings that could swing over the top of the fire to heat pots for cooking. To her left, at the side of the fireplace, there was an old leather case. *No, not a case, a chest*, she corrected herself. Kimberly walked over to it and lifted the lid. Inside there was nothing more than an old and broken black-and-white picture frame. The frame held an image of a creepy-looking old woman, dressed all in black. The only contrast was a lacy white blouse, barely showing through at the neck. It was odd, but Kimberly thought she recognised the face.

The room had been visited by vandals, who had continued their spray painting on the walls inside the house. There were all sorts of things written, including a few words she had never seen before. She wondered what 'contúirt' and 'rith' meant[1]. The windows were now boarded, but ivy had made its way through from the outdoor walls. It was creeping through the top of the window. This gave the room an even eerier feeling – if that were possible.

Kimberly made her way into the kitchen. There was a shelf full of musty old books. She avoided touching them. There was an old-fashioned pantry with walls covered in mould. Lying on the floor of the pantry were some music sheets. Some kind of Scottish waltz that Kimberly had heard of but she didn't know the tune. A damp box was home to old comics and magazines, dated from 1952. She opened a couple of the wooden pantry cabinets, and inside were all sorts of trinkets. There were a couple of tins of old buttons. And she also found a Bible. Not moving the book, Kimberly lifted the front cover. The first page was blank, except for a simple message: 'To Florence, from Davina.'

Kimberly walked out of the kitchen and into what was once the bedroom. There was a broken old bed. It had been dismantled and what was left of it was leaning against the wall. Below the window, there was a heater that looked like it belonged in the dark ages. It had an enormous old plug with round pins.

---

[1] Contúirt' and 'rith' mean danger, run.

There was a phone next to the bed. It was one of those dial phones with a curly cable that connected the handset to the base. Kimberly heard a noise. She looked around but there was nothing to be seen. Only old, damp and peeling wallpaper caught her eye. There was another box on a table in the bedroom. This held all sorts of weird and wonderful stuff. Empty bottles of lemonade, an unopened corned beef tin and a can of metal polish.

Kimberly heard a noise again. This time, she sensed movement and she headed back towards the front door. There was definitely no-one in the house, she was sure of it. Her heart was beating faster than normal.

The living room was empty. The kitchen was empty. The bedroom was empty. The only room she hadn't been in was at the end of the corridor on the left. Walking along the corridor, Kimberly noticed a small puddle of water on the floor. As she looked up, she could see light through cracks in the ceiling and in the roof above. She pushed the door to the final room. Her expectation was that it would creak like in the horror movies, and she felt disappointment when it didn't. In the corner, there was some kind of workbench, but no sign of a bed. The windows in this room faced the back of the property and looked out onto an overgrown garden.

For some reason, the boarding had been taken off the window. A pane of glass had been broken. The room was quiet, but draughty and cold as the winter breeze blew through the broken glass. Kimberly could see her breath – more so than she had noticed previously.

The colours of the old paint in the room caught her eye. She noticed the brass light switches. But, more than anything else, Kimberly still felt she wasn't alone.

Looking out of the window, she sensed movement in the undergrowth. It seemed almost as if the grass was moving. But this grass was not green. It was a dark grey.

As Kimberly stood looking through the window, the giant mass of grey made its way along the outside walls. It then started to move through the window. Heading towards her was a massive carpet of grey mice. Thousands and thousands of them.

Kimberly was a woman who did not frighten easily. She would bow to no-one. If she ever felt fear, she would not show it. Today was different. Today, Kimberly felt fear like never before. As this giant mass of mice started to pour in through the window, her feet were rooted to the spot. For a moment she felt like she couldn't move, so great was her fear.

As the mice moved towards her feet, Kimberly finally broke free of her paralysis and made for the door. As she ran along the short corridor, she sensed the grey mass of mice behind her. Looking round, she saw them pouring through the gap in the ceiling a split second before they started to fall on her.

The front door had swung closed. Kimberly grabbed the handle, but it came away from the rotten door.

Fortunately, there was a small gap between the door and the frame. Kimberly pushed her fingers through and, with an almighty wrench, she pulled it open to let her free. Her heart was racing, and blood was pumping into her arms and legs. The mice were running up her trousers and over her shoulders. She could feel them in her hair.

Kimberly couldn't contain the scream that had built in her lungs. In the split second it took to squeeze through the door, she let it out. It was an almost-inhuman scream. Fear had completely taken hold of her. Mice fell from her as she wriggled through the gap.

The door burst open, and Kimberly was at least glad of the fresh air and bright skies. Her legs carried her along what was once a path towards the old gate. There were still mice clinging to her. In her mind, the plants were moving to block her way and make the escape more difficult. Her pace became faster, causing her to trip over a long stem from a bramble bush. The prickly thorns bit into her leg. She fell head-first, instinctively putting her hands out in front of her to break her fall. Her senses told her the grey carpet of mice continued to get ever closer.

Kimberly was so full of adrenaline that she couldn't feel pain from the scrapes on her hands and knees. The thorny bramble cuts in her legs were ignored. She got to her feet and ran like never before. Had there been a record to be broken for the fastest sprint over woodland, it would have been smashed. She ran and ran, until her legs could carry her no more and her lungs screamed for oxygen. Kimberly finally reached the path and slowed, filling her lungs with air. She looked behind her to make sure the mice had stopped following. Her hands checked every inch of her body for mice. All gone.

Taking a much slower pace, Kimberly got her breath back. As she walked, the fear turned to fury. A call was made to her site manager, Alex: the person who would be overseeing the building in the forest. She insisted he meet her at the entrance to Devilla, right away. Her walking pace increased again. As she marched along the path, her composure started to return. Kimberly regained her thoughts, and decisions were being made in her mind.

By the time she got to the car park at the entrance to the forest, her mind was made up. The whole forest would be cleared of all mice and other animals. As she stood at the entrance to the forest, waiting for Alex, her fury came out. She spoke aloud to herself, outlining her plans. Kimberly stood below the oak tree as she waited. Her words were spoken through clenched teeth. 'By the time I have finished with this development, there will not be one mouse left in that blasted forest. Horrible, skin crawling vermin that they are.'

Thirty minutes later, Alex arrived. He was a big guy, but his years in the building trade hadn't given him a slender, muscular structure. Unfortunately, the daily bacon and sausage rolls hadn't helped his waistline. But he was fine with it, and that's all that mattered to him. He jumped out of his truck and walked over to Kimberly.

'What's all the panic, Kimberly?' said Alex.

'This forest is infested with mice. Thousands and thousands of mice.'

Alex was a bit confused. 'Of course it has mice in it. It's a forest. All woods and forests have mice. And probably rats. And definitely insects, birds, foxes, deer. You name it, it will live in the forest. Once upon a time, there were probably even bears,' he laughed.

'I know it's full of wildlife. But I want the wildlife removed. I can cope with the birds but get rid of the vermin. Get rid of the blasted mice. I don't care if you have to poison or burn them out of their nests. Just get rid of the mice. Oh, and if you don't, I'll find some bears and feed you to them.'

Alex knew better then to argue with Kimberly when she was in this mood. He knew the development plans were yet to be passed. Things like mice and forest creatures would be dealt with when the time was right. Alex was one of the few people who could handle Kimberly. He had a knack of always managing to say the right thing to diffuse the situation.

Taking a calm but firm tone, he said, 'Kimberly. When we start work in the forest the noise of the machinery will terrify the wildlife. And, as we build the lodges, we will ensure there are no mice around anywhere.' Rubbing his tummy, he added with a wry smile, 'And I've already eaten all the bears.'

Of course, Alex knew removing mice from the forest wouldn't be possible. You can never stop mice. But he also knew what he had said was partly true. When work got underway, the creatures would get a huge wake-up. He knew that life would never be the same again for the inhabitants of the forest.

Both Kimberly and Alex jumped into their cars and drove off.

As senior tree and guardian of the forest, Roburt had heard everything. He knew the mice in the cottage were there deliberately. The mice were smart. They had been told about the development and they were there to terrify Kimberly Parker. They had been partly successful. What they hadn't predicted was the revenge she would seek on the forest wildlife as a result. The situation had become a whole lot worse.

Back at the cottage, the mice were now all gone. A lone black cat with a stump for a tail sat on the windowsill of the back room. It was enjoying the warmth of the sunshine through the remaining glass. It had enjoyed the entertainment in the cottage today.

# Chapter 13

## Roburt

Roburt knew the situation wasn't looking good for the forest. He had heard everything Kimberly had to say, and he knew she was furious. He knew when the development of the forest got underway, it would be catastrophic. Not only for him, but for the other trees, the plants and the wildlife.

Through the woodland internet, Roburt contacted Sylvester and repeated everything he had heard. They agreed the forest would need to discuss this latest development. Sylvester arranged another meeting – all senior trees and animals. He sent a message out to the owls, rabbits and mice. He called on the crows and the foxes. He asked for the squirrels and the dragonflies and, of course, the otters, who would talk to the fish. Bonnie would need to attend the meeting, and it would need to happen sooner than anyone had expected.

Sylvester sent Chaff, the little chaffinch, to seek out Daley the fox, asking him to come over right away. Daley was a larger-than-average fox and was as cunning as you would expect. He had a home and family in the middle of the forest. When Daley got the message, he knew it must be urgent, even before Chaff spoke. She relayed the information to him in her usual, high-pitched and excitable fashion. There were few gaps between her words.

'DaleyDaleyDaleyyoumustcomequick. Sylvesterneedstotalktoyouabouttheforest. Hesaysitsveryurgent. GoquickDaleygoquick.'

Daley set off right away. His home wasn't far from Sylvester, and he was there within fifteen minutes. Sylvester wasted no time telling Daley the news. He was sent to Bonnie's house with a message. He had to get her to meet with Sylvester and the forest creatures urgently.

He knew that getting Bonnie's attention may not be easy. But he also knew that he could speak to David. All he had to do was wait for the right moment when a door or window was open, or for Bonnie to come out of the house.

It was late afternoon, and the winter sun was already setting. Bonnie ventured out of her house to give David a quick walk before tea. It wouldn't be a long walk, as he had already been out twice earlier in the day. She made her way up the lane and up to the gate, where she stood for a few minutes while David did his doggy business.

As Bonnie walked through the gate, David shot off, intent on sniffing everything for the twenty-seventh time that day. It was then that Bonnie heard another voice.

The fox introduced himself. 'Hello, Bonnie.'

This took Bonnie a bit by surprise. She was getting used to conversations with David and, of course, Iccuat the owl. But she wasn't prepared for new creatures in the forest coming to her for a chat.

'My name is Daley. We all know you in the forest now, Bonnie. We know you can hear us, and we know you can talk to us. We know that something terrible is going to happen soon. We know the plans for the holiday lodges are going to go ahead and it's going to be devastating for us all in the forest. We need you to come and see us early tomorrow.' There was a slight pause, then Daley added, 'Meet next to Sylvester Pine.'

Bonnie looked at the fox, as he sat there telling her this information. So much had happened in the past couple of days, and she still couldn't believe it.

'Why is it so urgent now? What's happened?'

'The mice tried to scare the bad woman Kimberly away. She was in the old cottage and all the mice from the forest ran into it. There were thousands of them, and Kimberly was terrified. But her anger kicked in and she's not one for backing down. She's going to do whatever it takes to kill the mice and any other forest creatures that get in her way.

'And the thing is, Bonnie, when they clear away so many trees to build their new homes, I'll be left homeless too. And not just me. There are all sorts of other creatures with homes in the forest. And any trees that are cut down will mean hundreds of us losing our homes.'

David had arrived on the scene. It was that strange David, who was much calmer. More composed. His tail was at level one.

'Hiya, David,' said Daley.

'Hiya, Daley,' said David.

'You two know each other?'

'We do,' said David. 'I know lots of different creatures in the forest. And sometimes we talk, sometimes we don't. It's just that you have never heard us speak before now. Anyway, what's happening?'

Daley repeated the story to David. He explained that the senior animals in the forest would all be at the meeting. And he explained how important it was. They arranged to be there the following morning. As they left Daley, David shot off to the nearest tree, peed on it and had a good sniff of a nearby bush. His tail was at level five by this time.

No-one had noticed, but a pair of orange eyes was watching them as they spoke and exchanged their plans. These were sharp eyes, and they could see a long way into the distance. And the creature had ears that could hear conversations from a long way away. Despite being a cat, it was able to understand every word spoken. Not just the animal words, but the human ones too. It knew that soon it would need to reveal itself to its rightful master.

Early on the Monday morning, it was still dark. But the moon was bright and – once your eyes adjusted – it was easy to see. Bonnie wasn't sure where Sylvester Pine was, as he wasn't near the other tree she had 'met.' But David said he knew where the tree was and he led the way into the forest.

Bonnie had told her mum she was awake early and wanted to get out with David for some fresh air before school. She wasn't happy about lying to her mum, saying she wouldn't go into the forest when it was dark. But there was little choice. It was a bitterly cold morning. Her pace was brisk which helped to get some heat flowing around her body

The girl and her dog chatted, with David speaking in a way only Bonnie could understand. To her relief, none of the other animals had popped over. There was only so much animal-to-human conversation one girl could take in a day.

Her thoughts had been premature, though.

'Good morrrning Bonnie. Thank you forrr helping us.' It was a deep, official-sounding voice. It sounded posh. Or 'suave', as Bonnie's granny would say. She imagined a James-Bond-kind of creature, with dinner jacket and bow tie. She also thought it had a bit of an unusual way of pronouncing some of the words. With some extra 'r's in them. Then she spotted it flying alongside her. A golden-ringed dragonfly. She happened to know this, as the bright yellow circles around the body had once terrified a six-year-old Bonnie into thinking one of its relatives was a giant wasp.

'My name is Rrrodger.' He spoke proudly. 'You prrrobably don't know this, but I'm a golden-rrringed drrragonfly. I'm one of the larrrgest species of dragonfly, and the larrrgest in the forrrest.

'You know a lot about yourself,' said Bonnie.

'Therrre arrre lots of naturrre walks. Lots of experrrts. Teachers walking with childrrren. All telling them about the differrrent crrreatures in the forrrest. I just sit and listen. I'm not norrrmally arrround at this time of yearrr, but I've eaten a magical mixturrre of rrrowan and holly berrries. That keeps me alive while the forrrest needs me.'

*The way he rolls his 'r's is not in any way distracting*, thought Bonnie. She repeated every sentence in her head, silently speaking it without the extra consonants.

'It's nice to meet you, Rodger,' she said, being careful not to add any extra 'r's in his name. 'Are you joining us for the journey?'

'I shall be delighted to accompany you and David.'

'Hiya Rrrrrrrrrrrodger.'

'Good morning, David. No need to emphasise the way I pronounce my "r"s, thank you.'

'Sorrrrrrrry,' smirked David.

Bonnie was thinking through what she had just seen. A smirking David making jokes at Rodger's expense, and a dragonfly that had gone into a bit of a huff.

At first light, Daley the fox joined Bonnie, David and Rodger. He walked the last couple of minutes with them until they all came face to face with Sylvester.

Bonnie could only talk to the animals and not the trees. But David knew exactly what was being said and would translate for her. She noticed that Sylvester was indeed a mighty tree. Not the biggest in the forest, but he was certainly imposing. She had never noticed a tree with a 'presence' before.

Iccuat was already there and introduced Bonnie to the others from the forest. Bonnie was expecting to meet creatures of great stature, such as deer or badgers.

The first creature she met was Beezy, one of the few smart rabbits. Typically, rabbits are a bit confused. They don't know which way to run, or where to go. They are forever asking directions and can never remember where they live. If you have ever shone a light at a rabbit, you will know that one of two things happens. They are either frozen to the spot, or they run away from it in a straight line. But Beezy was a little bit different. She was smarter. You could tell this was a rabbit with authority. And she was there, ready to help.

Next came a mouse. Bonnie would have imagined a small creature like a mouse to have a matching voice. But no. At least, not this mouse. This mouse had the deepest voice Bonnie had ever heard, even deeper than Rodger the dragonfly.

'Hello Bonnie,' said the mouse. 'My name is Burp.'

Bonnie could have sworn she heard chuckling in the forest.

'And, yes,' said Burp, in a fed-up tone, as if he had heard all this before, 'They all find it *hilarious* that my name is Burp. It means 'warrior' in our language. But everyone else knows it means something different when talking to humans.'

'It's lovely to meet you, Burp.'

Once again, Bonnie thought she heard laughter in the distance.

Next, Bonnie was introduced to Troben the crow. Along with Iccuat the owl, she was one of the senior birds. She was frank and forthright. Her colouring was described as black. But, if you looked closely, it was almost like a reflective blue colour. Bonnie thought it was beautiful.

Troben said everything as she saw it. Bonnie wondered if she was hearing properly … did Troben repeat the last one or two words of every sentence? Was Bonnie imagining that? Was that some side-effect of translating animal to human?

Some of the other forest creatures thought Troben could be rude, but that was her way. She meant no harm, but sometimes her manner could upset the other animals.

'Hello Bonnie,' said Troben. 'We are glad you are here to help us help us.'

Now that all the animals were gathered, Bonnie and David sat quietly. Sylvester called the meeting to order. It was a bit strange for Bonnie, as she could see all the animals listening to Sylvester, but she couldn't hear anything.

Sylvester continued to tell the creatures of the forest what the trees already knew. Every so often, he would stop and allow David to tell Bonnie what had been said.

It was clear that, as the human among the group, Bonnie was best placed to help the forest. She told them this had been in her thoughts non-stop, before she began to share her plans. Bonnie told everyone she would go to the meeting arranged by Firthshire Council. It would be here that the town's inhabitants would see the plans for the forest. Her mum and other people in the community would help her prepare. They would all object to the development plans and, if enough people objected, it would slow or stop the work. Bonnie had read all about the plans on the council website. Any objections to the development were to be sent by the following weekend. She said she would research everything that was going to be done in the forest. Bonnie had also found out that there were untrue statements in the plans. For one, many more animals and plants would die than the developers claimed. And the lodges were made of plastic containing illegal chemicals. She would ask about this at the meeting.

Her other plan would be to try and get help from her school.

Through David, Sylvester asked if she thought that would be enough.

Bonnie was honest and said she was worried.

'There's a lot to do, and I'll have to fit it in around my schoolwork. But I'll do everything I can to help.'

Bonnie had found out that the meeting to approve the development of the forest was only three weeks away. There had been a gap in the council diary and the slot for approval of the forest development had been brought forward.

That meant she had even less time to get support and put her plans into action. There was no way this could be done without getting help from her mum.

Bonnie asked if it would be possible for another human to be given the power to talk with the animals.

'Only once in a tree's lifetime is a human granted the ability to talk to the animals. And *you* are the one we have chosen, Bonnie,' said Sylvester.

# Chapter 14

# Video

Bonnie lived in a small ex-council property. It was in a long line with fourteen other houses, which all looked pretty much the same. Bonnie and her mum looked after the property. The garden was neat and tidy, although – like all gardens – it had taken on that rather drab winter appearance. The property was always well kept. Clean windows, nice bright front door, with polished brass handle and numbers.

As you walked into Bonnie's home you would remark that it was tastefully, if a little plainly, decorated. In the front room, there was a gas fire and a leather suite that was only a couple of years old but was already starting to look a bit tired. That annoyed Misty a little, as it still had about another year of payments on interest-free credit.

The kitchen had been renewed about nine or ten years previously but still looked modern. There was a little table, where Bonnie and her mum would sit to eat their meals. Upstairs there were two bedrooms, and of course David had his own comfy bed in Bonnie's room.

Bonnie loved her home. It wasn't as big as the homes many of her friends lived in, but she was happy there. Her mum worked hard to keep the house nice and give them a happy place to live.

Since that meeting in the forest, the next two weeks had gone by in a blur. Bonnie and Misty, along with a few others, had lodged their objections to the development. Bonnie had read about the development and researched all about the plans. She had also learned more about the lies that had been told. When you can talk to animals, it's amazing what you can find out. A well-positioned chaffinch or crow can learn so much about what's going on. Never use a pigeon though; they are so forgetful.

Bonnie learned about the materials to be used for the development. They were the furthest thing from green you could imagine. There would be no 'green sensitivity,' as it was described in the plans. The big machines would rip through the forest in record time.

The developers had promised that animals would be moved, and that great care would be taken. This was a lie. Bonnie learned about the bribes that had taken place. These bribes were either to approve things or to turn a blind eye. She heard how many different creatures would be wiped out, and about the damage this would cause to the animals. The forest inhabitants got along with one another. Of course, some of them would eat one another.

That's just the way it is. But if you take away one kind of creature, others will lose a food source. This was a crisis for Devilla Forest.

Her mother said to Bonnie, 'You've become a right little David Attenborough!' Bonnie had learned so much in such a short space of time about how the forest worked. Nature was so finely balanced, and everyone needed everyone else.

It took many late nights, but Bonnie pulled together a plan. It was all written out on her laptop. She pulled together pictures and stories of the great things in the forest. Many of these would be bulldozed, cut down or left to die out.

After school one evening, Bonnie was halfway through pulling her plans together when Misty called her into the kitchen.

'You know how I worked a bit of overtime in the lead-up to Christmas? And you know how your phone got cracked a few weeks before? Well, I've got a treat for you.' Misty then presented Bonnie with a new phone, making her one happy twelve-year-old. She thanked her mum and gave her a big 'squeeze your ribs' type hug. Their relationship had become so much better over the past few weeks. As they stood in the kitchen, Bonnie looked at her mum.

'I have something important I need to tell you about the forest.'

Bonnie realised this was the perfect opportunity to tell her mum about everything … well, *almost* everything … that was going to happen. But she would leave out the bit about talking to animals. She told her mum exactly what would happen if the forest was allowed to be developed into a holiday park. Explaining all about her research, Bonnie talked about the impact on the wildlife. She told her mum that what was on the plans was not exactly the truth. Explaining *how* she knew would just have to wait. 'More trees will be cut down than what they have said in the plans. There'll be so much devastation, harming all the animals and creatures that live in the forest.'

Misty looked through all the details that her daughter had pulled together on her laptop. There were updates on social media and a well-written speech that Bonnie planned to give to her school. She told her mum she was planning to go along to the council meeting, and asked her to come too. And then, Bonnie happened to mention that the woman behind the development was Rachel's mother – Kimberly Parker.

Misty told Bonnie how proud she was of her. 'The work you have done, the plans, they're all amazing. Your detail is absolutely incredible. I will help you with this every step of the way, Bonnie. And … one other thing you should know. The person who stole your father from me, then dumped him, was the same Kimberly Parker.'

This statement hit Bonnie like a sledgehammer. The woman trying to rip the heart out of the forest was the same woman who had ripped the heart out of her mother? This was another reason why their plans had to succeed. At this moment, Bonnie wasn't sure whether she wanted to cheer or cry. But, whatever she was feeling, it added to her determination to win this fight.

Misty resolved to do everything she could to help her daughter save the forest. 'If that woman has anything to do with it, everything about this plan will be lies and deceit. That woman is the biggest lying cheat I've ever met.'

Misty helped Bonnie make her school presentation as good as it could be. But she also said there were some things that needed to come out. 'You can't simply accuse someone of lying without proof,' she said. The plans were finalised. The next step was to arrange to go to the school for a meeting with the head teacher.

That evening, Bonnie started to share some of the beautiful things she had learned about the forest. Misty watched videos her daughter had made of the forest, which showed, in detail, the beautiful creatures that lived there. She was amazed at how close the creatures let Bonnie get.

There were videos with the owls, and one where Bonnie looked like she was having a chat with some crows. And there was also a video of her with rabbits, although they just sat there looking bewildered.

It was on this video that Bonnie had added her own voice, pretending to be the voice of the rabbits. What no-one could know, of course, is that Bonnie was merely repeating the words the rabbits had spoken. She said what they said, and spoke how they spoke. The end result was a funny video of six confused rabbits. None of them knew what was going on with anything. It was only yesterday that Bonnie had posted it on *TikTok* and within a few hours there had been over 50,000 views.

The date of the meeting with the school was set. Bonnie's plan was in place. The only thing they lacked was some evidence of the bribes.

As the interest in Bonnie's video started to grow, so did local concerns about the development. Word had started to spread about the damage it would do to the forest. Bonnie and her mum were seen as the two people fighting against the changes.

Word got back to Kimberly that there was growing unrest about the holiday park. And it was even worse when she learned who was behind it. Watching the video, Kimberly stood. Her eyebrows furrowed and she spoke with a menacing hiss. 'Do not cross me!' she said out loud, through clenched teeth.

# Chapter 15

# Riverdance

A couple of nights later, Misty's doorbell rang. She opened the front door, and who was standing there but Kimberly Parker!

Kimberly's opening line was polite and engaging, as always. 'I hear you're against our development in the forest?'

Misty stared at Kimberly. 'Yes, I am. I've never been more against anything in my life than this development of yours. You think you can stroll over here and just do what you want. But you have always done that, haven't you, Kimberly? You just see something and want it. Then you do whatever you choose to take it. So yes, I am against what you're doing. I'm one hundred per cent against what you're doing, Kimberly. Because you are nothing but self-centred, arrogant and completely unlikable.'

Kimberly stood on the doorstep, in an elegant dress and what was clearly an expensive coat. Misty stood in her hall, gripping the handle of her front door and causing her knuckles to turn white. Her outfit was gym leggings and a warm, oversized woolly jumper. The pair stared at one another, then Kimberly said, 'Look, I'm sorry. I could have started that conversation a bit better. And, for what it's worth now, I'm also sorry about your husband. I know you loved him. And I know I took him because I could. But things have changed, and feelings have moved on. I regret what I did all these years ago, and I apologise. There's no point in lying, I know I can be horrible. Always was, always will be. But this development in the forest will be good for the area. Yes, also good for *me*. But there are lots of livelihoods depending on this being approved.'

Misty was taken aback. At least Kimberly had apologised, but there was no conviction that any of her words were genuine – apart from admitting to being permanently horrible of course. But 'differences can't be resolved without conversation' is what she always said to Bonnie.

Misty knew that regret may follow her next action, but she invited Kimberly into her home. Walking through to the living room, Misty apologised that it was a little untidy. 'Would you like tea or a coffee?' she asked, more out of something to say than politeness.

'Yes please, coffee. Is it freshly brewed or instant?'

'Instant.'

'Just strong and black then, please. Two spoons of coffee.'

Kimberly was never great at small talk, but she made her best effort. 'Do you like it here? In Copsehead, I mean? Is this a nice part to stay in?'

Misty paused for a moment. Was this a polite question to get some chat going, or a loaded question aimed at belittling her?

'Yes. This has been my home for a few years now. It's the only home that Bonnie knows. We're both happy here.' There was a moment of silence, then she added, 'and it's close to the forest which Bonnie loves.'

Kimberly then spoke. 'Misty, if I may ask, a little more politely this time, why are you so opposed to the forest development? It's going to bring so much employment to the area, and it's going to be good for Scotland.'

'It may well be good for the area, Kim, but …'

'Sorry: it's Kimberly. Not Kim.'

'It may well be good for the area, *Kimberly*, but that's not everything. The forest is a beautiful spot, and it gives so much enjoyment to so many people. And, more than that, Kimberly, you must think of the animals … and the trees … and all the wildlife that lives in the forest. It's a home to them. And you're just going to rip that apart to build lodges?'

Kimberly tried to justify this. She explained a little more about her plans. She tried to win Misty around to her argument but could see it wasn't working.

Misty hated the way that Kimberly talked down to her. Every sentence was so patronising. Any time that she had been in her company, Kimberly had talked down to anyone and everyone. Misty continued, 'I believe that there are certain things in your plans that are untrue. And I reckon that you may have … what shall we say … *encouraged* some of those involved to be on your side. The problem is, of course, Kimberly, I can't prove it. Yet.'

Kimberly's face was like thunder. This had been a lifelong trait. She never could hide her emotions. *How could this even be suspected?* she thought. Kimberly made a mental note to speak with everyone involved to make sure no-one was blabbing.

'There are two ways this can go, Misty. One, you can go with my plans. Or two, you can fight them. If you choose option one, let's just say things will be nice and easy in your life. Things may even get a little bit better. If, however, you choose option two, I'm not sure what will happen next. But I do know the lodges will still be built. And your precious trees and animals will just have to step aside. And I also know that some of the plans may change. For example, the road outside your home has perfect access to the forest. I was looking for another road in. Maybe I'll make it a one-way system. All the traffic goes in the main entrance, and when it leaves, it comes along this road. Yes, I think that may be a good idea. It would be difficult, I guess, to live in a home that had traffic thundering by each day.'

Kimberly continued. 'And, heaven forbid we must buy some of the land nearby with a compulsory purchase. Some residents may need to be moved to local rented property. But, you know, you can't stand in the way of progress.' Kimberly smiled. 'I'm sure it won't come to that, Misty, but it's probably worth thinking carefully about your next steps.'

Bonnie had been listening to this from outside the door. To say she was furious was an understatement. Tears were welling behind her eyes. She now understood why Rachel was such an utter horror with a mother like that.

Then, from nowhere, David arrived. He walked into the living room and made his way over to Misty. She put her hand on his head and stroked him, gently tickling him below his ear.

David stared at Kimberly. Her attention was caught by the dog's eyes. They were hypnotic. She felt that she couldn't break away from his gaze. Were the eyes different colours, she wondered? Yes, they were. One brown, one blue. They were beautiful.

David continued to stare. He was getting ready to use superpower #2.

There was silence in the room for what felt like ages, but it was only a few seconds. Misty could see that David was 'applying the eyes'. She knew this could result in people becoming all gooey-eyed and offering him treats. But no-one was ready for what happened next.

Kimberly held David's gaze. There wasn't any other choice for her. David was working out what he would do first. *Let's have some fun with her speech*, he thought.

Kimberly started to speak, and the most ridiculous nonsense came out of her mouth. None of the words would come out right.

'Well, I've said my piece. That's something for you to think about.' At least, that's what she meant to say. But the words spoken were: '*Sell I've wed my piece. Thinkilus something for a tinkle twout.*'

Bonnie had now arrived in the room and sat down next to her mum. They both looked at Kimberly, wondering what on earth she had just said. Come to think of it, Kimberly was also wondering what words had just come out of her mouth.

'Did you put something in that coffee?' Or, as she said: '*Wild someput foffee come dingwat.*'

She tried again; '*I fluffi fingdoowa. Grumpla dufoosh dwee dwee.*'

Kimberly could *think* the right words, and her head was as clear as could be. But she was unable to say anything properly. David decided it was time to apply more eyes.

'*Shtinkin frubben glumps do fasa wawa.*' Or, 'Stop that dog staring at me,' she said.

Kimberly stood. Her legs felt an energy she had never experienced before. Her hands were on her hips. She shouted, '*Drivver shoogle, drivver shoogle.*' She meant to say 'Riverdance.'

Then she started to dance uncontrollably. Now, you must know that Kimberly was not a dancer. Never had been, never will be. But that day, her legs thought they were the best dancing legs that have ever been seen. Her legs thought they were about to give a solo show on stage at the Edinburgh Playhouse.

Her body was perfectly straight. Her hands had moved to her hips and were still by the side of her body. Her head was motionless. Kimberly's gaze made her look like she was in some kind of hypnotic trance. Her eyes were focused, staring at something beyond the walls of the living room. But it was her legs that were a sight to behold. For half a minute, Kimberly danced on the spot. She performed her own routine of Riverdance, making it up entirely on the spot. As she danced, she shouted at the top of her voice '*Drivver shoogle! Drivver shoogle!*'

David got up and left the room. It had been an excellent example of superpower #2, he thought to himself. 'My work is done here, for now,' he said to Bonnie, still watching in utter bewilderment. Kimberly stopped dancing and shouting. *She's back in the room*, thought David, as he walked away with what looked like a smirk on his face.

Kimberly had now broken free from David's hypnotic stare. She had two main expressions in life: stony cold or furious. But now, her expression was one of embarrassment. Her face, often red with anger, was now a puce colour. For once, Kimberly was speechless. Of course, neither Misty nor Bonnie knew about David's superpowers. So, they were also somewhat bewildered about what had gone on. They, too were embarrassed on Kimberly's behalf. The realisation of what had happened hit home. Kimberly grabbed her bag and said she must go. There were no goodbyes, no farewells and definitely no further pleasantries exchanged.

Kimberly walked out the front door, and seconds later Misty closed it behind her. She went back through into the living room, joined by Bonnie and David.

'What just happened there? I've never seen anything like it.'

David spoke to Bonnie. 'You need to tell her we can speak. Tell her you can talk to the animals and tell her what we know. And then I'll tell you about my superpowers and explain what happened.'

'Mum, I think I can explain this. But you are going to think I'm as crazy as that woman.'

'Go on,' said Misty.

'The day I was late home – the day I broke my phone – I was lost in the forest. I had some kind of encounter with a tree. I know it sounds silly, but the tree grabbed my hand. And, since then, I've been able to talk to the animals. I can speak to David. I speak to foxes and owls and all sorts.'

Misty wasn't sure what to make of this. She narrowed her eyes as she listened to Bonnie.

'David speaks to me all the time now. He's always been able to understand what we have been saying and doing. And it turns out that the other animals can as well – if they're interested.'

'You're telling me you can talk to David?'

'Yes.'

Misty was worried her daughter had become too involved in saving the forest. Now she was thinking that she could talk to animals, like some modern-day Dr Dolittle? This worried Misty greatly, so she tried to think of a simple question to test this. 'Before Kimberly arrived, I was in the kitchen with David. What book was I looking at?'

David made a few doggie sounds, which Bonnie understood. 'He says you were reading Jamie Oliver's 15-minute meals.'

David spoke some more to Bonnie. 'Or, as you muttered under your breath: "Jamie's two hour and fifteen-minute meals, more like. Who could cook any of this in fifteen minutes? And then you swore about him.'

Now it was Misty's turn to be speechless. 'I need a minute,' she said. 'I don't know what to make of all this.'

David said to Bonnie, 'You need to tell her we're able to hear anything that Kimberly says. And you need to tell her that I can talk to the animals like you. Let her know I can get people to do odd things. Things like you have just seen. Oh, and remember when you were at Granny Lilly's house, when I cleared the room? That's one of my other superpowers.'

'Mum, there's a little bit more, but it's all funny. David can talk to the other animals too, and it was him that made Kimberly do all that weird stuff. You know when we say he 'applies the eyes'? He's making people do stuff. And, that day at Granny Lilly's? He did that deliberately.'

Misty was starting to think clearly again. Still a little unsure of these new revelations, she said, 'We need to make sure this development doesn't go ahead, and that woman is brought back down to earth. If you really *can* speak with the animals, we need to get them to help us, Bonnie. And we need to think about how we do this. I can't get my head around how and why all of this has happened. But, if you can talk to the animals, and the animals can understand what is being said, then we need to add this to our plan. And fast.'

Bonnie made some tea. And she topped up David's water bowl and gave him a couple of treats. He had earned them. Bonnie and her mum sat at the kitchen table. David sat on the floor but was keen to be part of the discussion about to take place.

Misty started. 'First up, we've done lots of work. We – or *you*, Bonnie – have put together what we know about the forest plans. And you're going to share this with the school. But that's not going to be enough. You have quite a social media following with your videos, but again, that's not enough. And there is a council meeting shortly where we can make a nuisance of ourselves. But I still don't know if that is going to be enough to stop this happening. What we need is *proof*. Proof that Kimberly has bribed the powers that be into approving this work. So, the question is: how do we get proof?

'Oh, and who else can we get to help? Your friends? Granny? We need to get a team together, Bonnie, and we need it to happen quickly.'

Misty looked out of her front window as she spotted movement outside. Kimberly had been gone for five or ten minutes but was still not inside her car. The effects of the dance routine hadn't worn off yet, and every time she tried to get into her car, her legs would make an involuntary movement. It was entertaining to watch, and Bonnie wished she had been able to film Kimberly's visit.

As Misty and Bonnie watched, they fell into hysterics over her antics.

# Chapter 16

# Eyes

Until this point, the plan to stop work in the forest had been nothing more than 'OK'. But, following the events of Kimberly's visit, Bonnie and Misty's plan had become a whole lot better. Misty had taken some notes as they spoke, and she read aloud what she had written.

'One: get more people involved. Bonnie, speak to your friends Molly, Lucy and Jo. I'll get a couple of friends over, and hopefully a work colleague or two. And I'll give Granny a call and get her over. There's only one thing in this world more terrifying than me being angry. And that's Granny being angry.' Misty smiled and added, 'She may be small, but she's fierce.' Bonnie had heard this a hundred times before, but they both still laughed.

Misty continued to summarise the plan. 'Two: the animals. Get the birds, dragonflies or any creature that can understand you. Send them to all the places the developers meet. Tell them to find out where Kimberly does her talking and listen in. Find out who she talks to, follow them if necessary. And get more and more animals listening in. Find out who the decision-makers are and listen in on their conversations.

'Three: keep going with the videos. You can make one on the way to school, and another on the way back. Get them uploaded, and let's keep the interest going. Get your friends to like and share every post.

'Four: we need the school onside. They can help us because they are a louder voice. But they can't get involved in accusations. So, we need to keep it simple with the school.

'Five: the council meeting is a big one. We need evidence to prove there are bribes taking place. But we can't go shouting accusations – proof or no proof – at the council meeting. We need to make any objection at the meeting an emotional plea. We need to talk about the animals and the forest, and the damage the development will do. We need to get the people in the area onside.

'Six: we need evidence, and we need it quickly. As soon we have some kind of proof, then we can go to the authorities. When the animals think they have something, they need to let us know. Until then, we're not going to change anything.'

So, that was it, the plan. Bonnie went out into the garden and saw Daley the fox sitting patiently. She told him to relay the plan back to Sylvester. 'We need to have some ears listening to every conversation. We need to know what is happening, and fast.'

That evening, Bonnie's friends Molly, Lucy and Jo came round to the house. Of course, Misty was there, and so were two of her closest friends, Peter and Tracy. They knew one another from work but the three of them had been close for many years. And then Granny arrived. She was stern, ready for battle and carrying two jars of freshly made strawberry jam.

Bonnie told the assembled gang that they needed their help. The changes to the forest were explained, with details of how they would be less than green. And details of how they thought people in power were being 'encouraged' to agree to them. David sat peacefully among the group as they discussed what was happening. There was agreement not to share the 'animal talking' ability right now. Maybe some other time.

Not surprisingly, those in the room hadn't been aware of everything that was going on. There were so many other things happening in the world and in their lives. Something on their doorstep hadn't fully caught their attention. Of course, most of them had seen and laughed at Bonnie's videos. But nothing more than that.

They all agreed they would try and get as much support as they could to come along to the council meeting. The date was set for that Friday. It would be 'strength in numbers'.

Misty said, 'When we go to this meeting, we'll also try to get as many of the school pupils as possible along. If the school supports what we are doing, of course.'

Bonnie also explained how they would try to get evidence. But, because she couldn't mention having help from the animals, this plan may have sounded a bit weak to everyone.

The meeting with the school went well. The head teacher listened to everything that was being said. He was impressed with the work that Bonnie had put into her plan. He suggested that, the following morning, Bonnie should speak to the school at assembly. He said, 'This is a great thing you are doing, Bonnie, and I'm sure you'll have the support of the full school. You can have five minutes, so use the time wisely. Speak to Mrs Bell in English, and she'll help you. Think about what you're going to say, and practice saying it.

'Try to convince them this development is not going to be good for the community. Explain how it will destroy wildlife. Hopefully that will help you. Make sure you tell them they can help by joining the council meeting on Friday night. I'll speak to the teachers as well to encourage them to come along with their families. You'll probably only get the ones that live locally, but better some than none.'

After the meeting with the head teacher, Bonnie and her mum felt that it had gone well. This was as much as they could ask from the school. Even if they got fifty pupils along with their parents, that could be a hundred and fifty people at the meeting. Bonnie wrote down what she would say the following morning, at assembly. She wanted to make sure everything was as clear as possible.

Early next morning, as David was being taken out for a quick walk, Daley was waiting for them.

'Good news,' he said. 'I've been dying to tell you. We've got eyes everywhere. The whole area has been covered with all sorts of animals and creatures looking out for Kimberly. Where she goes, we're there. Iccuat followed her from her home to her office. She had a meeting with what looked like work people. They were all wearing boots and shiny yellow jackets. They sat in an office, and Troben the crow sat outside the window. She heard every word. As soon as Firthshire Council approve the plans, they are going to start work. The machines are booked and ready to be delivered, and they are going to put temporary offices at the entrance to the forest. It will be closed to the public soon after that.

'When all the people had finished talking, Kimberly went back home and Iccuat followed her. One of the dragonflies stuck herself to the corner of her window and listened. Only a few minutes after she arrived back, people in posh clothes turned up. There were four of them. They told her that everything was in place, and they expected no issues. There had been a few objections to the plans, but nothing they couldn't handle.

'They need the meeting to go well on Friday night. If it does, and everything is approved by the council, payments will be made at the weekend. They must meet somewhere secret, but no-one knows where that will be yet. They get half the payment when the plans are approved, and the other half when the work is finished.'

'That's fantastic work,' said Bonnie. 'You have done such an amazing job.' She then told Daley about everything they had done. Bonnie explained about her forthcoming talk to the school. She also spoke about getting lots of people along to the meeting on Friday night. But the conversation had to be cut short. 'I have to go now,' she said to Daley. 'I can't be late for school.'

None of them noticed the black cat that sat by the wall. It simply sat there, watching and listening.

# Chapter 17

## Stare

Bonnie stood in front of the whole school. Assembly was normally well behaved, and today was no different. Bonnie had watched videos of the best way to speak to an audience and had been coached a little by Mrs Bell. This would be her first time speaking to such a large group of people – many of whom she knew. The walk from the chair at the side of the stage to the microphone was a long one. She worried that her legs would give way. But they didn't. Bonnie stood on the stage and spoke to the entire school – pupils and teachers.

'Hello. Many of you already know me, but for those that don't, my name is Bonnie Banks. I'm going to talk to you today about the work due to take place in Devilla Forest. Large parts of the forest are going to be destroyed. And I need your help to prevent this from happening.' Bonnie was feeling confident now. She could no longer see individual faces in the crowd, which made her glad. The last thing she needed was to be looking into the eyes of Rachel Parker.

Bonnie continued. 'To build over two hundred lodges, twenty-four miles of roads will be cut through the forest. And to build twenty-four miles of roads, they will have to destroy hundreds of trees. And, of course, the lodges will need space. That will mean the death of another few hundred trees.' Bonnie paused and looked at her notes. She made eye contact with her audience, as Mrs Bell had told her to do.

'To put in electricity and water to all the lodges, they're going to have to dig up even more miles of forest. And to do this, they're going to have to clear even more trees. This means more wildlife killed or displaced.' Bonnie delivered this point in a firm manner, sounding like a natural speaker. Her confidence continued to increase.

Once again, Bonnie paused before she moved on to the next part of her speech. She had tried to make this part emotional.

'I have walked through the forest many times. We've all been there with our parents and grandparents, and we have enjoyed the forest for such a long time. We have enjoyed walks in all weathers.' Bonnie looked up at just the wrong moment. Her eyes caught Rachel staring at her. Her fists were clenched, and her mouth silently spoke the words, 'You're dead.' But instead of fear, this instilled even more confidence in Bonnie. Her tone became more assured.

'Yes, some of the forest will still exist, but it will be given over to holiday homes and to people coming to the area. Cars will drive through the forest. Barbecues will be lit. Tarmac paths will be created. It's for you to decide whether that will be better or worse.

'Tomorrow night, there's a meeting in the hall with the council. At that meeting, the plans for the development will be proposed and possibly approved. We've had plenty of time to object, but there have been few objections. There's not been enough interest in what's going on. We've not been interested enough in our local area.' Bonnie put a great deal of emphasis into that point.

'Tomorrow night is your last chance to make your voice heard. If you don't want this development to go ahead, please come along tomorrow night. Make your feelings known. Bring your mum or dad. Or, even better, bring your mum and your dad and your brother and your sister and your granny and your grandad.

'But, whoever you bring, please come along and show them you don't want the forest to die.'

Bonnie received fantastic applause from her classmates. And she spotted Rachel Parker again, sitting there staring with a look that could kill, just like her mother Kimberly.

Bonnie managed to avoid Rachel for the rest of the day. They were in different classes, so that was a relief. She received a few 'well done' comments from other pupils, both younger and older than her, over the rest of the day. Even more people were viewing her 'Forest News' updates on social media. The view count, likes and shares continued to rise. She was glad she had done so much work videoing herself in the forest. The funnier videos with the voice-overs were the most popular, rather than the more serious ones, but that didn't matter if it got people interested in what was happening. And all the better if it got them engaged in doing something about it.

Bonnie's first class of the day was English. This was one of her favourite classes, and it was Mrs Bell who made them so enjoyable. Just as the class was about to start, one of the school secretaries came into the classroom with a message for Mrs Bell. The head teacher wanted to see Bonnie. Hoping there was nothing wrong, she walked through the school to the headmaster's office. The secretary then asked a nervous Bonnie to go through into the office. The head teacher, who was always welcoming and had a good relationship with his pupils, invited Bonnie to take a seat.

'Well done on your talk to the school this morning, Bonnie. You did yourself proud, and the school is pleased to be associated with you in this activity. Now, what I need to tell you is that I have been contacted by Radio Firth, the local radio station. They would like to do a short interview with you, to ask about your thoughts on what is going to happen in the forest. And they also want to ask you about your video – you know, the one with the talking rabbits. It will be at three-fifteen this afternoon, and I thought it would help your efforts. I've spoken to your mum and she's OK with it, but what do you think, Bonnie? Are you happy to do this?'

Bonnie didn't hesitate for a moment. 'Yes, that would be brilliant. I'd really like to do that.'

At lunchtime, Bonnie tried to think what it was she wanted to say and wrote some notes. It wouldn't be that different from her words this morning. Three-fifteen arrived quickly and Bonnie was back in the headmaster's office. A few minutes early, the radio station had called and made sure Bonnie was OK, and still happy to speak. Then, just like that, she was live on air. 'Tell me about your videos, Bonnie, and why you think the forest development is a bad thing,' said the presenter.

Bonnie spoke well, telling the radio station all the things she had learned. Of course, there was no mention of anything about bribes or talking animals – this was neither the time nor the place. The presenter was particularly interested in the funny videos. 'Where do you get your ideas from, Bonnie?'

Bonnie said it was easy. 'I just sit and watch the rabbits and imagine what they're saying. Once you get the timing right, it's simple.'

In less than five minutes, the interview was over. Bonnie was feeling pleased with herself. The head teacher said she had done well and he promised to come to the meeting.

School was now over for the day, and everyone had gone home. Everyone, that is, apart from the teachers, and Rachel Parker.

# Chapter 18

# Fight

Bonnie's school was a well-behaved one. At least most of the time. There were always incidents and a bit of bullying here and there. But the school was on top of it. Any complaints or allegations were taken seriously. There was always a teacher or senior pupil on patrol, and they were straight over at the first sign of any incident. All that of course, was during the school day. At four o'clock in the afternoon, there was no need to patrol the school grounds, as everyone had gone home. All but two pupils: Rachel and Bonnie.

Bonnie was the bigger and older of the two girls. She was stronger as well. But what she didn't have was the one-line put-downs. Most fights and confrontations start with some form of verbal insult. In that area, Rachel was the master. Rachel was a pretty girl, always well turned out. Her school uniform pristine. As was Bonnie's. But Rachel always had a full face of make-up. She had to, as she put it: 'Look good and demand respect.'

As Bonnie made her way out of the school grounds, she heard the unmistakable voice of Rachel Parker. 'Feeling pretty pleased with yourself, are you? Radio interviews, school speeches, chats with the head and talking rabbits. You must think you're something pretty special. It's a shame they don't know you're a spineless loser. And a snitch. And you put weird things in other people's drinks. I think that's the sort of behaviour that should be talked about, don't you?'

Bonnie was confused about the 'weird things in drinks' comment. Then she remembered Kimberly dancing. Yes, David had applied the eyes. She couldn't help it; she smirked at the thought of Kimberly's Riverdance routine.

'You think it's funny, do you? I was all set to call the police, but my mother wouldn't let me. Messing with people's drinks is a serious offence. You're lucky you're not in some jail cell, you ugly loser.'

Bonnie drew breath. Outwardly, she was determined not to show she was afraid. And inwardly, she wasn't afraid – she was *terrified*. But still, she managed to steady her nerves, so her words were clear and assertive.

'Nobody put anything into anyone's drinks, Rachel. And there's nothing wrong in standing up for yourself or for something you believe in. If you want to call the police, go ahead. I'm sure they'll love to hear that your mum paid a visit to someone's house. And then performed Riverdance in their front room – speaking gibberish at the same time. I wish I'd been able to video it, it would have made a great post.'

Bonnie was surprised at her response. Perhaps she had it in her to have an argument with Rachel after all.

'Listen to me, Bonnie Banks.' Rachel spoke with serious menace. 'Keep your pathetic nose, your stupid mother and your scabby dog out of our business.' Rachel walked forward towards Bonnie, gritting her teeth. Her top half leaned in towards her schoolmate. Her arm was rising, but there was no sign of a punch. A pointed finger came out. Bonnie could smell Rachel's breath, which wasn't pleasant, she noted. The finger jabbed at Bonnie. Sometimes it made contact below her collar bone and sometimes the finger landed right on the bone itself. It was more annoying than painful.

'Do you hear me, Bonnie Banks? Girl with the most pathetic name. You think you're something. You think you're some kind of local celebrity.' Rachel shook her head as she spoke. 'Talking rabbits on the radio. Oh, that's hilarious. Think you're someone special, do you? See, if you even think about doing any more to stop my mum's plans, you and your pathetic mother, I'll … Yaaaaaaaaaaaaaaaaaaaa!'

Bonnie caught Rachel by surprise. She had snapped. The verbal abuse directed at her was one thing, but she wasn't going to tolerate it about her mum. The finger was just *there*. Prodding and annoying her. And it had hit her collar bone at the exact time that Rachel had uttered 'pathetic mother.' So, Bonnie had grabbed it, with all her might, and bent it back. For a moment, she thought it was broken, such was the yelp that came from Rachel. But, in that moment, it appeared to her that Rachel was small. And Bonnie felt big, strong and in control.

Still bending back Rachel's finger, Bonnie said what she felt. 'Don't you ever threaten me, my dog, my mother – or anyone else I know. You are a bully, Rachel Parker. But you are not going to bully me any more. I'm sick of you. You …'

It had felt to Bonnie like Rachel's finger was going to break, so she'd eased back on the pressure. Her knee suddenly felt a searing pain. She had made the mistake of not wanting to hurt Rachel. That was her nature, after all, she wasn't a bully and didn't like hurting anyone. But that wasn't Rachel's way. She'd seen the moment of weakness, twisted her hand and removed her finger from Bonnie's grip. In an instant, she had stepped back and launched a kick at Bonnie's knee.

With a sudden surge of anger, Bonnie was ready to fight back, like never before. But Rachel had already launched her next attack. The open palm of her right hand caught Bonnie right across the side of her face. It made perfect contact; the small vessels under Bonnie's skin reacted to the slap and her cheek instantly glowed red. She wasn't feeling so strong now. The smaller, more aggressive girl had become massive in Bonnie's eyes. Her confidence had started to crumble. Bonnie put her hands to her face as she saw another attack incoming. A second, open hand strike made contact with Bonnie, this time hitting her arm as she protected her face. As time slowed, she saw Rachel gearing up for yet another strike. Was her fist clenched? Then there was the magical sound of the headmaster's voice, booming across the school grounds.

'STOP THAT. YOU PAIR. STOP THAT IMMEDIATELY.'

Both girls stopped and stood back. Bonnie clutched the side of her red face while Rachel continued to intimidate with the fury in her red eyes.

'What's happening here? Why are you fighting? I would have expected better from both of you. Bonnie Banks, explain yourself.'

Bonnie was aware of Rachel's expression and continuing fury. Her earlier confidence had disappeared. 'It was nothing, Sir,' said Bonnie. 'We're fine now. Sorry. Just a silly disagreement.' She knew that telling the truth would only make the situation worse.

'What have *you* got to say for yourself, Rachel Parker?'

'Just what Bonnie said, Sir. Stupid disagreement.' She sounded almost genuine as she spoke. *Clever acting*, thought Bonnie.

'I want you pair to shake hands right now.'

They did.

'You'll both come and see me in the office tomorrow. Go home and think about your behaviour.

And I will speak to your parents about this. Bonnie, off you go. Rachel, you and I will stand here for five minutes. I don't want you pair near one another while your tempers are like this. A disgrace to the school, the pair of you.'

Bonnie made her way towards home. After a few minutes, she took out her new phone. Thankfully, there was no damage. She switched the camera to the selfie setting, using it as a mirror. There was a clear imprint of Rachel's hand showing on her cheek. Her hands were still shaking as the reality of what had happened hit home.

For a moment, Bonnie was proud of herself. She had stood up to Rachel, which was great. Only a little more courage and she could have taken complete control of the situation. Rachel was a bully. But, unlike most bullies, this one didn't back down when confronted. This one fought back. Then Bonnie became annoyed with herself for allowing feelings of fear and defeat to creep in. Her head shook with thoughts of what could have been. She hadn't expected the strength that had been awoken inside her.

As she walked in the other direction, Rachel plotted revenge. No-one stands up to Rachel Parker. No-one. Especially not Bonnie Banks. 'Pathetic, weak girl that needs taught a lesson,' she thought. 'At least she didn't grass me up to the head teacher. That's always something.' Rachel was an aggressive bully, but smart enough to know she needed grades. Like her mother, she wanted to make something of herself. And there were enough brains in her head for her to do it, without too much effort.

When Bonnie got home, the tale of exactly what had happened was relayed to her mum. Misty was proud of her. When Rachel got home and told her mother, Kimberly was also proud of her daughter. The characters of these four individuals were not set up for compromise. That much was certain.

The following day, Bonnie explained to the head teacher what had happened. The story was unchanged, and Rachel didn't say anything different either. The head accepted what they said. But he was experienced enough to know better. He knew the girls and their backgrounds. And he was certain that Bonnie had been on the receiving end of the other girl's temper. Yet they both seemed to show genuine regret for what had happened. He said he would be writing to their mothers and that he expected no further incidents. No further action would be taken. 'Now get back to your classes.'

Both girls left the office at the same time and walked along the corridor in silence. As they parted to go in opposite directions, Rachel spoke over her shoulder to Bonnie. 'Next time, it'll be out of the school, loser.'

# Chapter 19

# Grimalkin

The Chair called the meeting to order. This took a few moments, as the numbers in the hall were more than any meeting ever held by the local council. There were over three hundred people there. Many were pupils from the school, but they had brought along their mums and dads too. The hall was packed. All the seats were taken, and there was now standing room only.

The media were also there. Not just the local paper, but the BBC and STV News. People recognised a couple of reporters from the television. Bonnie was a bit embarrassed when STV News asked her a few questions for the evening news before the meeting started. But she stuck with the same script she had used over the past few days. She was getting good at it now.

'We're joined now by local pupil Bonnie Banks, who has caused something of a stir with her videos lately.

You're a bit of a local celebrity now, Bonnie?' said the reporter.

'I want the forest to stay as it is. They are going to cut down lots of trees. Hundreds of trees will go to make way for the lodges and their so-called entertainment hub. And cars will drive to and from the lodges every day in what's left of the forest. All this will harm the birds and animals that live in there and lots of them will die.'

'And what do your friends think about this, Bonnie? Are they against it too?'

'Most of them, yes. We've all grown up with the forest being nearby, and we all use it. So, I don't think it should be cut down for holiday homes.'

'You've caused a bit of interest with your videos as well, haven't you? You've now got over two hundred and fifty thousand views. That's very popular.' The reporter moved the microphone a little closer to Bonnie.

'It was a bit of fun, but it's made more people notice about what they plan to do with the forest, so that's a good thing.'

'And the way you describe the rabbits talking is funny. How do you work out what they are saying to one another, Bonnie?'

Bonnie laughed, to give the appearance she was joking. 'Oh, I just listen to what they are saying,' she said, before giving another little laugh.

The reporter ended his interview. 'Trevor Davidson for STV News, in Copsehead, home of the talking rabbits.'

The Chair of the meeting continued, showing a little more nerves than normal due to the size of the audience. 'The members of the planning committee for Firthshire were presented with plans recently. We were asked to give our approval on the proposed development within the Devilla Forest. Due to the increase of local and national interest in this story ...,' the Chair looked around the room at all the faces and the TV camera, '...we have decided to defer a decision on the matter for a period of fourteen days.'

'We will use this evening to explain more to residents about the development of the forest. The company behind it will show how they propose to be sensitive to the woodland and its inhabitants. And, once that has been done, there will be an opportunity for audience members to ask questions.'

Bonnie and Misty sat next to one another. Misty had spotted Kimberly and Rachel on the other side of the room, both sitting with faces of fury. Misty had been so proud of her daughter standing up to Rachel. But Bonnie still thought Rachel had got the better of her. 'So what, a letter from the school. No big deal,' said her mum. If it came to it, Misty would put up a robust defence of her daughter's actions. But best to let it lie for now. 'Choose your battles,' as Granny would say.

The chair invited Kimberly Parker onto the stage to allow her to explain the development. Kimberly had done this presentation many times and knew it inside out. The difference this time was that she didn't have the audience in her pocket.

Kimberly stood in front of the microphone and waited for the crowd murmur to settle. Then she spoke. 'Good evening, everyone. It's reassuring for me to see so many people here tonight. I love a community that is passionate, and cares about what is happening on its doorstep.' Kimberly introduced herself, making the point she was also a local resident.

Her talk covered lots of things about what was planned. She talked about more visitors to the area, bringing more jobs. Then Kimberly moved on to the main issue. 'I'd like to address one thing that has been raised in the past couple of weeks. This one thing has prevented the development from starting. It has slowed the creation of new jobs and investment.'

*Cleverly put*, thought Bonnie.

'This is what the council describes as 'permanent loss of habitat.' That, of course, means the removal of trees. And the perceived impact any removal will have on the animals that depend on them for survival.

'I would like to assure you all here tonight that I have the best interests of the forest at heart. I love nothing better than the woods and the trees, and all the little creatures that live there. I'm sure I've even made friends with an owl!' she said, laughing as she spoke. 'Every time I turn round, he, or is it she, is there.' There was a murmur of mild amusement in the room. 'I even got acquainted with a mouse or two the other day. There's a lot of them in the forest, but they hide themselves away.'

Kimberly continued, using what Bonnie described as 'big business words'.

'To mitigate any adverse effect of clearing away a few trees, we will plant twice the number elsewhere …' All Bonnie heard after this was: 'blah, blah, blah.' Big, boring business words.

It was now Bonnie and Misty's turn to have faces like thunder. Kimberly had handled the room so well. Every negative had been turned around. OK, so they knew there were lots of lies in what Kimberly had said. But they still had no proof. At least all the activity over the past few days had given them some extra time. The proof was out there. All they needed to do was find it.

It turned out that there were some good, and some tough questions. All of which Kimberly handled with ease. The audience walked away looking relaxed. Misty heard one couple saying to their son, an S6 pupil hoping to secure a place at university, 'You can get a job there over the summer. Get some money behind you. Sounds like it will be a great place to work.'

There were leaflets handed out to everyone on the way out. They showed artist's impressions of how it would look, and a section on The Parker Hotel Group's 'Five Principles of Sustainable Development':

- *Replace what you remove*
- *Rehome wildlife*
- *Tread carefully with every step*
- *Think green, act green*
- *Reuse or source locally*

This was going to be one hard fight, thought Bonnie. Kimberly had even been smart enough to pause her development and use the time to get local people onside. Everything had been going so well, but this had been a setback. At least they had more time on their hands now.

Kimberly and her daughter left the meeting happy. OK, so there had been a short delay. But it would be worth it if it allowed Kimberly's plans to go through without a fight. As they arrived home, they both noticed a black cat with deep-orange eyes sitting on the front step. It sat there, staring at them both. Kimberly noticed it had a stumpy tail. It reminded her of the cat at her father's funeral. As the pair walked towards it, there was no sign of fear – it didn't run off. Rachel walked to it, then kneeled in front of it. She reached and gently petted it. The cat showed no sign of affection and just sat there, motionless.

'Aw, isn't she lovely?' said Rachel, at once taken by the creature.

'SHOO,' shouted Kimberly, not feeling any more affection for animals than she did for people. The cat immediately crouched on its front paws, looking like it was going to pounce. It directed a venomous hiss at Kimberly as its fur stood on end.

'WHOA, MUM! What are you doing? You're scaring it.'

'I don't like the look of it. And we're not taking in stray cats.'

Rachel remained unafraid of the cat, despite its hiss. 'I don't want to take it in, I just wanted to pet it.' She moved forward again, gently and slowly moving her hand towards the cat. It sat still, watching her every move. Rachel stroked it again and, this time, it responded by leaning into her hand, as if enjoying the attention.

'I'm going in,' said Kimberly. 'Don't be long.'

Rachel and the cat were bonding, both enjoying the other's company. It was a strange sensation that Rachel felt as she petted the cat. It felt like she was lowing inwardly, and the word 'Grimalkin' kept entering her head. *Where is that coming from?* she thought. *Grimalkin? What an odd word to think. Is that what we'll call you little kitty? Grimalkin?* And, leaving her with that thought, the cat stood on all fours, turned and departed. Rachel went into the house and said to her mother, 'If it comes here again, don't frighten it, please. It's a nice cat. And I've called it "Grimalkin."'

# Chapter 20

# Recon

Bonnie and David went to see Sylvester first thing the following morning. They were there just after eight o'clock. Sylvester already knew what had happened. 'There were mice under the floorboards in the hall,' he said. 'They heard everything and now we all know.' Of course, this was all spoken to David, who translated for Bonnie.

He continued. 'You've done a great job, Bonnie. I know you're a bit disappointed. We're all disappointed. But you have bought us some valuable time.

'Let me tell you what we have in place. Iccuat and Troben know where all the decisions are taken. They know who the main people are, working for Kimberly. Rodger the dragonfly was also on her window for a while, so we also know the names of the people that are taking the bribery payments. At all the important places, we have recon in place.'

'Recon?' asked Bonnie.

'Reconnaissance. It means observing an enemy, so we can get information to give us a strategic advantage.'

'Oh.'

'Now, I've put Burp in charge of recon.' He heard some giggling in the forest but chose to ignore it. 'Burp, will you explain where we are at, please.'

'Thank you, Sylvester,' said Burp. 'As part of this briefing, I'm also joined by Rodger from the dragonflies who will be my second-in-command. Now, please pay attention. We have found six homes and one office that we need to watch. I have personnel in place in every property. They are hidden away, either under floorboards or in walls or attics. There are at least a dozen personnel in every location, all listening to what is being said. Once anything of any importance has been heard, we will contact you. Rodger, please explain what happens next.'

Bonnie was struck by the authority that Burp gave off. *He sounds like a military commander, not a little mouse*, she thought. *And that deep voice. Weird.*

Rodger flew forward and stood on one of Sylvester's branches. 'Thank you Burrrp.' He, too, ignored the giggling. 'We also have perrrsonnel in place. In each of the locations, we have a team of drrragonflies. They'rrre taking turrrns to ensurrre therrre is always someone therrre, alerrrt and rrready to fly. As soon as the mice have picked something up, they will give us the signal. We will then fly over to Iccuat forrr the locations on the west of the forrrest. Orrr if it's the east, Trrroben. Then

147

it's overrr to the birrrds to get the inforrrmation back to Sylvesterrr strrraight afterrr that. Iccuat will also let you know if something imporrrtant has happened, Bonnie. He will give you an owl call outside yourrr house. Should you be at school, a larrrge loft of pigeons will be making a lot of noise. Don't listen to anything they say, though, they talk a lot of nonsense. Just take the signal and get overrr to the forrrest as quickly as you can.'

'Thank you, Rodger,' said Burp. 'And may I just remind everyone that, where I come from, Burp. Means. Warrior.' It was quiet in the forest, making it easy to hear the little giggle in the distance.

'This is fantastic,' said Bonnie. 'But there's one more thing we need to do. One of my mum's friends, Peter, has given me these.' Bonnie held two little micro cameras. They were tiny, about the size and shape of a single chunk of chocolate. 'These are cameras, and if we can get them in place to record what's being said, then we'll have evidence. The problem, of course, will be how we get them where we need them.'

Burp stepped forward and asked for a closer look. He sniffed them, more out of mouse instinct than to achieve anything. He then picked them up with his little mouse claws. They were light, even for a mouse. Speaking in his deep, booming voice he said, 'We can do this. We'll get them in position. Where should we put them?'

'We've only got two. One needs to go into Kimberly's living room. The other needs to go in the office where the meetings often take place. They can't be visible; they need to be out of sight but still be able to see everything that's happening.'

'Leave it to us,' said Burp.

All they could do now was hope that the mice could get the cameras in place. It was going to happen that night, as soon as the people had gone to sleep, and everything was in darkness.

# Chapter 21

# Cameras

Iccuat the owl and Troben the crow took the tiny cameras in their claws and flew off. Iccuat headed for Kimberly's house, and the crow flew to her meeting office. The owl was first to arrive. It was further to fly for him than for Troben, but he had a bigger wingspan and a faster flight speed. This was not the easiest of meetings. The mice were afraid of Iccuat. He normally viewed the mice as a delicious meal, but all this was on hold. The needs of the forest were greater. Everyone's survival depended on what would happen over the next few weeks.

Iccuat knew the mice feared him, so he flew to the meeting point and released the camera from his grip. He then flew over and settled on a fence post a few metres back.

The mouse in charge at Kimberly's house was called Jesto. He was fearless, but, even so, a little wary as he ventured outside to speak to the owl.

Iccuat spoke first. 'Hiya, Jesto,' he said. 'How's things?'

'Errr, no bad. Jist sittin' aboot the hoose, waitin', ken.'

The owl and the mouse were no longer speaking with proper pronunciation. It was easier for Bonnie to understand the animals when they spoke without an accent. It translated better. But now they were chatting with one another, the local accents came out.

'So – see this 'hing. It's a camera. But it needs hidden. Like, totally hidden. Whar naebody kin see it. This bitty on the front, that's the bit that sees. Yi need tae point that at the room, so it kin see abody.'

The mouse understood. 'OK, I get it. Is it heavy?'

'Goanne pick it up an see.'

'Ye'll no try an eet us?'

'No, I'll no try and eet ye. No the noo anyway. Bit when this is ower, oan yer guard again moosey.'

Jesto crept forward and picked up the camera. It looked much bigger in his little claws. He turned round and shouted to the other mice. Two more appeared and joined him. 'Tak this tae the nest.' They did as they were told. Iccuat then explained to Jesto how the camera worked, and what he needed to do.

'I like it bett'r when yous owls dinnae try an' eat us ken.'

'Enjoy it while yous can.' And with these final words, Iccuat flew off.

Jesto went back inside the house and straight to the nest. The camera would need to be put into position, but accessible. When the mice got the signal, it would need to be switched on. Iccuat had told Jesto that the battery only lasted for a few hours, whatever that meant.

He moved along the inside of the house walls. There was a nice little path from the outdoor vents. It led to a little gap in the floorboards where they could get through. There had been a knot in the wood that had fallen out a few years ago, leaving a tiny hole next to the skirting board. The hole was plenty big enough for a mouse to get through unseen. It could then squeeze between the carpet and the skirting board. Jesto liked it in Kimberly's house and thought he may stay on once this was all over.

He needed to find out if the hole was big enough to get the camera through before they did anything else. Helping one another, the mice managed to figure out which way to twist the camera so it would fit through the hole. But they didn't put it in place – not yet.

Jesto could hear no-one in the house, so he went through the gap. He squeezed out from under the carpet and into the living room. The first thing he did was look around. It was enormous. Giant chairs that the people sat in. A giant screen in the corner that they watched, although it was just black today. He could smell food as well. But that could be investigated at another time.

His task was to find somewhere for the camera that was close by. When they got the signal to switch the camera on, he would need to be able to get to it unseen. And, of course, the camera had to be hidden away as well. It would be no use unless it was in a position where it could see, but not be seen. Jesto spotted the perfect place.

On the windowsill there was a black Harry Potter Lego model. It was partially covered by the living room curtains. All he would have to do is sneak under the carpet, then crawl for no more than the length of his body and tail. That would take him behind the curtains. He could then sneak out between the carpet and the skirting board. From there, he would be able to run up the curtains and jump onto the windowsill. Then it would only be a matter of pressing the button to switch on the camera to record. It was black in colour so it would match the Lego and be difficult to see.

Jesto was happy with this plan. He told the other mice what they would do. After dark, once the Parkers were sound asleep, the mice put their plans into action. Jesto carried the camera to the hole in the floorboards. With some help from the other mice, he twisted the camera through the hole. Then they pushed it along under the carpet. Getting it up the back of the curtains and onto the windowsill would be much harder. Jesto asked one of the other mice to do this. Dolly was chosen, as she had the longest tail.

Dolly wrapped her tail around the camera, and then climbed the curtains. She felt like she had a great grip of it as she made her way up. Jesto and another mouse followed close behind her. Dolly did a great job. It took her about four seconds to climb onto the windowsill. She put the camera next to the Lego and went back down the curtains, then headed to the nest. Her job was done.

Jesto now took over. He sat the camera on a little piece of black Lego, and it blended beautifully into the structure. The mice were delighted. 'Job done,' whispered Jesto. 'Let's get back to the nest.'

This had been remarkably easy. Jesto went outside and found the dragonfly. 'The camera is in place. We're ready when we get the signal.'

The dragonfly took off to report back. Now all Jesto could do was wait for his next instruction. *Oh, and there was also that smell of food. That's worth investigating now*, he thought.

A similar job had to be done at the offices. This time, the crow dropped off the camera and gave the mice the same instructions. Affa was in charge. Her assistant was Vic. They were two elegant lady mice. Always trying to speak posh, but often using the wrong words. They were the best of friends and had been since they were baby mice, over four months ago. They used to chat about how long they had been friends. To them, it felt like forever.

Affa and Vic took the camera back to the nest, which was found below the floorboards by one of the heaters in the office. Getting into the office was going to be more difficult. The mice could access it through the air vents or under the door, but the camera wouldn't fit. They explored the office in the early evening because it had been locked and everyone had gone home. They checked everywhere for gaps big enough to fit the camera through, but they couldn't find anything. However, there was a tiny gap at the side of one of the air vents. After some discussion they decided a little gnawing could make the gap big enough to get the camera through.

They were all proud of their work. It was difficult, although not impossible, to see the enlarged hole. They hoped no-one would notice the little bit of mess they had made on the floor. Chewing through wood and plasterboard can be a messy business. The office was large enough to fit about a dozen people. In one corner, there were cardboard boxes stacked against the wall. Next to the boxes was a small area to make tea and coffee. There were charts on the wall, giving dates when people were on holiday. Leaning against the wall were work tools and the cabinet where they would hide the camera. It wasn't the tidiest of offices.

The mice set to work with the camera. They squeezed it through the newly enlarged hole and carried it along the office floor. The cabinet was full of books and files and lots of other useless things. Based on the amount of dust in and around the cabinet, it wasn't used often. The mice had spotted the perfect place. The glass door of the cabinet was half open, so they could get in behind the glass. They could sit the camera in front of a black file, and you would hardly notice it.

Affa and Vic had figured out almost the same plan as Jesto. Vic would use her long curly tail to carry the camera up the side of the unit, then set it down. Next, Affa would join her and move the camera into position. Less than half a minute later, the mission would be complete.

There was a slight extra challenge here, though. It would be difficult to access the camera without being seen. They chatted about different plans. Affa suggested that, when anyone arrived at the office, one of the mice would need to get to the cabinet right away. They could hide there to wait for the signal. One of the chaffinches would be told to come and peck at the window. As soon as they heard this noise, one of the mice would go to the cabinet and hide. They would need to be able to get to the camera without being seen. That could be done by going along the back of the files. These were leaning at a slight angle, leaving enough room to get along the side of the last file. Then, a little claw could press the button. Vic thought this was a good idea. It was a little risky, but they would be careful.

Affa and Vic were organised, and they tested this approach a few times. One of the mice would tap, then the others would all have a go at switching on the camera as quietly as they could. Affa and Vic were happy. Plans were in place. They let the dragonfly know and the thumbs-up was given across the forest. Now, it was their turn to wait.

Timing was everything. The batteries in the cameras would only last a few hours. If they recorded something, and it gave them no evidence, they would need to take the cameras out. Getting them recharged and putting them back on a daily basis would not be easy. The mice were amazing. But they had to hope the cameras did their job sooner rather than later.

# Chapter 22

## Visitors

'Expect the unexpected' was one of Misty's sayings. If something important was happening at school, home or work, Misty would remind everyone: 'Expect the unexpected.' And that's just how it turned out, when Kimberly had visitors arrive at her house and office at the same time.

The visitors to her home had been seen before. They were known to be people involved with approving the project work. At exactly the same time, a worker in a high-visibility jacket and two men in grey suits arrived at Kimberly's office. Both cameras would need to be activated at the same time.

The signal was given, and the mice put everything into place. It all went like clockwork. At Kimberley's house, the camera was switched on and started to record. The mice would not switch on the camera unless there was more than one person in the room. And here they were, four visitors. The mice also listened carefully to what was being said. They all hoped to be the first to hear something important.

When the humans spoke, there was general chit chat: the weather, holidays, that sort of thing. In an unusual show of hospitality, Kimberly had made coffee and put out some expensive Waitrose brand chocolate biscuits. The visitors each took one, unwrapped it scrunched the wrapper into a ball and sat it back on the plate.

Kimberly said to one of the visitors, 'Gerry, I don't mean to be rude, but would you chew a little bit more quietly.' It wasn't a question; it was an order. 'You sound like a cement mixer going round. And, for heaven's sake, will you chew with your mouth closed. It's disgusting to watch you eat.' Poor Gerry. He wasn't sure where to look, or even how to continue eating. But he did, only quietly and slowly. And with his mouth shut.

Kimberly was in discussion with the councillors. They chatted about how they thought the meeting had gone a couple of nights previously. 'It was a wise call to push back the decision for a couple of weeks,' said Gerry. 'Make them think we are there to help them. Convince them that it's all above board.' One or two biscuit crumbs sprayed from Gerry's mouth as he spoke. Kimberly had to close her eyes and look away. 'And, if I may say, I thought you presented the plans and handled the questions well.'

For the next hour, they talked a lot about the plans. How the lodges would be shipped and constructed for the lowest cost was a point of discussion. The best way to get access for the machinery was another important topic. They chatted about how to make the central leisure area as good as it could be. Many things were spoken about, but there was no discussion about money. There was no mention of any payment in return for planning approval. Nor was there anything said about the Devilla Woodland Council giving up control of the forest. Soon after the discussions ended, the visitors left. The mice knew there had been nothing recorded that would be of any use. All they could do was hope the others in the office had better luck.

Over in the office, the two men in grey suits sat next to the man with the high-visibility vest. The mismatched chairs offered varying levels of comfort around the small square meeting table. The heating had been left on overnight, so the office was a bit stuffy. Mr High-Vis Vest opened a window. There was a similar chat to the one held by the visitors to Kimberly's house.

'How do you think the meeting went on Friday?' said Mr High-Vis Vest.

The portly gentleman in a grey suit with a receding hairline listened. His shirt had sweat stains under his armpits. 'I thought it was OK, to be honest. A bit frustrating to be held back, but these things happen. Anyway, it's not long now. A couple of weeks and we'll get cracking.' He smiled at the other two, 'And, of course, a little sweetener to help us along will be no bad thing!' He smiled and clapped his hands together, giving them a little rub.

Vic and Affa had the camera switched on and recording. Vic was hidden away in the cabinet and Affa had found a secret little spot behind the air vent. They both knew that this was going well. In the background, they heard the noise of another vehicle arriving. A couple of minutes later, the door to the office opened. Someone else walked in – someone they had never seen before. The mice guessed it was another member of Kimberley's team.

The person who came through the door was tall – around six feet four inches. A very tall woman indeed, who towered above the other bodies in the room. When she smiled, her entire face wrinkled, and Vic noticed that the woman's gums were massive … and a bit scary. She was smartly dressed and carrying a large bag. Whatever was in the bag was heavy, as the tall woman used a bit of effort to lift the bag and lay it on the table.

'Sorry I'm late,' she said. I had to take this one to the vet this morning. And, as she opened the top of the bag, she lifted out her pet cat. This was no ordinary cat. It looked like a mini tiger. It was monstrous. The tall woman scooped the cat up. 'This little monster has not been well. He's had to get tablets from the vet. And now he needs lots of rest and lots of cuddles. And we're going to get you home soon, aren't we?' she said cradling the cat in her arms like a baby.

The two men in grey suits reached over and stroked the cat's head. The cat had been enjoying the attention when, suddenly, it tried to wriggle free of the tall woman's arms. Its eyes were wide open, and it began to search the room. The cat knew that smell – it was *mice*. He finally broke free from the tall woman's grip and jumped onto the table. The cat gave his head a shake, then had a giant yawn. Or maybe the yawn was just an opportunity to show off his sharp pointy teeth to anyone willing to look. He gave his head another little shake, then jumped off the table and strolled over to the cabinet.

Mr High-Vis Vest, the grey suits and the tall woman returned to their discussion. The tall woman was being given details of some future meetings. They explained to her some of the items that would be discussed. The mice were no longer able to pay attention to anything that was being said, though. Both had their eyes on the cat.

As he strolled over to the cabinet, the cat noticed that some of the wall had been chewed away, next to the air vent. He gave the area a little sniff, and then moved his nose to the vent and sniffed again. The cat peered through the metal slats of the air vent. On the other side of the vent, Affa peered at the cat. Their eyes met. The cat swiped its paw off the metal vent three or four times, as if to make it clear to the mouse that he was coming for it. Affa shot back as fast as she could towards the safety of the nest, her little heart racing. The cat looked round the office and knew there was another mouse nearby. He could sense it. And he could smell it.

The attention of the people in the room had now moved on to the cat. They wondered why it was swiping at the air vent. Then they noticed the mess on the floor and the tiny little gap at the side of the air vent. 'Looks like you've got mice,' said the tall woman.

Mr High-Vis Vest agreed with this. 'And it looks like we've got a cat that knows where the mice are!'

The group of four sat watching the show. The cat jumped onto the cabinet where all the files were kept. It was looking at something, but they weren't sure what.

The cat could smell the mouse. He knew it was close; he could sense it inside the cabinet. Clever cat that he was, he had figured out that there was only one way in and out of the cabinet. And he worked out that the mouse was hiding in the far corner.

Vic's little heart was beating as fast as it ever had. She was terrified. All she could do was think of her partner and children back at the nest. And, of course, her lifelong friend Affa. But no-one could help her now. Her only escape was to be fast. To get past the cat, down the side of the cabinet and into the air vent.

The cat was also making plans. He pushed his way inside the open glass and reached his paw along the front of the glass. He was dangerously close to where the camera was. He stretched his long paw out towards the corner of the cabinet, which he could almost reach. He did this at lightning speed, along with a sharp and angry hiss. He knew he would never catch the mouse at this side of the cabinet. But he also knew it would be terrified. His guess was it would run along the back of the cabinet, and right into the claws on his other paw, which were already out. Waiting.

His plans fell into place as Vic shot along the back of the cabinet towards the door. Just as she was about to escape, the cat's claw caught her. 'Eeeeeeee' screamed the mouse. It was the last noise Vic ever made. The cat held the mouse in his jaws, making sure it was dead. He jumped back onto the floor.

The people around the table were on their feet now and they were applauding. 'The cat got the mouse, the cat got the mouse!' They were all chanting and celebrating this as a great victory for the cat. The tall woman opened the door and the cat strolled out with his prey, dropping it at the bottom of the steps.

'Don't worry,' said the tall woman. 'He'll come back. He's a house cat and doesn't go outside much.' And the cat did just that. Once he had dropped the mouse, he sprang back up the stairs and back into the office. He found a chair that looked comfortable, curled up and went to sleep. His dreams were of his tiger-like achievements.

The other mice made their way outside to see if they could see anything. It wasn't long before they discovered the body. A lifeless Vic – a great leader of the mouse horde in their little nest and always good fun. But now she was gone. The mice were devastated. Mice get caught by other animals every day. And they understand that. But this cat had caught and killed her just for fun.

They all knew Vic was playing such an important role in their future. And she was such a friendly and likeable character. They would miss her.

A message went out to the forest that the mission had been a failure. And that they had a mouse down. Affa was already plotting her revenge.

# Chapter 23

## Tall

The camera in Kimberly's house would need to be removed and recharged. The mice didn't want to risk removing it during the day, so it just sat there. It would record nothing of importance until the battery ran out. The camera in the office was much the same. Everyone had had high hopes for this little plan, but they all agreed it was going to be too difficult to get the cameras in and out on a regular basis. Plus, they would need to be recharged and put back in place. And, even once they were in position, there was no guarantee they would be able to record any evidence. In the conversations heard so far, there had been 'nods and winks'. But no-one had actually said anything about 'payment for approval', or anything like that. They had obviously been told to be careful.

There was a small village nearby called Hollypoint. It overlooked the river Firth and had picturesque views over the estuary. The village looked like it was stuck in a time warp. There were old, cobbled streets and houses from a different century. Someone had decided, many years previously, that they would keep the traditional look and feel of the village. And it was all the better for it. There were a few coffee shops, and midway down the main street was a traditional village pub.

Hollypoint was also home to the tall lady and her cat. The tall lady was called Alison Forsyth. The stripy grey cat went by the name of Rudi. In her younger days, Alison had been a great fan of ballet, and had even won a few local competitions. She had tried to compete at a higher level but was always told to work on being a bit more graceful. Alison had put this lack of grace down to her height. Eventually the ballet lessons stopped, and her time was invested in foreign language study instead. She became fluent in six different languages. French, German and Spanish were her early specialities. A few years later, she had added Russian, Urdu and Chinese to her repertoire. Alison had interpreted for many different companies. She had even been to meetings with high-powered politicians across the globe.

As a translator, she had got to know Kimberly Parker. Kimberly had needed someone to help her in discussions with foreign suppliers. Alison had even been involved in helping with the research. Kimberly hadn't been looking for a mainstream producer; a supplier that would build and ship lodges for a much cheaper cost was needed. These producers often had basic websites – if they had one at all. A good old-fashioned phone call was often required, to understand capabilities. Alison's worth had been proven quickly. She had become involved in the project – not that she had any issue with that. Earning a few thousand pounds for what would amount to no more than a couple of months' work was a good thing.

Alison had become aware that not everything was above board. She had noticed that the lodges were being built using low-cost plastic material made to look like trees. They were not from a company with any green credentials. And there were also the people of an official nature who had to approve the holiday lodge plans. Alison was aware they had been incentivised to do so. She had approached Kimberly on this matter, saying this was making her consider stepping back from her work. Kimberly had persuaded her otherwise.

'It's like this, Alison. You are now a main player in the development of the forest. We need you. You have built relationships with our suppliers that we never could. You understand what's going on. And, yes, sometimes I need to "pay a little extra" to make sure things happen. But that's just the way of things with some of these foreign suppliers and planning authorities.

'I'll tell you what, Alison. We are nearly finished with our overseas purchases. I was going to give you a good performance bonus anyway. How about you stay on until we wrap things up, and then I was thinking of an added ten thousand pounds at the end? I may even manage to get that to you in cash, so you don't have to worry about tax. Just as a "thank you", you know.'

*It all seems OK*, thought Alison. *It's not as if I'm involved in any significant way. I just translate. And an extra ten thousand? That would come in handy.*

Alison had agreed. Kimberly insisted she sign a form promising everything she knew would be kept a secret. *But that's fair enough*, she'd thought.

After the trip to the vet, and the little bit of mouse hunting earlier on in the day, Rudi the cat was pleased to get home. He was looking forward to a sleep in his own bed. Rudi liked a bit of sleeping and would nap at any given opportunity. He was feeling proud of himself today. His display of mouse catching had been particularly impressive. He deserved some tasty food and a nap. But first, a quick visit to the garden.

As his owner made her way into her house, Rudi headed towards one of the garden borders. He much preferred 'going' outside. He had always thought the cat tray was a bit common for his liking. Outside felt so much more natural to him. And there he was, hole dug and midway through his business, when an owl landed on the fence nearby. It was a big bird; he had seen owls before, but this one he had never met.

'Do you mind?' said Rudi. 'I happen to be in the middle of some private business.'

'I'll look away if you would prefer,' said Iccuat.

'Some of you still live in the wild, finding your own food, sleeping outdoors. But others prefer warm beds, and for our food to be brought to us by our human servants. So, why exactly are you interrupting my private time, owl?'

'You killed a mouse a few hours ago.'

'So? At least I didn't eat it, unlike some other species I might mention.'

'I would eat a mouse for food. I wouldn't kill it for fun.'

'Well, I killed it for fun, so get over it,' said Rudi, filling in the little toilet hole he had made in the garden.

'Look, I'm not here to argue. My name is Iccuat, by the way. I came to ask you to leave the mice alone, at least for now. They are helping us with … something.'

'Helping you with what?' The owl drew breath and thought about his response.

'People are going to destroy parts of the forest. We have homes in trees that will be cut down, there are nests and burrows that will be destroyed. There will be creatures killed just because some human doesn't like them. And they are going to let cars into the forest.'

'Oh dear,' said the cat. 'That's such a terrible shame. Anyway, was there anything else?'

*Hmmm*, thought Iccuat. *A sarcastic cat.*

'Yes, I can see you are gutted. I should have known better than to trouble a deadly hunter, such as yourself,' mocked the owl. 'Perhaps you should get back inside?

Your servant will want to give you cuddles. Oh, and I'm so sorry to have interrupted your private time.' As the owl departed, he added, 'Which stinks, by the way.'

Iccuat had hoped to talk some reason into the cat. He should have known better. Domesticated cats. They do their own thing and only think of themselves. He flew off, taking with him a despondent account of the day's events.

Once back in the forest, Iccuat sat on one of Sylvester's branches. Roburt, Stoor, Sorbus, Cupar and Krab were talking with Sylvester across the wood wide web. Nothing was private, of course; all the trees were connected to it. They were all listening in. The holly trees, Jabs and Rebery, were unusually quiet. Troben had been sent to give a message to Bonnie to say they needed her in the forest in the morning. The mood was gloomy.

Sylvester tried to rally some fighting spirit. It wasn't easy as there was a sense of hopelessness. The younger pine trees were saying, 'What's the point? There's nothing we can do. They're going to cut us down. We'll all end up as firewood.'

'ENOUGH!' bellowed Sylvester. He was a big tree, and when he spoke with anger, the vibrations went through the roots of every tree. Silence descended over the forest.

Sylvester spoke, and all the trees and creatures in the forest listened. There were no birds in the sky. They had all landed on a branch so they could feel the vibrations of what Sylvester was saying.

'Please, everyone, listen carefully. You must understand that if you think there is nothing we can do, then you're probably right. If you think there *might* be something we can do, then you're probably right. If you are *absolutely certain* that something can be done, then you're right. So, *please* focus on a positive outcome. Negative thinking will help no-one. Let's remain positive.'

At a moment like this, we humans would take a deep breath to get a little more composure. But what Sylvester did was release a large amount of oxygen through his leaves. He then said what was on his mind. 'My fellow trees and woodland creatures, I know this is a difficult time for the forest, it's a difficult time for us all. So many of us in the forest face being cut down, killed or, at best, being moved from our homes. And I understand your fear.

'But I have been here for over two hundred years – long before it became the forest we all know today. Some of the other trees have been here even longer. And we don't plan to go anywhere soon. This forest has faced many threats in its time. Sometimes these threats come from disease. Sometimes they come from fire. And sometimes, like now, they come from humans. But through all these threats, over many years, the forest has always survived.

'If it should happen that machines enter the forest, then we'll still survive. We'll adapt. But I don't want to think about that. None of us can think about that. We must remain positive. We must stick together. The machines have not arrived yet. So, there is still time. We can still fight back.'

Sylvester's voice became more powerful than ever. Every inhabitant of the forest felt the vibration of his voice as he spoke. In each and every living being in the forest, a seed of hope began to grow.

'No-one has ever won a battle if they have gone to fight believing they will be beaten. No-one has ever won a battle if they believe in only the worst outcome. No-one has ever won a battle if they do not know about their enemy.

'But we – and that's everyone in this forest, every tree and every creature – are a massive army. We can listen to every conversation. We can see every movement. We can watch every path. And …' Sylvester paused to help emphasise his next point, '… and we have a human who can help us. A human who is prepared to fight for the survival of the forest.

'But this young human needs our help – our positive commitment. She needs to know we are doing everything to help her, and that we are brave, not beaten. We are strong, not weak. And she needs to know that, at every turn, we are ready to help her in this fight.

'So, I call on you: every tree, mouse, bird, insect, or whatever creature you are. I call on you all to make the work of these people coming into our forest as difficult as it can be. Annoy them. Swoop down upon them. Deposit your business on them. Listen to every conversation and let the holly trees know what you hear.

'If we're going to stand a chance of winning this battle, we can only do it as a team. Only by standing together do we have a chance of fighting back. Together, we WILL win this fight.

'So please, animal, tree or insect, do your best. Do something. Do *anything* you can to make it difficult. Feedback every scrap of information. Don't leave it to someone else. *You* are responsible. *You* are part of this team. And this team, this forest team, can, and will, win. WE. WILL. WIN. THIS. BATTLE. TOGETHER.'

Across the forest, there was stunned silence. Every living thing had heard Sylvester's speech. His rallying cries. And now, the atmosphere in the forest was changed. It had changed instantly. There was now optimism and hope. And a team filled with optimism and hope is a formidable team. A dangerous team. This was a forest that was ready to fight.

# Chapter 24

# Attack

The forest development needed planning approval before any work could begin. But there was nothing to stop teams of workers measuring, surveying and mapping. And, today, this work was getting underway. A minibus containing various workers arrived at the forest at nine in the morning. Their official start time was eight thirty, but the supervisor had decided on a stop-off in Hollypoint. It was the perfect place for some tea and morning rolls. *They always work better on a full belly, so it's worth the investment*, he had thought to himself.

The minibus was full. There were thirteen in the team, all with different skills. The supervisor had already given them their brief but now issued another reminder.

'OK, let's all remember this is a tough, demanding client. She has big plans, but now needs the detail. We need to get our spots in the forest and take our measurements. Then we produce the surveys, the maps and all the relevant reports. You know what you need to do, so let's get going. We'll meet back here at noon.'

Debs was one of the survey team. She was good at her job and was looking forward to this one, thinking it was nice to be out of the office. Debs was accompanied by Dani, a young surveyor with only a couple of years' experience, but Debs knew she could trust her. She was able and the pair of them made a good team. Like Debs, Dani was looking forward to this job. It was something a bit different.

The pair made their way into the forest. They had a long walk to get to the spot they were responsible for. It was a bit of a dull morning, but not wet and not too cold. They were both struck by the beauty of the forest.

'Squirrel!' said Dani, in one of these hushed, but half-shouty voices. 'Red squirrel. Wait, no, *two* red squirrels.' They both stopped to watch as the squirrels ran up a tree, then paused to stare straight back at them.

Dani laughed and said, 'Who's watching who?'

The pair continued their walk and noticed an increasing number of pigeons in the trees.

'Ever feel like you're being watched?' said Debs.

'Yeah, there's a lot of pigeons, eh? I noticed them a few minutes ago. I would say they were staring at us, but their eyes are on either side of their head. So, who knows what they are looking at!' They both laughed at this.

The surveyors continued their walk along the path.

Scorrop was in charge of the pigeons. He was new to the role, having taken over from Commander Mertu only four days previously. Mertu was one of the oldest pigeons and very experienced. But, unfortunately, he had a wing injury and wasn't able to fly far so couldn't take charge of this mission. He had to sit in the tree doing nothing other than make the pigeon call – hoo hoo hoooo, hooo, hoo hoo. Over and over again.

Being pigeon commander was a great honour. Well, among pigeons it was. Scorrop was proud of himself. He was taking the job seriously. He knew that, on their own, pigeons could get a bit bewildered. They weren't sure what to do, or where to go. They just sat about making 'hoo hoo' noises. It wasn't a communication, or a nice song. It was a noise that meant nothing, but they all did it. No-one knew why. Scorrop had tried a couple of times to make a different noise, but it had made his eyes go all funny. He'd lost his balance and fallen off the tree. He wasn't keen to try that again.

As a team though, pigeons could be a serious force. They weren't the sleekest of birds. In the air, they were more bomber than stealth fighter. Although, they could produce a bit of an aerobatic display when they needed to. It was helpful, however, that they were more of a bomber shape. Because bombing was what they had in mind. They had all been instructed not to 'go'. A toilet bomb would form part of Sylvester's 'Project Nuisance.'

This instruction was starting to pose a bit of a problem for two of the birds, Glage and Geoys. As they sat waiting for the command, Glage confessed, 'I need to go. I don't think I can hold on much longer. My eyes feel like they are bulging, I'm so desperate.'

Geoys agreed. 'I know. It's a nightmare. I've not been since mid-afternoon yesterday. I should have gone last night, but I thought I was doing the right thing. Now I'm struggling to fly. And I'm a bit windy.' Glage flew around the other side of Geoys. She was now on the right side of him: upwind.

Geoys was about to make another complaint when the command was given. Scorrop loved this bit and spoke like a military commander.

'Commander Scorrop to pigeon platoon. Stand ready for briefing. Follow my lead. Fly forty-five degrees vertical for twenty seconds. Full left-hand swoop. Swing back ninety degrees. Assume attack formation. Targets below at ten o'clock. Wearing high-visibility vests. On my command, release attack substance.'

Glage and Geoys looked at one another. Glage said 'What is he talking about? Left-hand swoop? Attack substance? I've no idea what's going on.'

'Look, follow Scorrop, and poop on the humans,' said Geoys.

'Ah, OK, got it. I'll be glad to get going. In more ways than one.'

'Platoon ready, and airborne,' said Scorrop.

Around fifty pigeons took to the sky. It was a sight, and it caught the attention of the surveyors. They stood watching the pigeons as they swooped in the sky. Then the birds changed their position and swooped back around so they were now behind Debs and Dani. The pair turned around to watch them.

'They look like they are heading straight over us,' said Dani. 'I wish I had my cam …'

Unfortunately, Dani was unable to finish her sentence. A giant amount of pigeon poo was released from desperate birds and made a direct hit on the two lady surveyors.

'Commander Scorrop to pigeon platoon. Direct hit. I repeat, direct hit. Return to base. Repeat, return to base at once.'

Debs and Dani were covered. Absolutely covered. 'Oh. My. God,' said Dani. 'Oh. My. Actual. God.'

On the other side of the trees, their colleagues Steve and Alfie had arrived at the edge of Grindmill Dam. This was a large area of water, some distance into the forest. In the middle of the water sat Oilthigh Island. Steve had seen this as an attraction on the plans but couldn't remember what they were going to do with it. Anyway, that wasn't his task today. He needed to take measurements around the dam. This would include measuring slopes and looking at ground stability. And a bunch of other things that the client had asked for. He had to be careful. It was boggy at the side of the water.

On the banks of the dam sat two young otters. They had been playing away in the water. One would race the other, then they would chase some fish. The otters were enjoying their day. They knew Steve and Alfie were on their way. One of the crows had alerted them. They called the people 'shinys'. The bright yellow jackets they wore reflected the light.

The otters were called Grunt and Aaaalp. They were great friends. They would boast about who was the fastest, and who could catch the most fish. And they were always joking and playing pranks on the other otters. Only yesterday, they had hatched a plan to torment Pop, one of the older otters. Pop had been swimming away, making his way onto the bank. Grunt had sneaked up behind him and given his tail a gentle but firm bite. Pop had got such a fright. He had shot onto the bank, and no sooner had he made dry land, than Aaaalp had sprung out of nowhere. He was doing the otter equivalent of 'Boo!' Pop nearly popped; he was so frightened.

Grunt and Aaaalp had a little plan in store for the shinys. But, as they sat at the water's edge, they were more intent on fooling around.

'What do you think the shinys are saying to one another?' said Aaaalp.

Grunt did his best human impersonation: 'Ah, it's a lovely day, but looks like rain.'

They both laughed. They knew that people talked endlessly about the weather. And they wore strange clothing or funny hats and boots. They put different things on their bodies all the time.

Aaaalp took over: 'Would you like a sandwich. I fancy a sandwich. I'm hungry. Have some water. Sit down. Take your jacket off, it's warm. Put your jacket on. It's cold.'

Grunt was on his back laughing now. 'Haha, that's exactly what they say.' He stood on his back legs and walked towards the water, mimicking a human. He dipped his hind foot into the water, pulled a cold face and said, 'Brrrrrr, that water's freezing.' This was possibly the funniest impersonation Aaaalp had ever heard. They both fell about laughing at their own jokes.

'Shinys inbound,' said Aaaalp.

'Where?'

'Follow the line of my claw.'

'Got them. Shiny as ever.'

'Ready?'

'Ready.'

The otters got their plan moving. They went into the water and swam across the dam, then climbed onto the bank. They were close to the shinys. They both stood on their hind legs and waved.

'Steve. Pssst. Steve. Look. Over there. Otters.'

'Wow. They're close. Haha, they look like they're waving!'

Steve and Alfie waved back. The otters played the game. They made it more interesting by waiting for the shinys to wave first, then waving back.

'Watch this,' said Grunt. 'I bet they've never seen an otter juggle before.'

He picked up two little pebbles and lay on his back, moving the stones around in the air like a little juggler.

Steve and Alfie's jaws dropped. 'Get your camera,' said Steve. 'Follow me, I'm going to get closer.'

The shinys walked slowly towards the otters, who continued to play with the pebbles. Grunt said to Aaaalp, 'Time to get extra cute.'

What Steve and Alfie saw next was a cuteness overload. The otters let them get close enough to tickle their bellies, as they rolled about on the bank of the dam. The otters kept giving the hands of the shinys a little snuggle with their heads. All of this was being videoed by Alfie. Grunt then shot into the water, leaving Aaaalp to be as cute as he could be. Steve was chatting away to Aaaalp, like a parent would talk to a newborn baby. He was so focused on his new otter friend, he didn't see Grunt sneaking out of the water, right behind him. 'Watch,' shouted Alfie, still filming. 'The otter is at your feet.'

Steve spotted the otter, and lifted his foot so he didn't hurt it. As he did so, the otter grabbed his trouser leg with his teeth and pulled. He didn't pull hard. But it was hard enough to get Steve to lose his footing. He did that thing where you try and prevent yourself from falling backwards. He swung both of his arms in circles, getting faster and faster. Alfie reached out to grab his workmate, but it was too late. There was an almighty splash, and Steve fell in the water. In the loch water. In the cold, January loch water.

Steve had never moved so fast. The sudden shock of the cold water hit him, and he scrambled back onto the bank. Alfie knew he should show more sympathy but didn't. He laughed hysterically. All he could do was point at his phone and say, 'Video.'

'You had better not post that online,' said Steve.

'As if I would do such a thing,' replied Alfie.

On the other side of the forest, a massive flock of birds was gathering …

# Chapter 25

## Fightback

The shinys couldn't continue. They had to go back to the van, as Steve was soaked and freezing. Alfie had stopped laughing, knowing that he had to get his mate warm – and soon. Without delay they headed off. Alfie was still chuckling under his breath. He couldn't wait to see – and share – the video. They looked back and saw the otters on the bank. They looked like they were celebrating. Of course, they couldn't be, they were wild creatures. But it did look like the otters had high-fived one another.

Meanwhile, surveyors Lynsey and Patrick were walking along one of the paths. They were headed towards one of the non-signposted entrances to the forest. The developer wanted one way in and one way out. This was one of the options: to create a road in from another direction. Or was it the road out? Patrick could never remember. It was one of the sides of the forest that looked into the little village of Copsehead. There was less of a view here, but it was still nice enough.

Patrick was annoying Lynsey as he had just consumed two bacon rolls that morning. These had been washed down with a large bottle of Coke. And now he kept burping. 'No wonder you have indigestion,' said Lynsey. 'You rammed those rolls down your neck and hardly chewed them. Then you guzzled a gallon of Coke. No wonder you are burping for Scotland.'

'It was only half a litre of Coke, not a gallon. Anyway, you sound like the wife.'

'That reminds me. I need to order that medal from Amazon, don't let me forget.'

'Medal?' quizzed Patrick.

'Yeah, for your long-suffering wife.'

'Hilarious, aren't you?'

'I do try,' said Lynsey.

'We're here,' said Lynsey. 'This is the area we need to map out. Then we need to walk through the gate over there and get some photos of the road and nearby housing. Which do you want to do?'

'Eh, I'll get the photos and stuff.'

Lyndsey had known Patrick would take that choice. 'Least amount of effort the better,' was his mantra.

Patrick had no sooner taken a few steps towards the gate when a giant fly-like creature whizzed past him. 'What's that? A giant wasp?'

'I think it's a dragonfly,' said Lynsey.

'It was black and yellow. I think it was a queen wasp.'

'Nah, too long and skinny for a wasp. Definitely a dragonfly.'

Lynsey was already on her phone Googling images of dragonflies. 'Look, dragonfly,' she said, pointing at an image on her phone.

Patrick barely had time to acknowledge what Lynsey was showing him when the sky darkened. They both looked up. They had half expected it to be more dragonflies, but Lynsey had just read that it wasn't the season for them. What they saw was a massive flock of birds. Little birds. Sparrows, robins, chaffinches – every little bird you could imagine. All flying around Lynsey and Patrick. They weren't being attacked, as such, but the birds were swooping from all angles towards them, getting closer and closer every time. The robins were the worst. They had no fear and even bumped into the couple a few times. Both Lynsey and Patrick were terrified.

'Back along the path,' shouted Patrick. They both half walked, half ran, back on the path in the direction of the car park.

Within a few minutes, all three teams had arrived back at the car park. The welfare van had arrived, which was a relief to Patrick. It was an even greater relief to Steve. He found a warm, if a bit smelly, old jacket he could wear. There was also a pair of wellies to replace his soaking boots. Debs and Dani wiped their jackets as best they could. Both were disgusted with the task they were performing, but glad they had been wearing hats. Clearing that mess out of their hair would have made them both sick.

Everyone shared their stories. Each was shocked about what had happened to the other groups. Even more so, they were surprised at the coincidence. Every group had had some unfortunate encounter with animals. It was bizarre, and none of them could have continued working.

Next to arrive at the car park were the drone teams. The others called them 'the dronies' – and many other names which gently mocked what they did for a living.

'Here they come, Spielberg and Co,' joked Steve, feeling a bit warmer now. 'What's happened to you lot?'

It was Musta who answered. 'I've never seen anything like it. We sent the drones into the sky and had just started filming. Then, out of nowhere, these massive birds …'

'Red kites,' added Jas, one of the other drone pilots.

'Then, out of nowhere, these massive red kites came out of the sky and attacked the drones. They're all broken, all three of them. We've at least got two back, but the third one has ended up in the lake somewhere.'

'Loch,' said Patrick. 'England has lakes, we have lochs.'

'Whatever,' replied Musta. 'But it's thousands of pounds of equipment. Do you think the insurance will cover it?'

Debs was shaking her head. 'Never mind insurance for a minute. There are six groups of us working here. Six groups and thirteen people. We've all gone into the forest to do a job, and each and every group has been attacked by animals. That's what has happened, isn't it?'

'Well, technically, we weren't *all* attacked, but I get your point,' said Steve.

'What's going on here?' asked Debs. 'Have the animals been trained or something?'

Musta spoke up. 'I don't think you could train pigeons. Or robins and sparrows. Otters? Maybe. And perhaps the red kites saw the drones as some kind of threat? I've heard of birds attacking drones before. Are they nesting?'

The others shook their heads. 'Not nesting season,' said Dani. 'It's certainly a bit odd. Feels like more than coincidence to me, but what else can it be?'

The minibus driver had arrived back to return the group to their offices. They were all glad to be leaving. Everyone remained bemused about the events of the morning, although they did have a good laugh at the otter video. The biggest laugh came from Steve's language as he went into the water. It was somewhat colourful.

Kimberly was furious, actually, fury wasn't even the best word to describe it. She was incandescent with rage. Her face was a reddish shade of purple.

'We have delayed this project by two weeks already. And now, you are telling me thirteen contractors, *thirteen*, were attacked by birds. Is that what you are saying?'

As the lead contractor, Debs had been nominated to speak for the group. Debs dealt in facts, and wasn't easily intimidated, by Kimberly or anyone else. 'No, that's not what I'm saying to you, Kimberly. What I'm saying is that we went to carry out our work, and there were six teams of us. Thirteen people. Two of us, me included, were pooped upon by pigeons. And I mean totally covered in pigeon poop. I can show you pictures if you want.' Kimberly drew breath, but Debs continued. 'Another two were dive-bombed by a giant flock of birds. They're fine, though. Thank you for asking. One ended up in the loch, and he's also OK. So, you don't need to worry about him either. And then the drone pilots have lost thousands of pounds' worth of equipment – their livelihoods. Attacked by birds of prey. But, like I say, Kimberly, no need for you to worry about us.'

Kimberly paused. It's not often someone stands up to her in this way. But OK. Maybe Debs had a point. And they were all needed onside and back at work. She calmed a little, if only for show. Her tone remained pointed.

'OK. So, everyone is back, and everyone is OK. There's equipment damage, but insurance will cover that, I'm sure. It can only be coincidence, Debs. Why would a bunch of birds attack you like that? There's no reason for it. You've been in the wrong place at the wrong time. The flock of little birds must have been moving together, and you've got caught up in it. And the otter incident. That pair should have known better than to get so close to a wild animal, for goodness' sake. As far as the drones go, it's a well-documented hazard. Goes with the territory, I'm afraid. May I suggest that you all chill for the rest of the day, then return tomorrow? We need this work done.'

Debs left the office. *What an utter witch*, she thought. But Debs knew that a shouting match wouldn't resolve anything. She had stood her ground and would not be talked down to by anyone. Anyway, as much as she hated to admit it, Kimberly was right. There was no other logical explanation. It was a combination of coincidence and occupational hazard.

The forest creatures were delighted with their efforts. Planning started at once for a second wave of 'Project Nuisance'.

# Chapter 26

# William

Bonnie heard the news about the activity in the forest. Chaff had been waiting on her returning from school and couldn't get the story out quick enough. Anyone watching Bonnie would have wondered what was going on, as she stopped to stare at the little bird. There looked like some kind of conversation going on. The bird would chirp, then Bonnie would laugh. Then it would chirp some more, and Bonnie would nod or shake her head, as if hearing some juicy gossip. Little would they know that this was exactly what *was* happening.

Bonnie was delighted with what had happened that day. But more would need to be done – what that was, exactly, she wasn't sure. Sylvester's rallying call had worked. There was now an army of nature, and it was at war with any workers coming into the forest. *And rightly so. You can't make others feel pain for your own selfish enjoyment, so it serves them right, she thought.* Although the surveyors in the forest didn't know half the story.

Bonnie and Misty sat at the table for their evening meal. 'Knee teas,' as they called them, where you sat on the couch and ate, were banned. Well, most of the time. They were reserved for something special. Misty had always been taught by her mum that you sat at the table to eat your meals. Anything else was rude. And mobile phones were banned at the table. *Fair enough*, Bonnie thought. She had always preferred a teatime chat anyway. David would sit by her side, ever hopeful of a sneaky snack.

They had finished eating, and were about to clear away the dishes, when there was a knock at the door. Misty answered it. A stranger in jeans, work shirt and crew-neck jumper stood there. He had a body warmer on, and beautifully polished shoes, Misty noted. 'Hello, you must be Misty Banks. My name is William Clinton. Definitely "William", not "Bill", or "President", for that matter! I'm so sorry to arrive unannounced, but I've been following the story of the forest development. I work for the Forth Courier. I wondered if we could do a bit of a story on your daughter? It's Bonnie, isn't it? We'd like to know more about what she has been doing to help save the forest.' William raised his hands, palms open in front of him, and offered another apology. 'Sorry again for the intrusion at teatime. I can smell food, so I've chosen a bad time, I know.' He then flashed a warm smile. His appearance came over as being genuine.

'Eh, OK. Bonnie, there's someone at the door who would like to talk to you about the forest development. He's from the Forth Courier. Called William.'

Bonnie arrived at the door. 'Hi, Bonnie, yes, my name is William, I, eh, well, your mum just told you. Are you happy to have a chat?'

'Yes, of course. Do you have some ID or something?'

Misty cursed herself under her breath. Sometimes Bonnie was so responsible; of course she should have asked for ID.

'Sure, here you are.'

Mother and daughter studied the ID badge. Both were happy and they invited William in.

'I'm sorry about the mess,' said Misty. 'We've just eaten. We were about to have a cup of tea. Would you like one?'

'Yes, that would be lovely, thanks. Strong and milky, please.'

William must have been in his late thirties, early forties, thought Misty. Around her age, anyway. He was a pleasant chap, easy to chat to. They all sat in the living room, David at Bonnie's side as always.

'Thanks again for agreeing to speak with me, Bonnie. It would be good if your mum stayed with us, as you're under sixteen, is that OK?'

'Yes, that's fine.'

William got straight to work. 'And what's your interest in the forest Bonnie. Why are you so keen to see the development stopped?'

'It's a bit of a long story, but put simply, they are going to cut down hundreds of trees. And when you cut down trees, it means the wild animals will need to get new homes or they'll die. Those that survive get stressed, and stress is harmful to them. And less trees means less places to live, so birds could die because they'll not have enough trees for them all in the area they call home. And it will reduce the amount of food available for the birds. So, less food for the same number of birds also means a greater chance they'll die.'

'Won't they just fly off elsewhere?'

Bonnie knew the answer to this. She had done her research. 'Yeah, sometimes that can happen. But mostly they die. And the loss of habitat has much the same effect on things like foxes, deer and rabbits. Even mice. I know most folks don't like the thought of mice. But they are a vital part of the food chain – the ecosystem – in the forest. Everything that lives in there plays a part, whether it's the trees, the birds, the mice or even the wild grass.'

'And tell me about your videos Bonnie. The talking rabbits.'

*Here we go again*, thought Bonnie. *A pointless exercise. All they want is a story on the talking rabbits.* Anyway, she answered. And William was happy. And then it all changed.

William put his pen down and sat back in his chair. He had pensive look on his face. There was silence for a few moments.

'I shouldn't say this. But I'm going to. We're hearing stories that the forest development might not be as good as it's being made out to be. We're hearing stories about the person behind the development – one Kimberly Parker. There's a lot of talk about her making payments to people in power to get the development approved. There have been some suggestions of more trees and vegetation being cut down than is on the plan. And we are also hearing that the lodges are plastic imports from China and are not particularly …' he seemed to be struggling to find the right word, '… "green".'

'There's more, Bonnie, but that's enough for now. May I ask, and I'm not writing this down, have you heard anything?'

Of course, Bonnie had heard lots. But she couldn't tell him she had been told by a tree and an owl. 'We've heard things said, just chit-chat, you know? But we've never heard anything from an official source or anything like that.'

William spoke again, 'I've been trying to set up a meeting with Kimberly Parker, but I've never been able to. I've turned up at her home, but she's never in, or if she is, she doesn't answer the door. I know she has an office somewhere, but I'm not sure where – there's nothing listed.'

'I know where her office is.'

'You do? Would you mind sharing with me?'

Bonnie told William the address.

William continued, 'There's another meeting in a few days, and I think the plans are going to be approved at that one. I've spoken to lots of residents, and the general feeling is they think it will be good for the area. I don't see the existing objections being upheld. I think you are going to see work starting on the forest soon, if I'm being honest.

'I'd like to help you with your protest, Bonnie. I used to work for a different newspaper, a few years back. We were in Glasgow, and I investigated The Parker Hotel Group back then. There were accounting irregularities – and a few other things. I couldn't get anything to stick. But I've done this job for a while now, and I know something is not right. There's something wrong here, and I'd like to find out what it is.'

'What do you want me to do?' asked Bonnie.

'OK, so here's the plan. And it will take a bit of time, but hear me out. You have posted how many videos on *TikTok* – twenty, twenty-five?'

'You mean about the forest?'

'Yeah, just what you have done in the past couple of weeks. I'm guessing that none of Kimberly's closest followers are supportive of what you are doing. But maybe some of them are. Maybe there are one or two I could speak to.'

'Sorry, I don't understand. What do you want me to do?'

'First of all, go through all the comments you've received on *TikTok*. I assume that's the main site you use?'

'Yeah.'

'OK, so go through all the comments, and see if there is a recurring name that makes comments. I don't mean the odd one or two, I'm talking about someone who has commented or said something on almost every post. It's a bit of a long shot, but it's a place to start.

'Also, the office where everyone meets. I need to find out who has been coming and going there over the past couple of weeks. That way, I can see if I can link any names and find someone who is approachable. Would you happen to know anyone nearby that might have seen anything?'

Bonnie thought of the camera. It must still be in the cabinet, abandoned. She couldn't explain how it got there, but put that to one side for the time being.

'I may be able to get you something, some information. Tell me your number and I'll message you.'

'OK, let me know as soon as you've been through your posts, Bonnie, and if you have anything on the office visitors.'

'Will do.'

Misty showed William out, then returned to the living room.

'Sounds positive, maybe a bit of a long shot, but better than nothing. As a matter of interest, how do you know where the office is, and who do you know there?'

'The animals told me. And we had a camera in the office to try and record something. The ones we got from Peter. The recording all went wrong, but the cameras are still in place. They might have something on them.'

'I'm not sure how we'll explain that,' said Misty. 'But let's just go with the flow for now. What do you want me to do?'

'Why don't you start looking at the *TikTok* comments, and I'll let the animals know we need the cameras back.'

'On it.'

# Chapter 27

## Pirouettesandcats

M isty had been searching through all the comments on *TikTok*. Searching for recurring names was tiring on the eyes. There were thousands of likes, so she had stuck to people who had commented. Misty had set up a little five-bar-gate system, as she looked for names of people who said something sensible. *Haha. Go Bonnie. Lol.* Anything like that, she ignored. Anything that read like it had come from a well-meaning adult was what caught Misty's eye. Comments like: *Well done Bonnie. There are lots of us supporting you. Keep up the good work.*

She was getting through the comments quickly now. There were four names that stuck out: *EnglishBell70*, *TheWalkerman*, *Stromboliisme* and *Pirouettesandcats*. All four left regular comments that were meaningful.

'Bonnie, come and see what I've found. Do these names mean anything to you?'

Bonnie had a look. '*EnglishBell70* is Mrs Bell, my English teacher. The other three, I've never heard of. But four people, out of thousands of comments. Already?'

'It was easy, once I got going. Not foolproof, but it will give William something to start work on. There's still a lot to go through, though. How did *you* get on?'

Fine. We'll get the cameras back.'

Misty sent the four names over to William. She got a 'thumbs up' emoji back. Nothing much happened that evening. Misty and Bonnie chatted about what else they could do and mulled over a couple of suggestions.

Bedtime arrived, and the house was locked up. David settled into his bed.

Bonnie was awoken at 2.33 am. *Tap, tap, tap. Tap, tap, tap.* The sound was coming from the window. She noted that David, the ferocious guard dog, was still sound asleep. Bonnie wandered over to the window and peered through the curtains. It was a crow making all the noise. Bonnie opened the window, and Troben spoke first.

'Hello Bonnie. How are you, are you?'

'Oh, hi, Troben. Yes, I'm good. Sleepy. But good. What is it?'

'We've got the cameras the cameras. Here, take this one this one.' Troben flapped her wings. Moments later, another crow arrived with the other camera. Bonnie took them both and said her thanks.

'You're welcome, Bonnie. See you later,' said the other crow.

There was nothing that could be done now; she would message William in the morning. Drifting back to sleep, Bonnie wondered two things. Number one: what was it with Troben repeating the last two words of every sentence? And, more importantly, number two: would there be anything on the cameras they could use?

# Chapter 28

# Netflix

Before Bonnie had breakfast, she messaged William to say he could collect the cameras. His reply was almost instant, asking if they could be collected in the next thirty minutes. Bonnie replied that was no problem, as long as it was before she left for school. At about twenty-five past eight, William arrived.

'Hi, Bonnie. That's been great work from you pair, thanks! Just to give you a quick update – we're still checking the names on your list. A couple of them are worth following up. I've got someone in the office doing a double check as well, just in case it throws anything else up. It may be nothing, but let's see where we get to. What time are you home tonight?'

'After four. But I'll check my phone for messages in between classes.'

'OK, catch ya later.' And, with that, William was off.

'Morning, Pam!' William was always cheerful in the morning. Sometimes, this was much to the annoyance of his colleagues in the office. 'How were the pictures last night?'

His colleague, Pam, had only arrived moments previously. A coffee was needed before any conversation. 'Fine, yes, fine. And good morning.' Pam looked at William and held her hand out in front of her face, to prevent any further questions. 'Coffee.'

William took the hint. He followed Pam through to the cupboard-come-tea room and put some instant coffee in his own mug.

Pam took a sip of coffee, made using the milk William had brought in. She stood smiling as the hot coffee made its way into her system. The conversation from five minutes earlier was then restarted: 'The pictures were great, thank you, William. We enjoyed every minute. Well, apart from the old couple next to us who brought in all sorts of snacks. In the noisiest of wrapping. And the woman kept sniffing. Every thirty seconds. Sniff, sniff, sniff. I was ready to strangle her. Glen, bless him, sensed this and we swapped seats. Not that it made much difference.'

William smiled and gave a little laugh. 'But you had a lovely time.'

Pam ignored the mild sarcasm. Her lack of patience with other people was well known. She was grateful for William's gentle efforts to keep her smiling. There was no doubt he had prevented many a random strangling of a poor innocent stranger. He had a similar nature to her husband, Glen.

As the coffee flowed, Pam spoke about the comments on Bonnie's *TikTok* posts. 'I sat last night after tea and went through some of them. Then another hour, after we got back from Vue. Two hours, just scrolling. In my own time, I'll have you know!'

'You love it really. You could have been a detective – I've always said that.'

'Flattery will get you everywhere. Anyway, there are four names: *EnglishBell70*, *TheWalkerman*, *Stromboliisme* and *Pirouettesandcats.*'

'Bonnie's mum came up with exactly the same list, so that's a good start. And *EnglishBell70* is Bonnie's English teacher, Mrs Bell.'

'Makes sense. They were only ever supportive comments, so I think we can rule that one out. Now, the other three … *TheWalkerman*. He – and I found out it *is* a he – is quite angry. The comments tend to be about how much of a disgrace it is that they are doing this to a forest. Used to live here, apparently, but – judging by his recent posts – he's been away from the area for a long time.

'*Stromboliisme* is also an angry character. I can't find out much about him, other than he is angry about everything. Politics, football, education, the health service. You name it, he's angry about it – and he has great solutions for making everything better. Which normally involve sending politicians to barren islands in the cold.'

William laughed. 'Sounds like he should be in politics himself!'

'What do you think, keep or bin?'

'Put him on the list that says "unlikely", but we'll revisit if there's nothing else.'

'So, William. That leaves us with *Pirouettesandcats*. A comment on nearly every post that Bonnie has made. Seems a level-headed individual and the profile picture suggests it's a woman. Her comments tend to be in favour of the development. But, often, there is some sympathy. Things like saying tree felling will be kept to a minimum, and you can't stand in the way of progress. Cutting down trees is terrible but think of the jobs – that kind of thing.'

'OK, that sounds positive. Anything else on her?'

'She's a translator or interpreter, judging by some of her posts. There are posts of her in the local area, so I assume she's local. But her location is private on *TikTok*. And she is exceptionally tall and owns a cat.'

'I'd like to talk to her. Can you see if you can contact her, please?'

'To say what?'

'Eh, we're talking to local people about the forest, and what it means to them. For or against, kind of thing. Which is true. And also, we noticed she was a big commenter on the posts, so that's true as well.'

'Just miss out the Kimberly Parker dodgy dealings bit then.'

'You got it!'

William set about downloading the videos from the cameras. It wasn't going to be a morning binge watching Netflix, but it had to be done. Bonnie had also given him a connection lead, so it was all straightforward. Good quality sound and vision as well.

Videos uploaded, next came the task of watching them. He started with Kimberly's house but was uncomfortable with the legalities of how this footage had been obtained. He put these thoughts to one side as no one knew about the cameras. *Learn nothing, say nothing*, he thought.

Unfortunately, 'learn nothing' was exactly what happened with the first video. William was, in some ways, glad about that. A camera installed in a private property? It didn't feel right. He made a mental note to ask Bonnie how they had managed this.

Now, onto the office. Was a secret camera in an office any better, he wondered? He agreed with himself to stick to the plan: watch and see first.

'How's it going?' said Pam.

'Nothing much from the first video. I watched it on five times speed, stopping any time there was someone in the room. Just starting the second one now. Not sure about how much use this will be, though. I Googled about using cameras, and it's illegal if it's somewhere that you would expect privacy. If we learn anything here, we need to think carefully about how we use it.'

'Agreed. And best to tell that young lassie not to be installing videos in offices and houses.'

'Yes, I was thinking that myself. How did she get these in there? A question for another time.'

Pam made fresh coffee and opened a packet of digestive biscuits. The pair then sat to watch the second video.

'I'd better eat these biscuits quietly,' said William.

Pam threw him her legendary, but tongue-in-cheek, evil stare. 'This video is much the same as the other one. You can tell there's something not right. I mean, who reacts like that – clapping their hands, smiling and talking about a sweetener. It's not right, but no one will go to jail over it. Hang on, who's that coming in?' said Pam. 'It's her. The tall woman … *Pirouettesandcats*.'

They sat in silence watching the rest of the video. Apart from learning that the tall woman was involved in some way, they learned little else. But they did find out that her cat could catch mice and got a remarkable close-up of the cat in the cabinet.

As Pam and William discussed the next steps, Pam's phone pinged. It was a *TikTok* message from *Pirouettesandcats*. It read 'Thanks for the offer of an interview, but it's not for me. But thanks anyway.'

Some miles away, a black cat called Grimalkin sat quietly grooming its fur. This cat didn't think like other cats; it had human thoughts. It understood what people said and, if it chose to, it could put thoughts into their heads in the shape of words. Anyone looking at that cat would think it was two or three years old. But the truth was, the cat was over two hundred years of age.

It had been a loyal servant to a few witches over the years. Its most recent master was an old woman called Florence who had lived in a cottage in the forest. She had died many years previously. Grimalkin's job had been to wait for a new owner and finally, one had arrived. A young girl by the name of Rachel Parker. She was the daughter of an evil witch, who had never been granted a guardian. Grimalkin wasn't sure yet what kind of witch Rachel was: good or evil. What he *did* know was that her mother – Kimberly – was truly evil. He had lost his tail to her evil thoughts and he hoped she would never discover her true power.

# Chapter 29

# Stampede

The land surveyors had arrived back at the forest. There were only four of them this time. Two were going to use a drone. The others were going to get 'OS-map-accurate measurements', as was explained to Kimberly. They could only get two teams together, after the disastrous attempts the previous day. The others were booked onto other jobs. Despite Kimberly demanding these be rescheduled, a compromise was reached. Two teams it was.

The drone operators had to get footage to promote the development. The video edit would show what a wonderful job was being done. They would get pictures of different birds in a variety of trees. Words would flash onto the screen to suggest care for both the animals and the environment. This would be part of the advertising for the park, once completed. Musta and Jas were highly experienced with this type of work. They knew exactly the footage they wanted.

Lynsey and Patrick were the other team. Their equipment was all packed and they were ready to go. Both teams had decided that the previous day's events had to be some kind of coincidence. Everyone was looking forward to getting started; they were just waiting on the client arriving. Ms Parker had insisted she join them and was due to arrive at half past eight.

At 8.23, Kimberly arrived. An Audi A5 Quattro was her car of choice. 'Good morning,' she said, her tone flat, assertive and unwelcoming.

'Morning, Kim,' said Patrick. 'Nice car … I bet that's more gallons to the mile than miles to the gallon.'

'Firstly, my name is *Kimberly* and not Kim. And, secondly, I'm paying a lot of money for these services, so I'm not here for idle chat. Please tell me who is doing what, and how long it will take.'

Already being familiar with Kimberly's reputation, Lynsey went straight in with an explanation. 'I will be working with Patrick here, and we will be taking measurements to build an exact picture of the area. It will be brought up to date with any hazards or issues that need dealt with. Musta and Jas will be on drone footage. It's as simple as that. Will you be going with either group?'

'I might. But don't let that stop you. Go and do your thing and if I'm there, I'm there. You … drone person.'

'Me?' said Musta, pointing at himself.

'Yes, you. I want footage of this whole area. This entire area and the car park will change beyond recognition. I want before and after shots. And leave out that big tree there if you can. It will have to go, and I don't want all sorts of blabbering and badmouthing over a blasted tree.'

Roburt heard every word. He knew his time in the forest was coming to an end unless they managed to prevent the holiday park going ahead. In over two hundred years, he couldn't remember ever feeling fear. He could remember the war and hearing planes flying overhead. He recalled sensing the vibrations in his roots as bombs fell onto Scotland, but that was over a hundred years ago. He could remember it happening, but he hadn't feel fear then like he did now.

But he also felt angry. This person, this human woman. Talking about his life like it didn't matter. *Enough self-pity. I need to alert the others that they're here again*, he thought, as he put the wood wide web to work.

The land surveyors were already on their way into the forest. Glad to be away from Kimberly, at least for now, and glad to be enjoying such a beautiful, bright and crispy morning. The winter sun was already out, bathing the tops of the trees with its warm orange glow. The beauty of the forest even caught Patrick's attention. And normally the only thing that interested him was watching or playing football.

Lynsey and Patrick headed in a different direction from the previous day. The task was the same, but there were other areas of the forest more important to map. They were starting with what would become the main route into the forest. It was a large area off to the right that would become a giant car park.

'Seems a shame to cut down the old oak tree,' said Lynsey. 'If that thing could talk, it would have a story or two to tell.'

If only she knew.

Meanwhile, the animals were receiving messages. The 'www' spread the word far and wide. Squirrels were on alert. Every bird in every tree was on the lookout. Rabbits, foxes, deer, mice, you name it, they were all watching for the shinys. And, of course, Commander Scorrop assembled the pigeons.

Musta and Jas had not expected to lose three drones in one day. The drone they unboxed and set up now was an older bit of kit which they kept as a spare.

The drone was airborne. It captured footage of what would become the park entrance. It then journeyed above one of the wider paths that would become the main road into the centre of the park. Musta and Jas were happy with the footage they had recorded so far. They were due a battery change soon but wanted to get some nice shots of the entrance to the forest from high above. There was more than enough power remaining to get that done.

Roburt sent out another message. 'What's happening? Where is everyone?' Just at that moment, red kites appeared in the distance.

'Musta! Musta, bring back the drone!' said Jas. 'The big birds are heading over here.'

Musta didn't delay. The drone was brought down quickly as the red kites flew overhead. They made a few circles around the area before settling somewhere out of sight.

Jas changed the battery and decided to wait a bit before launching the drone again. 'They don't like the drones, do they?' he said.

Lynsey and Patrick were unaware of what was going on. They weren't far away, but far enough to be out of view. Equipment was unpacked and was being set up. Their high-visibility jackets occasionally caught the sun's mid-morning rays and reflected them. Lynsey was at the edge of the trees, her laser measuring equipment ready to use. Patrick was some distance away, in wide open space. Both were being watched by hundreds of pairs of eyes; the eyes of the forest – the eyes of Devilla. But the danger was not coming from the skies, this time. Many birds had gathered, but none had taken flight. They were all perched in the trees, watching.

Deep into the trees, forty sets of larger eyes were on Lynsey. Normally timid creatures, deer had gathered unseen in the trees. They walked forward with some caution, taking confidence from their leader. Wayne was one of the larger roe deer. He had the biggest antlers of the herd, but wasn't the horse-sized red deer variety. Not that *he* knew that. His sense of smell was unmatched by the other deer and his ears could hear a pin drop a mile away. He was the head of the herd. And Sylvester had instructed him to chase the visitors from the forest.

Wayne moved the herd through the trees and ever closer to Lynsey. She was facing the other way and couldn't see them.

Patrick was too far away to see anything. But what he *did* notice was how quiet the forest had become. The bird song they had heard on arrival had stopped. The forest had become still. Eerily so.

'Lynsey,' he shouted.

'What?'

He started to walk towards her. 'I don't want to spook you, but can you hear anything?'

'No, nothing. Why, what's wrong?' There was something about Patrick's tone that put Lynsey on edge. 'Patrick. What's wrong?' She was starting to feel panicky.

'There's no noise. And there's an atmosphere. Something's not right. Stay calm, Lynsey, but look behind you. Can you see anything?'

Lynsey looked over her shoulder before turning round. *This is ridiculous*, she thought. *I'm standing next to trees in a forest in Firthshire. In Scotland. It's not the blooming Blair Witch Project.*

And then, she saw the eyes. Whatever her direction of vision, there were eyes: to the left, to the right and to the front. And the eyes were getting closer … and closer. Lynsey was momentarily rooted to the spot.

'Run!' she screamed.

As they made for the path, Patrick had no idea what was happening. All he heard was Lynsey shouting 'Run!', and the sound of stampeding hooves. Over forty roe deer were running out of the trees towards them. Lynsey ran as fast as her legs would carry her towards Patrick as the deer, much faster than her, closed the gap. She caught up with Patrick just as he had started to run towards the path. They were running over rough ground, much better suited to the deer than to two middle-aged surveyors.

The deer were getting closer and closer. Forty deer in a herd, travelling at great speed and coming straight for you, is not a pleasant experience. But it would make you run fast. Lynsey and Patrick gathered speed as the land levelled out. But not for long. They felt the sensation of the weeds and the wild grass grabbing at their feet, slowing their progress. Patrick was the first to fall, knocking the wind out of himself. Seconds later, Lynsey fell. Both of her wrists were hurt as she reached out instinctively to break her fall.

The deer kept coming. The noise became louder and louder. Closer and closer. There was nothing either surveyor could do, other than curl into a ball and pray.

The herd of deer ran right over the top of them. Large heavy deer, with hooves hardened by nature. The noise of the running herd disappeared into the distance. Patrick stood, uninjured other than needing to get his breath back. 'Lynsey,' he shouted.

'Over here. I've hurt my wrists.'

Patrick went over and helped her to her feet. 'Are you OK? What's wrong with your wrists?'

'I'll be fine, I've just hurt my wrists falling forward. Nothing's broken, though. That was a close one. How they managed to run over us and not trample us to death, I'll never know.'

Patrick looked at Lynsey, eyebrows furrowed. 'What *is* going on in this forest? This isn't a coincidence – something's wrong. We need to get back to the car. Mrs Happy won't be pleased.'

'Mrs Happy', aka Kimberly Parker, was now standing next to Patrick and Lynsey, having watched recent events from just a few metres away.

*Splat.*

Commander Scorrop had scored a direct hit! Right on the head of the angry woman. 'You blasted thing,' she screamed. 'I hope you end up in a pie.' As she stared at the departing pigeon, she repeated her hopes for its future under her breath … eight more times.

'I've no idea what's going on here, either,' fumed Kimberly, ignoring the pigeon deposit on her head. 'But if some force of nature thinks it's going to stop *me*, it can think again.' Getting angrier and angrier, she started to shout again. 'Whoever you are, do you think this is funny? You'll think it's hilarious when the machines arrive.'

Her fist was clenched as she shook it and shouted into the open air. 'I'll flatten the whole blasted forest!'

# Chapter 30

## Progress

Kimberly Parker was fuming. She was on the verge of losing control. She wiped the pigeon poop from her hair, then wiped her hands on the damp grass, then on her jacket. Patrick thought to himself, *That's a rather expensive jacket for walking in the forest.*

Kimberly continued to shout obscenities at the sky and the trees. It would have been an odd spectacle for anyone looking on.

'I'll fly a blasted plane over here to do the surveys if that's what I need to do,' she yelled. Distracted by her own fury, she had still not asked Lynsey and Patrick if they were OK. Kimberly started to make her way back to the car park, cursing with every step. The land surveyors followed behind, not keen to progress with their task, nor were they in the mood for conversation.

Kimberly stood next to Roburt in the car park. His winter branches looked bare and vulnerable. She spoke to, or, more accurately, *at* Patrick and Lynsey. 'I need you to do your work in this forest. I need you to do your thing. I don't care how you do it, just get it done. And don't tell me you've been attacked by rabbits or anything ridiculous like that. You have a contract to survey this forest. And if you don't meet the terms of the contract, I'll damn well sue you.'

Arriving back at the car park, Kimberly was focused on getting her jacket off to check for pigeon droppings, so she didn't notice Roburt's low-hanging branch. It was a light branch, more of a twig, really, but she managed to get it caught in her hair. Already in a temper, she grabbed the branch and snapped it off the tree. Her temper wouldn't allow her to take the time to untangle it. She pulled it from her hair, taking a few strands with it. The branch was then used to hit the trunk of the tree. 'And I'll burn *you* to the blooming ground.'

Lynsey and Patrick had decided a coffee was the best next step. Musta and Jas joined them. They went back to the quiet little deli in Hollypoint, off the main square. Patrick spoke first. 'So, what now?

'I'm at a bit of a loss,' said Lynsey. We can't file "deer and otter attacks" as the reason not to complete the work. The other attacks were odder and only a little bit scary. But today? I thought I would be trampled to death.'

Musta replied, 'Yeah, I agree. I don't want to lose another drone, but what you went through must have been a nightmare.'

It was Jas that came back with a plan. 'Look, we've got another couple of weeks to complete the work. But we only need a couple of full days on site. What if we return later today with the drone and get an hour of work done at last light? It's not ideal, but if we try it at a different time of day, maybe …

'I don't know why I think this, but we should park at the other gate. I mean, surely we can do this without another animal attack? Maybe they see the equipment and it spooks them? And if you guys use the other gate as well. Don't unpack until you're right where you need to be, then get set up and go as fast as you can. Leave the high-vis jackets off and we'll have one last try and see how it goes. If it happens a third time, then we'll need to wriggle out of the contract somehow. But if it goes OK, we can get the others back, survey for shorter periods, later in the day and still get this wrapped up. Thoughts?'

It was as good a plan as any. No-one was comfortable coming back, but they had to try again. They also agreed they would enter the forest separately, to attract less attention. Although less attention from *what*, they weren't sure.

At three o'clock, the surveyors made their way into the forest. They looked like a couple out for a walk, so the trees and animals thought nothing of it. Patrick had even brought his dog, a golden Labrador called Copper. They wandered into the forest unnoticed by the creatures and were able to use their equipment in relative silence. Their chosen spot was visible to others enjoying the forest. But it was in a clearing a little bit away from the trees or any sign of wildlife. They worked for over an hour. Silently, diligently and successfully – but constantly looking over their shoulders, nonetheless.

Musta and Jas had similar success. They had parked as close to the forest as they could. The drone was launched from the side of the car, and controlled by Jas sitting half in, half out of the driver's seat. It had a good range, and they were able to get all the required data and footage. They flew the drone high. They kept the height and swept over as much of the area as they felt comfortable with. Musta had walked to the main flight path of the drone, and they had kept their mobile phones on. At the first sight of any birds, Jas would drop the drone as close to Musta as he could.

Both teams got together further along the road, away from the forest. Their plan had been a success. High fives were exchanged. They agreed they would return over the next few afternoons to complete the work. The lighting wasn't ideal, but it was more than workable. They would stagger the times, never arriving together. Plain clothes, no high-vis jackets. Everything would be agreed in advance. There were no conversations 'in the field.' The work had finally got underway. Kimberly was sent a message to confirm that progress was being made.

Deeper into the forest, there was great confusion among the pigeons. Commander Scorrop had been doing such a wonderful job, but he had disappeared. No-one could find him anywhere.

# Chapter 31

## Beezy

In the offices of The Forth Courier, William had been trying again to contact the tall woman. She was still resisting his request for a meeting, saying signed documents prevented her from talking to the press. William was getting nowhere and getting there fast. He knew he needed a breakthrough. But how? In his previous job, he had investigated The Parker Hotel Group. But this had come to nothing. He had invested a lot of time and effort into the story, sure that it would pay off. When it all fizzled out, his career went with it. His move to the Forth Courier was seen as a 'sideways step'. To him, it felt like a step down. But always being one to look on the bright side, at least he had freedom to do as he chose. If there were good stories, then paper sales went up and the website was clicked. He enjoyed it there. The salary wasn't as good, but it was a great place to live. He even ended up a bit better off – his house was the same size as the one he left behind in Glasgow, but it was much cheaper. And the views were way better. The only thing that kept William awake at night was a niggling feeling. He was sure he had been stitched up in some way. The Parker Hotel Group investigation was a blot on his otherwise unblemished career. If the development of the Devilla Forest *was* in some way unlawful, he was determined to find out. A great story, and it would offer something to clear his name. He began to come up with an idea.

Bonnie had arrived home from school. There was little time until the next council meeting. If nothing could be done, they would lose the battle and work would start on the forest. She was at a loss. Her mum was supportive but had no idea how to prevent the plans being approved. William had gone quiet – *probably lost interest*, she thought. Bonnie had spoken to Iccuat, who shared her despair. The forest was still on alert. But, other than dog walkers and photographers, they hadn't seen much else. Or so they thought …

Even the media interest had died down. 'So much for the world standing up to prevent forest destruction,' said Bonnie, out loud.

David joined her. 'Chin up. You've done everything you can. Don't blame yourself. Something will happen.' When Bonnie was halfway through thanking David for being so supportive, like her own personal counsellor, two things happened. The doorbell went, and David had a serious attack of the 'zoomies'. Bonnie made her way to

224

the front door as David ran from room to room, round and round furniture, and all at top speed. She opened the door; William was standing there.

'May I come in, Bonnie?'

'Sure. Please excuse David, though, he goes half daft at times. His head is full of mince and broken glass.'

William took a seat in the living room and started to speak as Misty joined them, cups of tea in hand. 'It doesn't need me to tell you it's not going well. We have lost momentum. I can't get to talk to anyone that might give us something to go on. We've only suspicions of bribery, no proof. So, I can only think of one thing.'

'Go on,' said Misty.

'The thing that got me interested in the first instance was Bonnie's viral video of the talking rabbits. That started everything. We need another one … an emotional one. Rabbits upset the forest is being cut down, crying, losing their homes – that kind of thing. Think of these appeals when there's been some foreign disaster. You know the ones? They have the sombre video with the sad music. Can you do that, Bonnie? Like, in the next day or so?'

This was an easy one for Bonnie. She knew exactly what she was going to do. 'Leave it with me. I'll have exactly what you need by this time tomorrow night.'

'You've got school tomorrow, Bonnie,' said Misty.

'I can do it,' she replied.

William left, happy with the discussion, and a bit bewildered about how they coped with that dog of theirs. It sped from room to room the entire time he was there. Daft thing.

Bonnie was up late that evening. There was lots of unused footage of the rabbits, all she needed was a voice-over. And now there was a theme, a plan to work to. She was happy with progress, but something was missing. What was needed was an interview with a rabbit, and to make it look like it was doing part of the 'voice-over.'

Bonnie took David out for a quick walk, and within minutes they were speaking to Chaff. She was as excited and as fast-talking as ever.

'Hiya Chaff, how's you?'

'HiyaBonnieI'mgoodhowareyouwe'reallstillworriedth oughdoyouthinkyoucanstopthework?'

Bonnie had had to get used to 'Chaff speak'. She wasn't always easy to follow.

'I don't know, Chaff. I'm trying. Look, I need your help. Can you get Beezy the rabbit here first thing tomorrow? I need to try and get fresh interest going. And I need her help.'

'SureIcanBonnieshe'llbehereatfirstlighttomorrowisth atok?'

'Thanks Chaff. It's our last try, so I'll make it a good one. Promise.'

Chaff flew off, David did his business and they returned home. Bonnie worked until one in the morning on her epic rabbit production. It was going to be a masterpiece. All she had to do was slot in an interview with Beezy, and it was done.

First light arrived, and Bonnie was good to go. She had made a little studio to create the look and feel of a chat show. Some of her old doll's house furniture completed the homely feel to the background. Bonnie stood in the garden and waited for Beezy to arrive. When she turned up, the pair had a quick human-to-rabbit chat, then went into the garden shed out of sight. This was easy for Bonnie. She asked the rabbit some questions, and Beezy answered them. What the rabbit said was open and honest, and – at times – moving. All Bonnie needed to do was put her 'rabbit voice' to the video.

School passed at a snail's pace. Bonnie was excited about her production and couldn't wait to get home. An hour's work and it would be finished. She had messaged William to tell him to come round about five thirty, when the video would be ready.

Ten minutes before the agreed time, William arrived. Seats were taken and teas were poured. Bonnie played the video on her laptop. It was amazing. Everything that William had hoped for, and more. It was a 'disaster appeal,' direct from the rabbits. Bonnie had even thrown in some new characters with new voices. There was an owl and a crow, along with an otter and a chaffinch. All unused video footage from her trips to the forest. And all held together by Beezy the rabbit.

The video was uploaded, and the views started to clock up. One view, followed by one like. Then, within a few minutes, there were fourteen views. Within an hour, it had hit over four thousand. This was *big*. It was going viral; this was happening before her eyes. The evening saw the numbers continue to grow. There were likes and comments from all around the world. At bedtime there were over fifty-one thousand views.

Bonnie slept well but woke early. She checked her phone while rubbing the sleep from her eyes. Over a quarter of a million views. *A quarter of a million.* Bonnie rubbed her eyes again and sat up straight. She pulled her thoughts together, doubting she had read the numbers right. But she had. It was 278,866, to be precise. David was awake, wondering what Bonnie was doing. As much as he was a talking and intelligent dog, numbers didn't mean that much to him.

'You know how you get fed every day?' Bonnie tried to explain. 'Well, imagine this was plates of food. That would be enough food to fill this whole room, the whole house – maybe more.'

David got it. 'So, that's good then?'

'David, it's brilliant. Absolutely brilliant. But the meeting is on Friday. I don't know if anything will work now.'

Misty had heard Bonnie's voice and was hoping this animal talking thing wasn't something in her daughter's head. *Stress can do strange things to people*, she thought. Knocking on the bedroom door, Misty waited for an answer. 'Somebody's learning,' Bonnie muttered, under her breath, then she said, a little louder, 'Come in, Mum!'

No sooner was the bedroom door open, than Bonnie announced, 'Over a quarter of a million views, and it's still rising.'

Misty was stunned into silence. 'Let me see your phone, please.' She thought there had been some kind of mistake, but no. A quarter of a million it was. 'There's nothing more you can do, Bonnie. You've done everything you can. And what you have done is wonderful. We'll need to leave it to …'

Misty jumped as the phone started to ring in her hand. 'Oh, it's William.' She instinctively answered it. 'Hello, William. It's Misty Banks here. I'm with Bonnie now. Have you seen the views?'

'Seen them? I certainly have! I couldn't believe what I was seeing. Have you been looking at the comments? They are amazing. The usual trolls, of course, pathetic specimens that they are. But there are great comments. All supportive. Not sure whether it's for Bonnie or that rabbit, though!' He ended his sentence with a little chuckle.

Misty switched the phone to speaker. William continued, 'There are about twenty-odd comments this morning, all from the national news looking to speak to you. BBC, ITV, SKY and even CNN have picked this up.

Bonnie, if you are going to use this to your advantage, you need to get a couple of days off school. I'm sure they would support it. It's great for them, and a wonderful story. Local pupil fights big corporate, kind of thing.'

'Leave that bit with me,' said Misty.'

'Why don't we meet to discuss what we do next,' said William. 'I could come round, or it might be more private if you come round here. I know the media, and they'll be at your house and at the school in no time.'

It was decided. They would meet at the offices of the Forth Courier later that day.

Showered, dressed, breakfast, quick walk for David, then off. While they were out, Bonnie saw Beezy. 'Hello, little rabbit. How are you?'

'Hiya Bonnie. Am I famous?'

'Famous? You're known worldwide!'

'Worldwide? What does that mean?'

'The world stretches way beyond the forest, Beezy. Further than your eyes can see.'

'Cool. Can we keep our forest, though?'

'That's another matter, Beezy. I'm trying. But lots of people seeing your video is a good thing. We need lots of people to support us, and this video helps more than you'll ever know. So, keep your fi … eh … *paws* crossed.'

'Why would I do that, Bonnie?'

'It's just for luck, Beezy. You go and tell the others. See you soon.'

At about quarter past eight, Misty called the school and spoke to the headmaster. 'Good morning, Mr Hayes. I don't know if you've seen the …'

'*TikTok* video?' He completed the sentence for her. 'Yes, I've seen it. You have quite an activist on your hands there, Ms Banks.'

'Misty's fine. Please call me Misty'.

Mr Hayes sounded a bit uncomfortable calling her "Misty", but he went with it.

'I'm guessing you want to take Bonnie out of school for a couple of days?'

'Eh, yes. If that would be OK? She will catch up, and it's so important for the area, and a good example to the school, too, I would have thought?'

'Misty, it's fine. A couple of days will be fine. Please know that if I or anyone in the school can help, you just have to ask. We also have resources here, printing and copying, that kind of thing. Shout if you need anything.'

'Thank you so much, Mr Hayes.'

'Please pass on my good wishes to Bonnie. Oh, and if they want to film her at the school, then that's also fine. You take care, Ms Banks.' He couldn't keep with calling her "Misty".

'Thank you, Mr Hayes, bye.'

And that was it. Bonnie had a couple of days to keep spreading the word. Local support had dwindled, so if they were going to do anything, now was the time.

The viral video had made its way all over the world. And one of the viewers of the video in Boston, America, had strong ties to Misty and Bonnie Banks.

# Chapter 32

# Jack

**B**onnie was on the national and international news. They all loved the story. It wasn't the first item, but it wasn't the last either. Calls came in from other radio stations looking for interviews. Bonnie was loving every minute. William looked after her, keeping her right with good things to say and things *not* to say. Yes, Bonnie was enjoying being in the limelight.

Over at The Parker Hotel Group, Kimberly Parker was 'unavailable for comment'. She wasn't interested in discussing things with the media. On the group's social media pages, it issued a statement that said:

*The Parker Hotel Group invests in local economies. We grow businesses and create employment. We bring tourism to Scotland. Like all our developments, the changes proposed to Devilla Forest will be ecologically managed by our teams of expert contractors.*

And that was it. More big business words. Bonnie continued with her press interviews. She was on the radio, on the TV and in print. Pictures were taken at the school and at the forest. They even had one of Bonnie pretending to chat to a rabbit in a nearby pet store. If only they could have heard what the rabbit said when he realised he could hear a human talk! It came as a bit of a shock, and Bonnie's genuine laughter made great TV. And Bonnie was pleased to hear that the rabbit didn't mind being in the pet shop. As long as he got a home soon, with plenty of space to run around. And no cats. He didn't like cats.

Bonnie, Misty and William had had a busy couple of days. The planning meeting was now only four hours away. Lots of great things had happened, and even local support had improved. But it looked like nothing was going to stop the work going ahead.

Bonnie heard from Chaff that the mood in the forest wasn't great. The woodland creatures loved everything she was doing, even though they didn't fully understand it. But they watched as the TV crews took footage of the forest with Bonnie. And they knew this was good. But probably not good enough.

It was coffee time in the offices of the Forth Courier. William had brought in cakes. He was pleased with the work of the past few days and, of course, he had exclusive coverage. He was writing a more in-depth article. It covered the development of the Devilla Forest and the longer-term impact on the area. Misty had read through the early draft and thought it made good reading. But, like the residents of the forest, they found their enthusiasm had drifted a little. It was all starting to seem a bit pointless.

Misty's phone rang. Unknown caller. She'd had several of these of late and could never figure out how these people got your number. *Pesky nuisance callers*, she thought. *No better than internet trolls.* Despite her reaction, she answered.

'Hello,' she said, curtly.

'Hi Misty. It's Jack.'

Misty's mind went into overdrive, processing all the Jacks she knew. Which were few. Although the voice was familiar. But it couldn't be, could it? Jack Banks? What did she feel right now? Was it anger? Betrayal? Or sadness? She opened her mouth to speak, but Jack beat her to it.

'Misty, I don't even know where to start. "Sorry" doesn't cut it, I know. So, I won't say it. I have nothing to offer you other than regret. Regret that has stayed with me for twelve years. Regret that I can't even show you my face, regret that I haven't even spoken to our daughter. Regret that I cheated on you. I know it's nothing compared to what you've been through, nothing even close. You've raised a fine and beautiful daughter on your own. You are part of a family. You have even kept in touch with my mum and dad, which I know isn't easy. So, for what it's worth, I've lived twelve years that have been nothing other than work and regret. And I'm more ashamed than sorry. But I'm also sorry.'

Wow. That was a statement. Misty was still lost for words. All she could say was 'Where are you?'

'I'm at Boston airport. I'll be home – well, at my mum and dad's house – later tomorrow.'

'What are you coming home for, Jack? You aren't part of our lives. Why are you calling? You can't call out of the blue like this. Bonnie doesn't even know you.'

Bonnie was watching the call take place and had figured out who it was.

'Misty, I need to talk to you. Face to face. I know you don't want to see me, but I have information to share about Kimberly Parker. It could change the outcome of her plans to destroy the forest.'

Misty was still numb. Hearing from Jack after all this time was not on her list of things that might happen. But she had to focus. The meeting was that night and her mind needed to be clear. Not that there was much that could be done now. There had been no further objections to the development. The community was supportive of Bonnie, and anyone she spoke to wished her well. But, deep down, it felt like everyone was OK with what was happening. It was 'one of those things'. Trees get cut down all the time in the name of progress. Why should Devilla Forest be any different?

The media stir had been an amazing experience, and Bonnie had done so well. Misty was so proud of her daughter. And the little *TikTok* video had travelled all the way over the sea and landed in front of the eyes of Bonnie's dad, Jack.

*All this, but still we'll have lodges and holiday makers*, she thought. *And the forest will lose trees and natural habitat. Little creatures will lose their homes and lives. But as long as holidaymakers can trash their way through the forest, then that's fine.* Misty admitted to herself that these words were perhaps a bit harsh, but that's how she felt.

Bonnie and Misty arrived home to an angry neighbour. Les was a retired joiner and had lived next door to them for years. He lived on his own, but always had old friends round for a chat. It was rare that he was anything other than cheerful. He would often help with the odd domestic chore that was beyond Misty's ability. She wasn't good at heights and would call on the help of Les if a gutter needed cleaned, or something like that. But, today, Les was grumpy.

'I'm glad you're back hame, Misty. That dug o' yours. It's been in oor bin. There's rubbish a' ower the place. You'd better watch 'im in a'. I've no idea whit he wis eatin' but it stinks. And I'm sorry if I'm grumpy, but I'm no' enjoying clearing it up.'

'I'll get that for you, Les,' said Bonnie.

'It's fine, lass. You've got your meeting the night. You do that. But you'll get a chore tae dae fur me to make up for this. You'll be raking leaves or cutting grass this summer.'

Les was starting to smile a bit now, having got the little rant off his chest.

'I'm sorry, Les. We'll give David a good telling-off.'

'Aye, keep that mutt oot o' my sight.'

Bonnie cornered David.

'What have you been doing? Why are you in the neighbour's bins? What were you thinking of, David?'

'We've a meeting tonight, Bonnie. You may need my superpowers.'

The penny dropped. 'David, you'll not get into the hall. They won't let you in.'

'I'll get in, Bonnie. You take me there in the car and then let me out. I'm going to try and buy you more time by clearing the hall. I'm building superpower #3 right now. You get me there … and leave the rest to me.'

Bonnie thought that she would leave it there and say nothing more. This information would be kept to herself, as her mum would only worry. But what was there to lose? David would come with them in the car, and it would be interesting or fun – or both – to watch his plan play out.

# Chapter 33

# Kerflumptulation

It was 7:20 pm. There were fewer people in the hall than at the previous meeting, although some of the big news names had arrived. Bonnie saw Kimberly with her daughter, Rachel. The two pairs of women – mothers and daughters – faced off with one another, steely stares all round. No pleasantries were exchanged.

They were about to take their seats when Bonnie announced she had left her phone in the car and would be back in two minutes. Shortly thereafter, she returned, with David now free to roam.

The meeting got underway. There were formalities and all manner of things were read out. Some questions were taken, including a couple of tough ones from the heavyweight media. But Kimberly was as cool as ever, handling the questions well. The answers were often untrue, but Misty couldn't prove that.

The meeting was approaching its conclusion. The couple on the door were there for show, more than security. They merely stood at the door, said 'hello', pointed the way, then said 'thanks'. Not that anyone would have been wary of an elderly gentleman in a brown cardigan and his wife in a 'Barbados Sun' sweatshirt anyway. At the end of the meeting, their job was to utter a simple 'good night' or 'thanks for coming.'

David arrived, a harmless dog on his own. 'Hello boy,' said the man. He reached over to give David a pat, which turned into a full-on affectionate rub down. 'Who's a good lad, then? You *are* a fine chap, aren't you? Come on, now … you can't go in there.'

The woman joined in. 'Not tonight, doggie, you'll need to come back another night.' David started to apply the eyes. The woman spoke again, 'Look, he's got different-coloured eyes. Isn't he beautiful?'

David set his eyes to 'maximum'. Full-on hypnotic beauty. The couple were transfixed, letting him past as they stood, smiling.

David was working to his own plan to stop the meeting going ahead. He would do this using superpower #3. He had consumed a leftover takeaway from Les' bin which had been in there for some time and was unique in flavour. It was now ripe within his belly. As ripe as he had ever experienced. He was loaded and ready to go.

Next, he had been working on his method of deployment. He would move into stealth mode, and deployment would be silent. But, as was so often the case, 'silent' meant 'deadly'.

Finally, he would use the 'crop dusting' method. He would start at the entrance to the hall. Then, he would walk along the centre aisle, kerflumptulating as he went.

This was a big hall, and he knew it would take longer than forty seconds to empty. He would give himself sixty. The countdown began.

**+1 second:** all systems go. He would remain in stealth mode for as long as he could.

**+9 seconds:** David was halfway along the aisle and had started to catch the attention of those in the hall. Stealth mode was turned off.

**+14 seconds:** kerflumptulation had started, and was already forty per cent complete.

**+16 seconds:** those sitting at the back of the hall were hit first. Mrs Henderson from the local newsagents made some kind of inhuman noise as she was first to retch. She then looked surprised, unsure if it had been herself that had made the sound. She hoped there was no-one else there from the golf club.

**+22 seconds:** seventy-five per cent deposit complete. David felt a sudden surge of gas strength towards the end of his release.

**+29.5 seconds:** the man from BBC Scotland shouted 'Herrrugh!'

**+30 seconds:** the audience at the back of the hall made for the door.

**+37 seconds:** David turned left at the top of the aisle and completed the deposit. An extra richness at the base of his belly tank was noted. Stealth mode re-engaged. He moved through the door to the canteen, and out through the fire exit. Mission complete.

**+38 seconds:** Mrs Henderson clutched the chair, her knees weakening. Mr Davis from the bowling club took her arm and led her out, his other hand covering his mouth with a handkerchief.

**+39 seconds:** the pace picked up as the back half of the hall evacuated.

**+41 seconds:** kerflumptulation waves hit the front half of the hall.

**+42 seconds:** Alfie Patterson, the lollipop man for the school, turned an odd shade of green. Tears started to form in his eyes. He wished he had his lollipop stick to aid his walking.

**+43 seconds:** The Chair of the meeting passed the plans for the development of the forest, gagging as he spoke. He declared the meeting closed. David's plan for a further time extension had failed.

**+44 seconds:** Kimberly Parker started to retch. She buried her face in her sleeve as she made her way to the door and started running.

**+46 seconds:** everyone was making their way to the main door or fire exits. This *was* an emergency, after all. Mrs Wilson was on her inhaler, unsure what was happening but following the crowd anyway.

**+48 seconds:** The doorways were jammed with people. All had hands to their faces, or their faces buried in their sleeves. David had left an aroma that could almost be sliced. There was much wailing and gasping for clean air. The chap from the BBC bumped into the wall; his eyes were streaming, and he couldn't see where he was going.

**+50 seconds:** David was pleased with progress. He decided he must change his superpower statement to 'I can clear a normal-sized room full of people within forty seconds. Larger spaces within a minute.'

**+58 seconds:** hall clear. David sat quietly by the car waiting on Bonnie and Misty.

**+60 seconds:** Kimberly found Misty. 'I don't know what kind of trick you think you are playing here, you and your manky dog. But the plans are passed. Work starts on Monday. You lose, silly girl.'

It wasn't the best end to the meeting. All Bonnie and her mum could do was laugh at the antics of everyone in the hall. There was nothing else for it, other than laughter. But the laughing would soon fade, and the reality of failure would kick in. On Monday, work would begin in the forest. On Monday, trees would be cut down and the habitat would start to suffer.

On that Saturday afternoon, Bonnie met her dad for the first time. Bonnie had often thought about this moment. She had imagined what he looked like, face to face. He didn't fit with any of her expectations. He was average height and had a Scottish accent with an American twang. It was a bit unusual, but not in a bad way. He was well dressed and looked like someone with money. Not that any of that was important. She was just glad to meet him. But she was also wary. He had left her mum when Bonnie was a baby and he had never been in touch until now. Bonnie couldn't start a daddy–daughter relationship without considering her mum's feelings. *Anyway, he's bound to disappear again soon*, she thought. But, she had to admit to herself, that also made her feel sad. Despite only having known him for a few hours, it also made her feel a little weepy.

They had agreed he would come round to Misty's house, so he could see where his daughter lived. They drank tea and had a 'safe' conversation. Work, school, hobbies – that kind of thing. Then, Jack started to open up a little and it became clear why he was there.

'Misty, Bonnie, what I said on the phone yesterday was true. I've lived with twelve years of regret. And I can't change any of that. I'm not going to sit and make promises to you now. I'm not sure whether it's too early or too late for that. But I have seen Bonnie's video which made it halfway across the world. And, since then, I have watched, riddled with guilt, all of your videos. I knew it was you, Bonnie – not because of the name – I just would have known you. And we both know there is a woman involved here that has crossed our paths in the past.'

Misty listened, saying nothing. But she could feel old hatreds rekindling in her stomach. Was that why she was so passionate about helping Bonnie save the forest? To get back at Kimberly?

Jack kept speaking. 'When I left you, the whole Kimberly thing, I … I… oh, I don't know. I felt ashamed and foolish. I became involved with her, even though I didn't want to. I *absolutely* didn't want to. But, for a reason I can't explain, I did. That's why I left. And, to cut a long story short, I started to work in finance in America. And what I want to share is confidential, for now. But in the next few days, it will come out. My company deals with a business called PHG Holdings. I won't bore you with the technicalities. But we have noted some financial irregularities with their accounts. Deposits and transfers. And payments to private bank accounts. And we've traced one of these back to someone in this area that handles the approvals for the forest plans. And some of these payments go back some years. It looks like Kimberly's business is built on dishonesty. So, I've reported it to the American authorities. And they've been investigating. It's now being investigated over here, too. And, I say again, you can't mention anything right now. But it *will* all come out soon.

'So, there you have it. In a nutshell, Kimberly is corrupt. And I'm trying to make amends. If I'm being honest, I would have reported this anyway. But it seemed fitting to let you know.'

'It's a small world,' said Misty. 'You're thousands of miles away, and you happen to come across Kimberly's business? Weird.'

'It's a coincidence, I'll grant you. But I deal in finance in America. And I investigate irregularities. So, if you are doing anything untoward in my neck of the woods, there's a possibility I will come across it. Not as much of a coincidence as you might think.'

The mood in the house relaxed. Jack stayed for another hour, and they shared stories of the past, and one or two highlights of the past twelve years. Bonnie chatted with her parents, feeling rather special. David had made an early appearance, but stuck by Bonnie's side, never going anywhere near Jack. It was all very civilised.

Jack left in the late afternoon. There were no hugs or handshakes, only smiles and a polite goodbye wave. Jack promised Bonnie he would keep in touch, but no such promise was made to Misty. *Probably for the best*, she thought.

Misty and Bonnie looked at one another. Misty spoke first. 'I wonder what Monday will bring?'

The newspaper headlines were a bit odd that weekend. There were all sorts of creative headlines about the meeting, although none of them made the front page. There were the factual ones from the more serious papers. 'Devilla Development Approved,' that kind of thing. The tabloid papers had more fun with the events in the hall. 'Atomic Dog Fart Clears Village Hall,' was the one Bonnie and Misty laughed at the most.

That evening, Bonnie took David for a long walk. She stuck to the paths around the forest, as it was dark. But she had her head torch on and felt safe in her big jacket, with David by her side. It was nearly seven o'clock, and David had been calm all day. No zoomies. Well, not yet anyway. But there was still time.

Iccuat was at the edge of the forest. Bonnie spoke with him, and the tone was sombre. 'I'm sorry Iccuat. I did everything I could. There was nothing else I could do. The plans were approved.'

Before she could get the next sentence out, she was sure she could see tears forming in the owl's eyes. 'Look, Iccuat,' said Bonnie. 'I don't want to build your hopes, but there was one other thing. It happened before the plans were passed, but I only found out about it a couple of hours ago. This might come to nothing, but you know how Kimberly Parker is paying money to get the plans approved?' Iccuat nodded. *He* could understand the principle of money, unlike David.

'Well, we think this is going to be reported to the authorities. It may be too late to stop the work, but we hope, really, really hope, that it will only take a few days. Will you let the others know? Oh, and please, Iccuat, I don't know for sure if – or when – this will happen. So, hope for the best, but you need to expect the worst.'

Outside Kimberly's home sat a black cat with a stumpy tail. He was trying to figure out if the young girl he had been assigned to was a good or evil witch. He made sure it kept out of the way of Kimberly, though. She had caused his tail to fall off, some time back, with a careless and unintentional spell. As it sat there, it placed a thought into the mind of Rachel Parker: *Grimalkin is your protector. Do not obey the witch, for she is evil. Follow your own thoughts, Rachel – they will show you the right path.*

# Chapter 34

# Cut

Kimberly Parker was furious. Again. 'That blasted dog has stolen the headlines.'

There was no fanfare of job creation, no tourism uplift for Scotland, nothing like that. 'Atomic Dog Fart.' That's what everyone would remember. Anyway, she would have the last laugh. The plans had been approved and payments were arranged for those involved. They were all safe payments. Everything was handled offshore from the parent company she had in America. All the approving committee were happy and had received a message from her to say: *Job done.* They would understand the message. 'Nothing incriminating in writing,' – as was said at every meeting.

Over in the forest, Sunday morning was quiet. It was early, and the sun hadn't risen yet. There were a few dog walkers and joggers out. They were all familiar with the forest and happy to venture out, knowing first light wasn't far away. The mood of the forest was still sad.

Word had spread quickly as Iccuat had let a few of the trees know. Before long, the www had informed everyone. Every living creature and growing plant knew. Each species reacted in different ways. Some were sad and many had tears. They may have been tears for themselves, or tears for their friends in the forest. Some birds were even upset for their prey. They all understood the principle of eating for food versus killing for fun.

Of all the creatures in the forest, the angriest was Burp. You've probably never seen an angry mouse. And, if you did, you may not notice. But this was one angry Burp. And he made it known. He had called on the other senior mice in the forest to say a meeting was needed. And these little mice sat together and hatched a plan. Unfortunately, this wasn't a plan to prevent the work getting underway. This was a plan of revenge. And, as they say amongst mice: 'The talons of the eagle are like feathers when compared to an angry mouse.'

The anger didn't stop with the mice. There was a lot of it about today. Kimberly Parker had also been thinking of ways to make her mark. Whatever was happening in the forest, she had to show she was in command. Change was coming and the development *would* go ahead.

Meanwhile, far overseas, the first batch of lodges were ready for shipment. They would be loaded onto a ship, sailed across the ocean and assembled in Scotland. To allow this to happen, two other things were taking place. An official in China had been paid to sign off the credentials of the lodges. He turned a blind eye to the materials they were built with. And, of course, no-one would mention the child labour used in the construction.

Closer to home, Kimberly had paid overtime to one of her contractors. They were at the entrance to the forest on Sunday morning at nine o'clock. Safety barriers had been erected and chainsaws were started. The animals nearby were afraid of the noisy machines.

Shortly before 9:30 am, Roburt was cut down.

Roburt had seen what was happening. He didn't see it like you or I would. Trees 'see' in a different way. They can sense all the vibrations in their roots and other trees share what they are feeling. All this is interpreted by each tree to build a picture of what's happening. There was little time for the forest to react. And the noise of the machinery was terrifying.

Roburt was an oak tree. He had been around for over two hundred years and had experienced life in all different shapes and sizes. Over a hundred and fifty years ago, he would watch people walk to work. They used horses to pull heavy loads from one place to another. He had lived in a time before electricity, when things were much harder for the humans. But no-one knew any different. That was just the way it was. He had watched as times changed: roads being built for motor car; lorries starting to carry goods, retiring the horses that pulled the carts. Tractors ploughed fields. Even the wars that took place in the first part of the twentieth century were picked up by his roots.

Roburt was admired in the forest. His years were many, but his thoughts were still young. One of the strongest trees, he was respected by everyone in the forest. Well, almost everyone. To Kimberly, he was an obstruction. A tree, nothing more, nothing less. A tree in the way of her plans. Roburt knew his time had come. He could sense the machines heading in his direction – and the vibration of their powerful engines. There was no physical pain as they began to cut him. But he could feel the emotional pain of his time at the forest coming to an end. He thought of his friends and the animals. He thought of his friend Chaff, who would sit in his branches and chatter away. And then there was Sylvester, who was talking to him through the www as the chainsaws did their work. Roburt thought about their great friendship. His only wish would have been that he had grown next to Sylvester and been able to get his thoughts strong and first-hand. As the chainsaws cut deep into Roburt, Sylvester assured him they would always have a friendship. 'The reach of your roots will remain in the forest for many years to come.'

By late morning, Roburt was in several pieces. His main trunk had been cut into different-sized parts, to allow loading onto a trailer, and taken away for machining. Larger branches had been trimmed and loaded onto the trailer. The smaller branches were put through a 'chipper' machine and sprayed over open ground. They would rot away over time. *At least that's something*, thought Sylvester. *Roburt will live on as parts of him become part of the soil. But it will never be the same.*

All the other senior trees were devastated. They had only ever known the forest with Roburt in it. And now he was gone. Forever. This was a sad day for them all. And they knew it wouldn't be the last. There *was* hope – and they all clung on to it. But they also felt the true fear of losing more of their friends.

Burp couldn't cry. He was too angry, and too busy plotting his revenge.

On the Sunday evening, Kimberly sat with her daughter in their front room. She had taken great satisfaction from the pictures sent in by the contractors. That giant eyesore of a tree was no more. Once the roots were removed, access to the forest would be much easier for the machines. The lodges were on the ocean now, and there was a lot of work to do to get the forest prepared for their arrival. They would take weeks to arrive, but there was still a lot to do to make up for lost time. Blasted contractors. *Expecting to be paid for the two weeks when they did nothing*, she thought. Was that a scratching noise she heard? *Probably just the central heating.*

Kimberly had made a celebration meal. And she had shared a couple of glasses of wine with Rachel – watered down with some lemonade. Being of the same stock as her mother, Rachel spoke for some time about her dislike of Bonnie Banks. She described everything about her that she didn't like. None of it was true, of course. All exaggerations from her own mind and a desire to be superior. But she was in good company. Her mother told her tales of taking away Misty's husband, then discarding him a few weeks later. She remembered he didn't want to leave his new wife, but Kimberly had felt like she was able to cast some kind of spell over him to get him to do it.

'Go out into the world and get what you want, Rachel. And if you can't get it, take it. If you want to succeed, take no prisoners. Take nonsense from no-one. Trample on them. You can use any means necessary to get what you want.'

Anyone listening in would be disgusted at the advice this mother was giving to her daughter. There was nothing about trust. Nothing about compassion or considering other people's feelings.

Rachel listened to every word spoken by her mother. For the first time in her life, she wasn't sure about the words she was hearing. Her life so far had been about demanding, asserting or threatening. But the events of the past few days had made her question herself. Was it the right thing to do – to bully other people? And why was it that the only feeling she experienced when seeing pictures of the fallen tree was sadness? As Rachel pondered these thoughts, another struck her: what *were* those scratching noises?

Kimberly had brought her laptop into the living room. She was showing Rachel her plans. This was quality bonding time, in her head, and a good lesson about business. She explained how to get around some of the regulations. 'If it costs a hundred thousand pounds to buy an environmentally friendly lodge, but only twenty thousand for one made of plastics, then you've got a lot of money to play with. You can then use the difference to solve your problems. So, imagine, you could spend another few thousand to, you know, encourage someone to turn a blind eye on the green credentials. Then you've only spent a fraction of the cost. Do you get it?'

Kimberly didn't mention the child labour used to build the lodges in China. As far as she was concerned, they were being given money for doing a job. The quicker they started to learn a good work ethic, the better.

Rachel got up midway through her lesson on Kimberly's version of good business ethics and went over to the wall. She put her ear against it and listened.

'What's up, Rachel?'

'I keep hearing scratching noises. They are coming from the walls. Do you hear them?

'I wouldn't worry about it, Rachel. Probably bits of insulation falling down the gap inside the wall, or something. I'd get it looked at, but once the profits start coming in from the forest, we'll move somewhere bigger. We'll get something built the way *we* want it.'

Rachel wandered back to her chair, still convinced she heard noises.

Meanwhile, in the walls of the house, a little mouse was giving orders. Burp had called the other MICs (mice in charge) to order. He spoke with authority. 'As you know, this is the house of the woman who is going to destroy the forest. We've already chased her out of the old cottage. *And* she was the one that killed Roburt. We know that killing us and removing us from the forest is her only goal. We are never seen in the forest as we are so spread out. But she hates us and will kill us all. So, we must act. Go to your teams. Tell them the story – they've heard it before but tell them again. Remind them how important this is. And remind them of the mission. On my signal, we'll pour out from every little gap in this house. And we'll terrify this evil woman and her daughter.'

It was nearing ten o'clock and Rachel and her mother had decided it was bedtime. Kimberly was pleased with herself and was looking forward to the week ahead. Rachel wasn't particularly looking forward to school. But she was already working out plans to sort out that loser Bonnie Banks. She had left some vile comments on her videos, but they were lost among the thousands of other comments. No, she would get her on her own. And she would have a couple of her friends with her. She knew that, when it came to bullying others, it was best done as a group. She wouldn't risk Bonnie getting the better of her, not after the last time. If anything, she felt there was a good chance Bonnie would have won that fight. No, the next confrontation would have numbers in Rachel's favour. And she would reduce Bonnie to tears. She shook her head, trying to rid herself of the feeling that these actions weren't right.

Teeth were brushed, jammies were on. The mice were in position, and Burp issued the command. 'Pile in!'

When you look closely at some buildings, it's amazing how many little gaps there are. Especially in older houses. Gaps in floorboards. Gaps next to central heating pipes. Gaps in storage cupboards. Gaps under the kitchen sink. And gaps under doors. When you are a little mouse, especially an *angry* little mouse, you can fit through these gaps easily. And that's what they did. Thousands of them. And they poured out from every little gap in the house.

Rachel was the first to scream. She was making revenge plans in her head when she spotted what looked like a grey snake. It came from behind her wardrobe. A large moving grey snake that was getting bigger by the second. A split second later, another grey snake appeared from under her bed. Bigger than the first one. Then, as it merged with the first snake, Rachel realised it was made up of mice. A seething mass of mice. Hundreds of them.

Rachel's first scream was so high-pitched, it could hardly be heard. Her heart was racing. She grabbed her quilt and stood quivering on her bed. There were mice everywhere. Her second scream would have been more audible, had her mother not screamed at the same time. Neither was heard, each wondering why the other hadn't appeared to offer help.

Kimberly's screams were *definitely* audible. There were mice on the curtains. On her bedside cabinets. She saw them pouring out of her wardrobe. They started to come through under the door of her en suite toilet. They were a moving, squirming grey mass and they were climbing the side of her bed. On the bed. At her feet. Climbing her legs. There were mice everywhere.

As Kimberly stopped screaming for a second to draw breath, Rachel's screams could be heard piercing the air. They were less prolonged. There was a scream for a few seconds, then a pause for breath, then a further scream. Despite Kimberly's evil streak, she knew she had to get to her daughter. Jumping off the bed, her feet squashed a couple of mice as they hit the floor. Word went back to Burp: *casualties reported.*

Kimberly ran through to Rachel's room and found her still standing on the bed, shrieking. She grabbed her hand and shouted: 'Rachel, come on, let's get out of here. Run! Run with me.'

Together, the pair ran along the short landing and down the stairs. There were thirteen steps and the mice were everywhere. They took the few remaining steps to the front door, Rachel still screaming. Kimberly couldn't find the key. It was on the shelf next to the door, but in her panic, she couldn't see it.

'There. There! On the shelf,' shouted Rachel. There were mice gathering at their feet. Kimberly grabbed the key and fumbled for a few seconds – which felt like hours – to get the key in the lock. Finally, key in, door unlocked. And they were out into the cold. They had nothing on their feet, and only nightclothes to keep them warm.

In his deep, low voice, Burp gave the command to the mice troop leaders. 'Everyone back. Mission complete.'

And the mice disappeared as quickly as they had arrived. There were thousands of them, all heading home to their own part of the forest. As a force, they were terrifying. But as little mice, spread across the large area of the forest, they were harmless. Nothing more than mice playing their own part in keeping the balance of nature together.

Kimberly had to get into her car: somewhere warm for her and her daughter. She had instinctively grabbed her phone when fleeing from the house, but who to call? Contractors, business associates, friends? It was at that point Kimberly realised that, other than Rachel, she had no-one.

Her first call was to the police. Concerned for the welfare of a young girl stuck outside her home in the winter, they came round quickly. They checked the house, and apart from a couple of dead mice in Kimberly's bedroom, there was no sign of anything. Kimberly asked the police if they would stay for a few minutes while she grabbed some clothes and the car keys.

Kimberly pulled away from her house feeling drained, as Rachel sobbed in the passenger seat. One of Kimberly's hotels would be their home while her house was fumigated and put on the market. They would never go back there.

# Chapter 35

# Rudi

Burp was pleased with the evening's work, resulting in only two casualties. He had hoped for none, but that was a hazard of being a mouse. You didn't live for years. There were casualties every day, for a variety of reasons. Burp would have preferred it if the mice had a better reputation. After all, if they didn't clear the mess left by humans and other animals, who else would? And, as much as they hated it, they knew that the bigger animals in the forest relied on them for food. That's the way it was. But that's not to say they couldn't be feared, as they had proven tonight.

But the night wasn't over. Burp had a different team on standby over at the tall lady's house. He needed to get there before the night was out. His taxi was waiting. Sitting on the back of an owl was a thrilling experience, and it made him feel even more like the warrior he truly was. For now, there was mutual trust between owl and mouse. For the owl, it was a short flight with Burp on his back, but he would manage it no problem. Off he flew at great speed. There was no need to stop for a rest. At around three o'clock in the morning, Burp arrived at the tall lady's house.

There was a different squad assembled here. Burp had no reason to settle any scores with the tall woman. But he *did* have one to settle with Rudi the cat. This wasn't something he would normally do. It's risky business, exacting revenge on a cat. But the forest was on the warpath and tonight a point would be made. A point that Rudi could share with his other domesticated friends. After tonight, they would all know: 'Don't kill us for fun.' Yes, Burp was on a mission tonight.

The mice at the tall lady's house had already checked everything out. Access would be easy through the cat flap. When he arrived, Burp was given a full briefing. How to get into the house, where the cat was, how long it had been asleep – everything he needed to know. Burp had no intention of causing the cat harm. He just wanted to make a point. Mice are not there to be a cat toy. And, within the next thirty minutes, Rudi the cat would know this.

They were an unlikely hit squad. A mouse, a dragonfly, a badger and a fox. But Burp was still in command. The badger was keen to go in through the cat flap and sort out the cat. 'A quick bit of wrestling, pin the beast to the ground, then give it what for,' was Austin's plan. But that wasn't what Burp wanted.

'No. We need to do this properly. I want him spoken to. I want him to change his ways. No need for violence, although we may teach him a lesson or two,' he laughed. 'Here's the plan …'

Half an hour later, everything was set. The first challenge was to lure Rudi outside. This would be the job of Rodger the dragonfly.

Rudi was in his basket, sleeping. There were occasional purrs coming from him. He was a big cat, of the Scottish Fold variety, and he used most of his basket. His ears folded back, which gave him the apt name. His fur was grey and stripy. He liked to think he was more tiger, and often imagined himself patrolling through the forest. In his cat dreams, he saw all the animals bringing him food and bowing to him as he made his way through the trees. He was majestic in his appearance, and the envy of all the forest creatures.

Unfortunately for Rudi, the truth was a bit different. He was afraid to go outdoors. Anywhere nearby was fine, as long as he was within reach of his servant – the tall woman that brought him food. He wasn't afraid of mice, or at least, he wasn't afraid of one or two mice. Any more than two and he would leave them alone. And he didn't like birds. He would leave them well alone too. He'd tried to sneak up on a young crow once. He hadn't know that the crow's mum was nearby, and she had swooped down and pecked him right below the eye. Since then, he's kept well clear of any birds.

Rudi felt a tickling sensation on his nose. It was an odd sensation and, in his deep sleep, he thought he was dreaming it. He resisted opening his eyes, holding on to his sleep for as long as possible. But then the tickling sensation spoke to him. 'Wakey wakey, Rrrudi.' Rudi's eyes were open, scanning the darkness in the room. He locked eyes with the dragonfly. Smaller than a mouse, so not frightening, he thought. But it had wings, and he didn't like wings.

'I'm so sorry to waken you, Rrrudi. You werrre sleeping so peacefully.' The dragonfly stared at Rudi. His eyes were mesmerising. And scary. But Rudi felt a sudden surge of courage. With his left paw, he swiped out at lightning speed towards Rodger. It wasn't his fastest-ever strike, as he had only just woken. But he was proud of it.

*I am the tiger*, he thought. He was looking for a squished dragonfly but saw nothing. He then felt a tiny tingling sensation on his head. Then he heard the voice. 'You'rrre a bit slow forrr a cat, arrrent you, Rrrudi?' The dragonfly was on his head. Rudi went low on his front paws, sticking his bum in the air. He then started to walk backwards out of his basket, trying to reverse away from the voice. 'I'm here, Rrrudi. On yourrr head.'

Rudi swiped his paw again, managing to do nothing more than hit himself on the back of his ear. He was now reversing around in circles.

'Overrr herrre,' said Rodger. The cat looked towards the voice. 'No, overrr herrre.' The voice was coming from a different direction now. Were there two of them? he wondered.

Now the voice was coming from all directions. Not at the same time. But the voice teased him for a split second and was gone before he could turn his head. *This dragonfly is fast*, he thought.

Rodger decided he would say a bit more. 'Who's been a naughty cat then? Killing a little innocent mouse forrr fun. You need to learrrn, Rrrudi. We don't kill forrr fun. We kill if we need food. You don't need food Rrrudi. You arrre serrrved yourrr food. You kill because you arrre a bully.'

Rudi knew the dragonfly was faster than he was. He had worked that out right away. But was he smarter? 'Yes, I killed a mouse. So what? I'm a cat. That's what cats do.' There was an air of menace in his voice. *I'm not such a scaredy-cat after all*, he thought. 'I'm not frightened of *you* either, little dragonfly. I could squish you with one swipe of my paw. I've done it before, you know.' Rudi tried to edge closer to Rodger, who was sitting on the floor next to the table.

Rudi was trying to annoy the dragonfly so he could catch him with a paw swipe. 'Oh yes. All sorts of dragonflies come by here in the summer.' He edged even closer to Rodger. 'I go into the garden and swipe at them for fun. Some I catch, some I miss.' Closer still. 'It's a great feeling when you catch them in your claws,' said Rudi, his voice now a low hiss. 'You feel the razor-sharp nails sink into your prey, then discard them … dead.' It was at that point that Rudi pounced. He had positioned himself with most of his weight on his back legs. All his power transferred from his hind legs into a forward motion towards the dragonfly.

It was one fast movement, expertly executed. Rudi then felt a searing pain across his nose as he hit the table leg with full force. The cat spun around to find Rodger in mid-air, hovering and laughing. 'Ah, the deadly cat sprrrings on his prrrey. But he is so slow, a lazy house cat. Can only kill a corrrnered mouse. Big, scarrry, lazy cat that he is.' Now it was the dragonfly's turn to tease the cat.

Rudi was angry. He lunged again at Rodger. And again. And again. 'I'm overrr herrre,' sang Rodger. 'No, overrr herrre. Pussycat. Pussycat. Can't catch a little drrragonfly.' Rodger hovered in front of the cat-flap. Rudi made one final leap to try and catch the annoying flying insect. Too slow. But his leap took him straight through the cat flap. As he landed, Rodger flew through the gap as the flap swung backwards and forwards a couple of times.

Rudi sat up and looked around. The dragonfly looked at him. He was sure it winked. There was no point in getting cold though, he would go back in the house. *Oh-oh. Problem*, thought Rudi. He looked the other way only to be met by a badger. A big, angry badger. He looked to the left and saw the dragonfly. To his right, a mouse sitting next to a fox.

Burp was about to speak when Rudi let out a wail, before saying, 'Please, please, please don't hurt me. I didn't mean to kill the mouse. I'm only a house cat. I don't kill anything. They bring me food. All I do is sleep and eat all day. I don't even go outside. Let me back in the house. I'll never do it again. Please. I promise. Please.'

'Enough grovelling,' said Burp. His voice was as low and authoritative as ever. 'If you do as we ask, you'll not come to any harm. But you need to learn a few things, cat. And don't look around. You can't escape. The fox and the badger are faster than you. And stronger. And they're not frightened of the outdoors. So, sit and listen.'

Rudi heard the voices in his head. They are the same voices we all get from time to time. The ones that tell you whether you can or can't do something. Rudi didn't know that whichever voice he chose to listen to would be the one that came true. So, he chose the weaker one of the voices – the one that said: 'You're a house cat. Just do as they say. You'll never get away. You deserve this. You brought this on yourself.'

'First of all, let me introduce myself. My name is Burp.' It was faint in the distance, but the cat thought he heard laughing. 'I am one of the senior leaders of the forest creatures. You have already met Rodger, the dragonfly. A hundred times faster than you will ever be. And, at the door, we have Daley, the fox. In front of you is Austin the badger, preventing any stupid dash into the garden.' The badger and fox nodded at Rudi. Rodger appeared to wink again.

Rudi sat rooted to the spot. His little cat heart was pounding, as he knew that he was in a dangerous position.

Burp continued, 'What we have here, little house cat, is a situation. For those of us that live in the forest, we are threatened with losing our homes. Many of the trees will be cut down. And many of us will die. In the forest, we all depend on one another for survival. And when we are threatened, we pull together and help one another. And then, on the other side, we have lazy, good-for-nothing creatures like you. You take everything you are given. The only thing you do in return is kill innocent creatures, one of whom happened to be a friend of mine. And you sit in your luxury basket and do nothing to help the forest. You do nothing to help your fellow animals. What do you have to say for yourself? AND DON'T GROVEL.'

Of all the things Burp couldn't stand, it was grovelling he hated the most.

Rudi spoke. He felt a bit more confident now. He sensed, if he said the right thing, he would get away with no harm done to him. 'I'm sorry your forest is being cut down. I didn't know. You're right, I'm a house cat. I don't need to do anything. But that's not my fault. I was born a housecat. And she brings me food. And it's warm.

But yes, I did kill your friend. And I'm sorry. I won't do that to another mouse. Or anything else. I promise.'

'Easy words, house cat. But I need more. I need to know you won't harm any of the forest creatures for fun. And I need to know you are there to help us if we need you. How do I know you aren't trying to worm your way back into your home?'

'What else can I do? asked Rudi. 'I've promised you I won't do it again. I don't want you turning up here in the middle of the night, threating me.'

'We're simply teaching you a lesson, house cat. We're teaching you that you can't bully and kill and there be no consequences. What do you guys think?'

Daley said, 'I think we should shave him. Maybe not all of him, but definitely bits of him. Make him look ridiculous.'

Austin was a bit more in the mood for a scrap. Typical badger. 'Let's see if he can last seconds with me without screaming for mercy. That's what we should do.'

'Chuck him in the loch,' offered Rodger.

Burp had told them to say these things. He wanted the cat to feel some of the fear that Vic had felt when the cat killed her. And it worked. Rudi started to beg some more. 'Please don't hurt me. I promise you. I won't do it again.' The voice in Rudi's head kicked in again. 'You're useless. You deserve this.' But then he heard the other voice. Stronger this time. Offering better advice. 'Accept it. Don't plead. Offer something, stand by your mistake but still be strong.'

The cat listened to the second advice this time. He looked the four creatures straight in their eyes in turn.

'Burp. Rodger. Austin. Daley. You are condemning me for instinct. I'm a cat. I chase mice and birds. And anything else. One of the guys wearing those yellow work vests had me chasing a laser pointer for thirty minutes a few weeks back. I didn't know what it was, I chased it until I was so tired, I could chase it no more. But I'm sorry. I know I don't need to kill mice. And if there is a way I can prove it to you, I will.' He sounded much more self-assured now. He had started to believe himself. 'Let me know what I can do to help, and I'll do it.'

Burp felt that the house cat was now starting to sound genuinely sorry for what he had done. 'OK, you're starting to convince me. But you are not getting away without punishment.'

The cat sat silently, awaiting his fate.

'At the end of the house, there is a large barrel which collects rainwater. It's not been emptied for a while and it's a bit smelly. We will accept your apology and we will believe you if you go and jump in the barrel. You may feel bullied by this, but that's a small price to pay if it teaches you to be a better cat.'

Austin and Daley stood to add a bit of menace to the situation. They were reminding Rudi that he could not wriggle out of this with no consequences.

Rudi knew he had no choice. And he was starting to truly regret what he had done. He knew he had it easy. Much more so than the forest creatures. This was his moment. As much as he hated water, and especially cold and smelly water, he knew he had to do it. There was no escape. He heard his little internal voice again. The one that was more encouraging. 'Get it done. Take a deep breath, jump in. Turn around and jump out. And show no facial expressions.'

It was good advice from the more positive voice. The house cat walked over to the barrel and jumped in. The cold hit him like a thousand pin pricks all at once. He hated the cold, but he stayed brave. He took his punishment and climbed back out of the barrel. Rudi shook the water from his fur, but still looked bedraggled and sorry for himself.

Burp spoke again. 'We may need your help soon, Rudi. If we do, we'll be back. Stay out of trouble.'

And with that, the mouse hopped on the back of a squirrel, and disappeared into the darkness. He was followed by the badger, the fox and the dragonfly.

Rudi made his way over the garden, his wet paws collecting some mud along the way. He was frozen and feeling miserable. Tonight, Rudi knew he had been brought down a peg or two. But he had admitted his mistake, and that helped him come to terms with the humiliation. He crept in through the cat flap to be met with the kitchen lights on and the tall lady standing over him. *Oh no*, thought Rudi. *That's all I need.* He made his way back to his bed, leaving muddy paw prints behind him. He did his best to shut out the telling off he was getting from his cat mum.

It had been a bad day for Rudi but, in the back of his mind, a plan was forming.

# Chapter 36

# Mighty

Sometimes words make no difference. Sometimes words can hurt. And sometimes words can change everything. They are powerful things, words. Jane Mullins was shorter than your average woman. 'Five feet on a warm day,' she would say. Jane was the proud mother of Misty Banks, and even prouder granny of Bonnie Banks. Jane had been a worker all her life. She had managed to raise her family when times were harder and had worked, in one way or another, throughout. She had started out as a secretary then, when Misty was young, she had taken on part-time jobs to give her flexibility. When her children were old enough, she went back to doing what she knew best – being a secretary. Or, as it was now called, a 'personal assistant'. *And rightly so*, she thought. Jane enjoyed her work and had quickly learned all the changes that had taken place in her few years away from what she called 'the 9 to 5'.

Early retirement arrived for her at sixty-three, with her having 'done her bit', as she put it. Not that there was any danger of taking it easy. Jane had lots of friends and interests to keep her busy. And, of course, her beloved granddaughter, Bonnie. Any help needed where Bonnie was concerned, and Granny was there. Regular 'girls' days out' were arranged and these would always involve shopping and a nice bit of lunch.

Jane was proud of what Bonnie had done with her fight to save the forest. And she was gutted to hear it had been unsuccessful. That woman, Kimberly, had blighted her family before, and here she was again. And it sounded like her daughter was every bit as bad. Bonnie had told her granny about the fight at school. Her gran would care and give advice, but never interfere or make things worse. But, this time, enough was enough. The feelings of anger towards Ms Parker and Rachel had spilled over. She knew it was unlikely that words would make much difference now. But these words were inside her and they had to come out.

Kimberly was in the suite at her five-star hotel. The couple who had booked the room would no doubt give a scathing review for having been moved to a different one. But needs must. It was her hotel, and she needed the room.

Meanwhile, back at Kimberly's house in Copsehead, a small woman had pulled up in a Vauxhall Corsa. The woman got out of the car, only to be met by two men from Verminout Ltd. Jane asked to speak to the owner but was told by the older of the two men: 'sorry, she's off to her hotel. Bit of a problem with mice here, so best to try her there. It's the Parker Hotel in Glasgow. Does that help?'

'That's a big help,' said Jane, 'thank you.'

According to the sat nav, Kimberly's hotel was forty-three minutes away. There was no going back for Jane now, she was in the mood.

Forty-seven minutes later, the Corsa arrived in the hotel car park. It had taken four minutes longer due to a misunderstood navigation instruction. It was now half past four on the Sunday afternoon.

Jane had bottled her anger for years. The events of the past couple of days meant that the release valve had to be pulled, and steam needed to be let off.

The receptionist asked Jane if they could help her as she took a seat in reception. 'Thank you, but no,' said the sweet lady in her sixties. 'I'm waiting for a friend. I'll give you a shout when she's here.' That was nothing out of the ordinary, so a glass of complementary water and lemon was served. Jane sipped her water as she waited.

Forty minutes later, Jane's patience was rewarded as Kimberly arrived at reception. Jane could see she was heading out somewhere. The release valve was pulled. An audible Jane Mullins had her say with, or, more accurately – *at* – Kimberly.

Jane opened with a tone of derision. 'Well, well, well. Look who it is. The woman who lives in the mouse-infested hole. I hope you keep your hotels better than you keep your house.'

There were only about six or seven people in reception, but they all tuned in.

'You can't help yourself, can you Kimberly? First, you destroy the lives of two people perfectly happy with one another. You *had* to have Jack Banks, didn't you? Then you dumped him. Leaving him devastated. And leaving my daughter on her own to raise her daughter … *their* daughter. After you use what you need, you throw it away. Is that what you do with everyone, Ms Parker, is it?'

Everyone listening in had now slowed down. They didn't want to leave the area; they needed to hear what would happen next. Kimberly was about to open her mouth when Jane said, 'And don't even think about saying anything, lady. Your pathetic whimpers aren't fit to be heard by my ears. But everyone else should hear. You've lied about the forest development. I know, I can see it in your face. Your pathetic, lying face. And you don't care about anything, do you? Nature, animals, people. You only care about yourself. Who's building your lodges for you? Kids aged eight and over, is it? Anything to save a penny. Who cares about anyone else? What about the mice, Kimberly – does your fancy new development come with free mice in every lodge? Or is that just your house? Oh yes, I've spoken to Verminout earlier. Worst infestation they've ever seen, apparently. What were you doing, feeding them? Your poor daughter should be taken into care, living in conditions like that.'

Kimberly's face had turned puce. 'GET OUT!' she screamed. 'GET OUT, NOW! Or I'll call the police.'

'Don't you worry, lady, I'm going. I don't need to do anything else. Karma will get you, it always does. And you are well overdue a visit.' And with that, Jane Mullins left. She'd said all she wanted to say, and she felt much better for it.

Kimberly couldn't find any words; she stood in silence. But not for long. She marched to the reception desk, all eyes on her next move. 'You. What's your name?'

She saw the receptionist's name badge before the young woman could reply. 'Celia. Is that what you do when your employer and owner of this hotel is accosted and threatened, is it, Celia? You stand there looking stupid? Lies and accusations are hurled at me, and you don't intervene. You don't call the police. Why didn't you call the police? Call them, at once, and let me know when they arrive.'

Celia's eyes were filling now. Undeterred, Kimberly continued, 'This was basics today, Celia. Basics. Do you hear me? You have a long hard think about your incompetence today. You be at my office for nine tomorrow morning while I think about your future.' That did it. Celia started to cry. 'And stop your blasted snivelling.'

She marched over to the lift and headed for her suite on the top floor. 'Karma. Karma? I'll show you karma.' Kimberly knew the only way to get her revenge was to make the development happen. And happen it would.

# Chapter 37

# Spooked

It was now Sunday evening and Jack Banks had returned to Misty's house. He was heading back to America in a couple of days' time and wanted to spend some more time with Bonnie. He also wanted to spend time with Misty, but knew it was too soon to even think about that.

They spent the evening talking. Bonnie was upset about the forest plans going ahead, not to mention how she felt about Roburt being cut down. She was clinging on to hope that the information her dad had found would be enough to prevent work starting. It was unlikely that it would happen quickly; these things can take weeks. Or so she believed.

The doorbell rang, and it was her gran. Jack braced himself. He had thought Misty's mum was formidable a few years back, but he had always had a good relationship with her. He knew better than to cross her. Then, foolishly, he had seen something in Kimberly Parker and the rest was history. He steeled himself for a dressing-down, but it never came. Jane merely said 'Hello' and threw him one of her famous looks. If looks could kill, he would have evaporated in a split second, but nothing was *said*.

Jane told her daughter and granddaughter what she had done. 'Left her without a name, I did. And everyone heard. Serves her right. Marching into people's lives, thinking she can do what the hell she wants. Karma will get her, though, believe you me.' Jane was a great believer in karma.

The evening was only slightly strained. Jack felt like he was the 'elephant in the room'. He knew at some point Jane would give him a telling. But he knew it was only to defend Bonnie and her mum. They told Jane about what Jack had found out, and what might happen next. To say Jane was pleased about this would have been the understatement of the week. Karma was coming. Jane could feel it.

By almost nine o'clock, Jack had left and Bonnie had taken David out for a quick bedtime walk. Jane was putting her jacket on and about to head home. 'It's going to be another full-on week,' she said. 'Do you think Bonnie is coping OK?'

'She's like you, Mum. Made of strong stuff.'

'Yes, but that's no guarantee. You make sure that lassie is OK. She's had a lot to deal with, newspapers and TV cameras and everything.'

'I will, Mum, I will.'

'And what about 'Jack the lad'? What's *his* plan? Showing up after twelve years. You don't need him, Misty. You know that, don't you?'

'He means well, Mum. And he's sorry for what he did. It was a long time ago. And he *is* Bonnie's dad.'

'He's been Bonnie's dad for twelve years. That didn't start yesterday. If he even thinks about upsetting you again, he'll get it from me. Both barrels.'

'Yes, Mum. I think that's all highly unlikely, though. He's only back, and he's away again on Tuesday. I don't think you need to worry.' The truth was, Misty hoped that something *would* happen. She had expected feelings of anger towards Jack, after all this time, but anger was the last thing she actually felt.

On the outskirts of the forest, Bonnie was caught in conversation. Iccuat sat perched on a fence post, waiting for her and her canine companion to arrive. He spoke to David first, with sarcasm in full flow. 'Well, well, well. It's the furry one. How's the fleas?'

'I haven't got fleas, thank you very much,' said David.

'So *you* say. Bet your fleas have fleas. What kind of dog are you, again? A manky mongrel?'

David snarled at the owl.

It was Bonnie's turn to speak. 'Iccuat, please. We're all meant to be on the same side here. Why are you winding him up?' Iccuat stared at Bonnie. 'What's the point? We're going to lose our homes. I'll not be here tomorrow. May as well have some fun.'

'Iccuat, that's not the attitude. We fight until we know we are totally beaten. We fight until our breath runs out. And then we fight some more. Are all the animals on standby? The second the workers arrive, we launch a full-on aerial assault. Annoy them at every turn. Prevent work going ahead. Make everything as difficult as possible.'

'Yes, I know, Bonnie. But you've seen the machines. They're scary. And we're all feeling a bit, you know, "what's the point?"'

Then David spoke. 'Iccuat, Bonnie. There may be another way.'

The girl and the owl looked at the dog, as he began to explain his thinking …

It was eight thirty on Monday morning. In the car park of Devilla forest, a large area had been cornered off. Site offices were due to be delivered and built. Notices were posted saying the public walks would be inaccessible while work was underway.

Footpaths would close. The transition from public woodland to holiday park had begun.

An articulated lorry arrived with a Portakabin on the back. This would serve as the offices for the team in charge of the build. It would become their permanent place of work for many months to come. The site supervisor was pleased. Of all the places he had worked in over the years, this was one of the nicest. An office with a view. And a great project to work on. He was looking forward to getting set up and starting work, although that would be a few days away yet.

The supervisor hoped that he wouldn't see too much of the client, the owner of The Parker Hotel Group. She was a tough cookie, and not easy to deal with. But if he could keep her at a distance, it would be a great project to work on. And he expected little in the way of issues. There were a couple of sensitive sites that needed to be left alone, and the usual rules and regulations. He also noticed there were a few things that would normally be forbidden – but many of these restrictions had been lifted. Odd. *But, whatever*, he thought. It made his life easier.

The supervisor hadn't paid much attention to the forest creatures and the trees. He noticed the freshly cut oak tree at the entrance. This left him a bit puzzled, but other than that, all was normal.

He didn't spot hundreds of pairs of tired eyes in the branches of the trees and the outskirts of the woods. He didn't notice them, because they were all blending into nature. And if he *had* noticed them, he wouldn't know that they were tired eyes. Tired, because they had been awake all night. Tired, because a dog had spent long hours teaching them how to 'apply the eyes.'

These hundreds of eyes now had the power to control anyone that looked into them. They were eyes with the power to control humans and get them to do the oddest of things. Eyes that were the last chance to save the forest.

More people were arriving at the forest. A combination of different skills, all needed to turn the plans into reality. Equipment arrived: generators to power the office, lighting, fencing, signage … you name it, it had started to arrive. By 2 pm, there was an office in use. Chairs, tables, computers – all the equipment needed by the site workers. And a kettle. A well-worn, well-used kettle. Nothing had happened on site that day other than preparation.

In the afternoon, another smaller Portakabin arrived. This was for security. As more and more equipment arrived, twenty-four-hour surveillance would be needed. The Parker Hotel Group had contracted Allwright Security Services to look after the site.

In charge of security was retired police sergeant Alfie Wright. Alfie had been used to being part of a busy police office in Wolfscraig and was glad of the change of pace. His friends would ask, 'Are you enjoying retirement, Alfie?' His reply was always the same. 'Livin' the dream, pal, livin' the dream.' Alfie had been an excellent police officer. He was always one for detail. If there was something unusual, he would spot it. And it was a skill he had never lost.

'What's with all the birds in the trees?' said Alfie. 'You don't normally see that many. Owls as well. Very unusual for daytime. And they're all quiet. It's eerie.'

The supervisor, Alex, hadn't spotted the birds. 'Did you hear about the surveyors? Attacked by birds and chased by deer. The lads think all the animals know we're here to cut down large parts of the forest.' He laughed as he said that last sentence, mocking the suggestion. 'I'll put up a notice – Dear birds, we're coming to cut yer trees doon!'

Alfie laughed along with this. 'Yeah, I'd heard that. All seems a bit odd. Anyway, I'm sure it will be fine. Still a bit weird, all these eyes watching you, though. Have you seen them?'

Alex looked at the trees. The eyes were difficult to see, but with a little bit of concentration they came into focus for him. And once he had seen one, he started to see hundreds of them.

'Looks like they're watching us. I didn't notice them earlier, but now you point it out, there are lots of eyes. Good Lord, they're everywhere. I'm starting to feel a bit spooked.' As they both stared into the trees, they didn't notice the flock of pigeons coming in from behind them.

# Chapter 38

## Antics

Alfie Wright was having an interesting evening. He had been pooped on by a flock of pigeons. Fortunately, he'd been able to clean off his high-vis waterproof jacket easily enough. He'd then sat in his Portakabin located near to the forest entrance. By 4:30 pm, everyone else had gone home. When the site was a bit busier, he'd bring in more security. But, for now, there would be one on site at any time, working a twelve-hour shift for four days straight. He found that was the best way to supply security. He had a few former colleagues who worked for him. Some only worked twenty-four hours a week, but doing that over two days gave them a decent wage to top up their pension. And then five days off. Everyone was happy.

Alfie checked the other Portakabins every couple of hours. They were lit and visible from his office; no need to wander out every time. He could see them from his window. And there was no point in having a site patrol yet. There was nothing for anyone to steal or vandalise, other than what lay in the car park.

He couldn't see the trees properly. The light from his Portakabin reflected off the glass. Anything that wasn't lit was difficult to see. And, if he was honest, he wasn't feeling at ease. This was a strange feeling for retired sergeant Alfie Wright. He had been in some scary situations over the years, and there wasn't much he hadn't dealt with. He tried to shake off the feeling. Anyway, another couple of hours and he could go home. One of his team, Gary McWilliams, was due in at eight and would look after things until the next shift change.

It had been quiet outside earlier, but now a wind had started to blow. It made the trees sound like they were wailing for help. He laughed at himself as he thought: *This is like I'm on the set of a spooky movie. Get a grip Alfie, get a grip.*

On the other side of his office sat the generator. It was a modern piece of equipment, generating electricity for the Portakabins. A sticker on the side boasted it was one of the quietest available. It still made a gentle hum in the background, but you had to be close to hear it. That was almost the only sound in the car-park-come-site-office. That, and the wind journeying through every gap in every tree across the forest. There was also a constant scurrying sound. Not that anyone was likely to hear the scurrying of squirrels. There were around sixty of them, all red squirrels. And in charge was Wizzbush. He had set the other squirrels a task: 'Drop anything you can carry through any little gap in the generator.'

For the next hour or so, anything they found and could carry was dropped into the generator vents. Eventually the machine clogged up and stopped working.

The lights went out in the Portakabins. *This is unusual*, thought Alfie. *These little generators are pretty reliable.* There was nothing else for it; he had to take a look. Alfie was equipped with a high-power torch. It was one of those rechargeable ones, and it brought a lot of light – blinding if you were silly enough to look at it. He put his jacket on, made sure his phone was in his pocket and went out to check what was happening. It was a bitterly cold night, and the breeze was stiff. He was glad of his gloves and his hat which covered his ears. Both were a present from his grandson. If he was warm and dry and could see, he always felt in control.

Alfie made his way over to the generator. The shiny, well-maintained machine of earlier on in the day looked a bit different now. It was covered in all sorts of twigs, bits of grass, mud – you name it, it was there. He took a photograph of how he had found the generator, before clearing away all the loose debris. He then saw the problem: a clogged exhaust. This wasn't your old-fashioned diesel exhaust; this was much more concealed. But still accessible, and still clogged. Alfie took a twig and cleared out the worst of the debris, which allowed the generator to work again. He restarted it and the lights came on, bringing a feeling of comfort and security.

Alfie instinctively stood back to look around the generator to see what he could see. There were boot prints all around the machine, but that could have been from when it was set up earlier in the day. No way to tell. He walked around the Portakabins, shining his torch around the base and walls. He tried the door handle, which was locked and secure. He walked to the other equipment that had been delivered that day and inspected it. There was no sign of anything unusual. *Nope, everything looks fine*, he thought. Although, there was still that odd sensation of being watched. Alfie was more in tune with this feeling than most. He had spent many years patrolling the streets at night.

He gazed into the forest, his torch beam illuminating the trees. It took his eyes a moment to adjust to the distance and the change of light. He blinked a couple of times, squeezed his eyes together, then rubbed them with the back of his glove-covered hand. No, he wasn't seeing things. The eyes were all still there. He shone his torch to the left, and it reflected dozens of pairs of eyes. He shone the torch to the right and, again, there were dozens of pairs of eyes. He pointed the torch into the woods, and every few meters apart, there were eyes staring back at him. He would never have admitted it to anyone else, but he felt uneasy. Not afraid, as such, but the hairs on his skin were tingling ever so slightly.

Alfie backed off. He made his way back to the Portakabin, glad of its four secure walls and a lockable door. The lights were back on, and the heater had again brought warmth to the office. He made an audible 'uuuh' sound when there was a knock at the door. 7:40 pm. Gary. Phew.

'Hey Gary, you're early mate.'

'Aye, first night on the new job. Just wanted to be here in plenty time, get familiar, you know.'

'It'll take me about three minutes to show you round, Gary. Nothing much happening yet. The generator went out a few minutes ago, though. Covered in rubbish, it was. Must have been a freak gust of wind or something, I've no idea. It clogged the exhaust, though, so it cut out. I've fixed it, but I'll let you see it. Anyway, coffee?'

'You know me, Boss, never refuse a brew!'

The pair laughed and Alfie made a coffee for them both. Strong and milky. No sugar. They exchanged stories and the latest family news with one another. They had spent many years together in the police force, so always had lots to share. There was never a shortage of memories to recall.

It was now about 8.15 pm. Alfie had promised his wife he would be home on time. Although she knew, if there was anyone to talk to, Alfie would be late. He liked a blether and catch up.

'Right Gary, come on and I'll show you this generator. Oh, and I don't want to freak you out or anything, but the animals in the forest have taken a bit of interest in what we're doing.'

'Eh? Animals? What you on about, Boss?'

'Jacket on and follow me.'

They walked over to the generator, which was purring away. Alfie showed Gary the pictures on his phone. 'This is what it was like earlier. Odd, eh?'

Alfie showed Gary around the area, although there wasn't much to see. 'Fairly straightforward. It will be a bit more involved when the work starts, but that's no meant to be for a few days yet. There's one other thing though. Not a problem, but just so you know.'

'Uh huh. What's that?'

Alfie shone his torch at the forest to be met with reflective eyes from every direction. He saw a less-than-comfortable look on Gary's face.

'Man, that's spooky. What's that all about then?'

'No idea, mate. But aye, it's spooky all right. Look, it's just birds in the trees. And in the forest, it could be foxes, deer. Badgers, even. But they're probably just nosey. I know you don't get freaked out easy, but if there's anything you're no happy with, just gie me a shout. You've got the moby. And I don't mind. Honestly.'

'Mate, it'll be fine. Sleepy birds and nosey foxes or something. That's all. Off ye go, and I'll see you 8 am for changeover. Or 7.45 am for coffee, blether and changeover.'

Alfie laughed. 'Sounds like a plan to me. See you, then.'

Gary was a light sleeper. This had been a burden to him for many years. But since retiring and taking up overnight security, it was the perfect solution for him. He could pull up a chair and sleep. But the slightest noise would waken him. This allowed for a night of half-work, half-sleep, meaning more time for him on the golf course.

By 9.15 pm Gary was sound asleep. Around 11 pm, he was wide awake. He thought he had woken in an aviary, there was so much bird noise. Birds chirping. Crows cawing. The pigeons doing their 'hoo, hoo, hoo' noises. He checked his watch. He thought it was morning at first, there was so much noise. But no, 11 pm. 'What the hell is it with these birds?' he said out loud, to no-one in particular.

The night passed with no further events, and at 7.45 am Alfie was met by a tired-looking Gary. 'What's the matter wi you then, mate?' said Alfie.

'Flaming birds. What a racket. There was no chance of any napping last night.'

Gary then remembered that Alfie was now his boss, and no longer a work colleague. 'No that I'm napping on the job like, ten-minute shut-eye at break time. That's all. I set my alarm and everything.'

Alfie ignored Gary's comment, knowing full well that he was prone to a little nap now and again. 'So, a noisy lot of birds, then. But nothing other than that?'

'Naw. Not a cheep.'

'That's no even worth a smile, Gary, never mind a laugh.'

The pair of them enjoyed their morning coffee. Both men appreciated the way it made them feel slightly more awake. Gary left before eight o'clock, glad he was heading home for some proper sleep.

The site supervisor arrived as Gary was leaving. Alfie walked over to meet him, cup of lukewarm coffee still in hand. Just the way he liked it. 'Morning,' said Alfie.

'Any trouble last night? I'm guessing everything was pretty quiet?'

'Nothing for you to worry about, Alex. You should see this, though.'

Alex scrolled through the pictures of the generator on Alfie's phone. They both agreed it was a bit odd and could find no explanation.

'And my overnight security said the noise of the birds went on most of the night, but I'm not even sure why I'm telling you that.'

'Ah, no worries. I'll keep an eye on the generator, but it's going fine now. As for the birds, they've got another few days in these trees then they all get cut down. That'll sort that one.' They both laughed.

'Aye, that'll do it right enough. Anyway, just thought you should know. They can be pretty strict on disrupting birds these days.'

'You're telling me. Flaming nightmare. Albeit this job's been fine. Permission has been granted to crack on!'

'Right, I'll leave you to it,' said Alfie. I need to start getting the wider security arrangements in place for you.' He switched to a posh accent. 'Should you need my assistance, I shall be in my palatial mansion. Otherwise known as the Portakabin.' And with a laugh, off he went.

Alfie noticed that the eyes were still watching him from the forest.

# Chapter 39

# Testing

Kimberly arrived on site at 10 am. She was looking for a detailed schedule from the contractors. What was arriving and when. What work would start. In what order things would be done. Her mindset was already preparing to get the contractors to up their game. They needed to know who was boss. She needed to ensure they were clear that delays would not be acceptable in any way. 'Don't *ever* bring me problems – tell me your solutions,' would be her opening line. The overused cliché spoken by her father also came to her mind: 'If you give them an inch, they'll take a mile.'

Alex Moss, the site supervisor, was one of the few contractors that gave her confidence. He spoke his mind, said what needed to be done, and got on with it. That earned her respect. But it would do no harm to remind him who was boss. Kimberly parked her car next to the biggest Portakabin. She grabbed her laptop from the back seat and locked the car by remote control. A dirty great 'splat' landed at her feet. Fortunately, it missed her, other than a little splash on her shoes. *If I didn't need some trees as part of this resort*, thought Kimberly, *I'd remove every single one. That would keep these blasted birds away.*

Kimberly refused the offer of tea or coffee. She had no desire to drink out of a mug that some unknown worker had used before her. *No, thank you.* Sitting at the table in silence, she had no wish to engage in any small talk. And Alex made no mention of the generator, thinking there was no point. Sitting with his senior team, he opened the meeting.

'Thanks for coming along, Kimberly. Now, I know you are looking for an update. So, this is how it's looking …' Alex gave her the full overview of plans, timelines and issues. He knew how Kimberly could be and was ready for her. He gave all the detail and got straight to the point.

Meanwhile, the creatures of the forest had been working away. Their ability to 'apply the eyes' was working. They had tested it on a few innocent dog walkers and early-morning joggers. The owls were good at it. The pigeons struggled a bit, probably with their eyes being on either side of their heads. All they did was look confused. Rabbits were also good, as were the deer. The smaller birds and the mice were no use at all. The eyes weren't big enough. But, even without the little birds, mice and pigeons it was a big army.

The animals tested their newfound skills on unsuspecting folks who were enjoying the forest, minding their own business. The results were amusing.

Neil was out bright and early to walk his dog. Sabre was an obedient Labrador who normally stayed close by his side. This morning though, Sabre had wandered off the track a little, following the trail of a new scent he had picked up. He was a bit startled when a deer came by and he barked at it. But the deer spoke to him: 'I'm not running away today, Sabre. I need to help the other animals save the forest. They're going to cut lots of the trees down. I'm not going to hurt your owner, but I need to look at him. I promise you, it will be funny, and what happens next will wear off shortly.'

'Fair enough,' said Sabre, barking to get his owner's attention. Neil walked over to see what Sabre was barking about and came face to face with the deer. He was about to chase it off, when he stopped in his tracks. The deer stared at him with its dark, hypnotic eyes. He was applying the eyes, like he had been taught.

Neil was unable to move. He stared at the deer, drawn into its eyes. Sabre sat a few feet away from him, enjoying the show. Neil couldn't work out what was happening. When the deer finally broke his gaze, it ran off into the woods. Neil made his way back to the path and all was well for the next few moments. Then, unable to stop it happening, he stuck his bottom out. His arms were tucked by his side, occasionally flapping like wings.

Every so often, he would jerk his head forward and make a chicken noise. To the animals, applying the eyes was a tool to save the forest. To anyone else watching, it was the most unusual of sights. Neil was aware of what he was doing, but he couldn't stop himself. Sabre found it funny, too.

On the other side of the forest, Brian and Elsie were out for their early-morning walk. It was nice and bright, and the sun had risen. They were both in their early seventies and were always up early for a walk – rain or shine. They loved the outdoors. Until a few years previously, Brian had driven past the forest every day on his way to work. Now, he could spend time enjoying it with his wife of over forty-five years. It set them up for the day, and they both looked forward to getting home for a hot, freshly made coffee after their walk. They loved seeing nature and would often stop to point out the simplest of things to one another. 'Look, a robin,' Brian would say, as they both stopped to watch and appreciate the little bird.

Today was a special treat, though. Elsie spotted it first. An owl. It was close by, sitting on a tree branch. *Hang on*, she thought. *There are two owls. No, three!* This was fantastic to see. 'Brian … Brian!' Elsie was speaking in a low whisper, keen for her husband to see the owls, and she didn't want to disturb them. 'Look, over there. Do you see them? Three owls.'

Brian raised his eyebrows. What a sight! Three beautiful owls, perched on a tree. What a picture that would make. He removed his phone from his pocket. After a bit of fumbling – his grandchildren said he had fists of ham – he got his camera on. He snapped a few pictures as the owls sat, almost like they were posing for photographs. He walked closer, Elsie by his side. He couldn't believe this; they were *so* close. Another couple of pictures. 'The family are going to love this,' he whispered.

But that was Brian's last photo of the morning. A strange sensation came over him as he looked into the owls' eyes. He was so focused on seeing into the birds' eyes, he was unaware that the same thing was happening to Elsie. It was all over in about half a minute. The owls flew off. Brian turned to Elsie and his soldier-straight back became curved. His arms bent at the elbow, and his chin stuck out. He started to beat his chest like a gorilla. Then came the gorilla noises. He was aware of what he was doing, but unable to stop. Elsie took it upon herself to walk to the tree, also adopting a gorilla-style walk. The tree made a great back scratcher as Elsie also made gorilla-like sounds. She used the tree, to great effect, to relieve the itch on her back. The pair then reunited, as Elsie crouched low and allowed Brian to check her hair for little beasties.

The gorilla noises continued as bemused dog-walkers and joggers passed them by. Roddy, busy working on his time for a cross-country 10k, had seen this couple out many times before. He'd always thought they looked a bit daft.

The forest creatures were happy with the tests they'd carried out that morning. They had applied the eyes to six different people, in total. The people had all been out minding their own business, but they had all ended up performing odd and embarrassing tasks. Now it was time to get onto serious business.

# Chapter 40

# Madness

Alex was in full flow, presenting detailed plans and timelines of the forest development. From time to time, Kimberly would challenge him: 'Are you sure? That had better not be delayed. What happens if …?' and so on. But Alex was an expert at his game. He dealt with everything thrown at him. And, to be fair to Kimberly Parker, she was pleased Alex was in charge. He sounded like he had everything in order. It took a lot to impress her, but he managed it.

The mood relaxed a little, and there was even some casual conversation when they broke for coffee. Kimberly drank water out of her own bottle. Alex turned up the radio a little as Madness played 'Baggy Trousers' in the show's 'three of the best from …' slot. 'I love this,' he said. 'Was brilliant in the eighties. Still brilliant today. I saw them in Glasgow a few years back. Unbelievable live. What a night.' Alex gazed towards nothing, as he remembered hearing the band in his youth.

One of the others in the room was called Tommy. As his deputy, Alex would tell Tommy he was always 'reliable and supportive.'

Tommy stood at the window and noticed four deer standing outside. *That's unusual*, he thought. 'Guys … Guys! Come and look at this.'

They all looked through the window at the deer. It was an unusual sight, as deer were normally afraid of getting too close to people. 'I'm going out for a closer look,' said Tommy. Without thinking too much about it, they all filed out of the Portakabin into the car park. The radio station was now on the second song from Madness, as 'Embarrassment' started to play.

Tommy got close to the deer. He was slow and cautious in his approach, but the deer weren't afraid. And what was that next to them? In the trees? Owls! *Wow*, thought Tommy. *Three, no four. Five. Six! Six owls in the trees. And four deer standing staring.*

Everyone, including Kimberly, was now out of the office. They gathered only a few metres from the deer. Then the owls flew from the trees and perched on various objects nearer to where they were all standing. Photos were taken. They were all mesmerised. None of them realised it, but they were, in fact, rooted to the spot. The gaze of the deer and the owls caught them whichever way they looked. Everyone was drawn into the eyes of the animals, unable to look away. It was a strange sensation that washed over them all. A happy, joyous feeling. Like they had all had a little too much wine. They were smiling and happy.

The radio station started to play the third Madness track as the DJ tried to convince her audience that this was the best of the three songs.

It was a lovely moment. Fabulous music was drifting through the car park. People and nature were interacting with one another.

Kimberly was the first to break. In perfect time with the tune, she sang at the top of her voice.

'NIGHT BOAT TO CAIRO!' She then started to sing along to the wordless start of the tune. 'Ta da da daaa daaaa, ta da da daaa …'

Without a second's hesitation, the rest of the workers joined in. There were six of them in total. All in the car park, loving every minute of the Madness hit 'Night boat to Cairo'. Kimberly took the lead. And what a performance – she was a total natural. At least, that's what *she* thought. The workers had lined up behind her, following her made-up-on-the-spot dance routine. All were being serious with their moves but also enjoying every minute.

The dog walkers and those out to soak up the forest were also enjoying the show. They were too far away to hear the radio. All they could hear was a woman belting out tuneless shouts of 'Night Boat to Cairo!' every now and again. As for the dancing, it was without doubt the most bizarre thing they had ever seen. They were suspicious about what the workers had been doing in the Portakabin. They suspected alcohol had been involved.

One of the onlookers was Toni. He was due to start his shift at a tyre depot in Collistown in an hour and had been out for a morning stroll. He was glad he had filmed what was going on, as no-one would have believed it otherwise. These were the hashtags used by Toni when he posted his video on Instagram and Facebook:

#devillaforest

#forestmadness

#nightboattocairo

#workiesgonemad

#2tonedancing

He liked to dabble on the various social media platforms with funny videos. He would like, share and create. Toni had quite a few followers – several thousand of them. And many of these followers also had thousands of followers. And, by the end of the day, he'd had over 80,000 views of his post #forestmadness.

Toni wasn't the only one to have captured the antics of Kimberly and the workers. There were a few others that saw it and took photographs or video. The local paper led with the same headline: Forest Madness. To be fair, it did look like a bunch of workmates taking a break and having fun. To Kimberly though, the antics matched the name of one of the songs, 'Embarrassment'. She had no idea why such a thing had happened. *It was like the night at Misty Banks' house with that stupid dog.*

Brian, Elsie and Neil had also seen the video. They felt relieved that their actions weren't captured and had worn off after ten minutes or so. But the antics that had taken place that day did seem odd to them. They would let it pass, though. No point in getting themselves into the public eye.

The woodland creatures were treating the whole episode as a great success. Sylvester Pine had sent a message out through the www, to congratulate everyone involved. He got word to Bonnie and arranged a meeting of the forest animals. It would start as soon as she got there.

Bonnie popped into her house after school to get changed, then, along with David, she made her way into the forest.

By now, friendships had been formed with many of the forest creatures. There were lots of 'hello's exchanged on her walk. She arrived at Sylvester's spot in the forest. As always, David would translate what the tree said.

'Thank you for joining me, everyone. As you know, we're still in a difficult situation. The people are not yet out of the woods. We've had setbacks, and recently we lost Roburt – one of the finest trees that had ever grown.'

'And now, there are all sorts of human machines arriving every day. Our latest weapon to delay the start of work, taught to us by David here, has been a great success. It won't stop the work, but anything we can do to delay it will be helpful. So, we must keep on with that.

Every person that comes into the forest with one of those shiny jackets must be tackled. Pigeons, keep doing your work. Deer and owls, keep doing your work. Whatever your role in the forest, please keep at it. Make life difficult for the shiny-jacket people. Now, I think you will all have heard about Bonnie's words of hope. Bonnie, would you like to share these with the forest again? It would be nice for us to hear you say them.'

Public speaking was becoming a 'thing' for Bonnie; here she was, again, in the middle of the forest, trying to give nature hope. She had no desire to overpromise them anything. But she had to leave them with something, some kind of hope. These were important words that Bonnie was about to speak, as a hush descended over the forest.

'Thanks Sylvester. What you have all done is brilliant. Like Sylvester says, you *must* keep doing it. Every little bit you can do will help. Even if it slows work for only a few hours, that could be crucial. You've all seen or heard about the woman responsible for the changes to the forest. Money is being paid to people to approve things that wouldn't normally be allowed. She is bad, and doesn't care about you, or anything in the forest. But we have someone who knows she is doing this, and they have reported her. Now, all this takes time. And I'm sorry, but I don't know how long. It may be tomorrow. It may be in six months. But it *is* happening. As soon as I know anything else, I will tell you. I'm sorry I can't be more upbeat than that. Meantime, we've all got to keep doing what we're doing.'

'Thanks Bonnie,' said Sylvester – through his interpreter David the dog. 'So, that's it. Keep at it. Whatever you did today to be a nuisance, do the same again tomorrow. But do it more. Keep applying the eyes. I know that's going to be difficult when they arrive in machines but do what you can. And – one final thing. We don't harm the humans. I know that may seem odd to you. Especially when our own lives are at risk. But we can see the harm and the pain that hurting one another can do. So, we don't become the same. We disrupt. We annoy. We get in the way. But we don't harm. We can win this fight without hurting. Stay strong, nature, stay strong.'

# Chapter 41

## Embarrassing

In the tall woman's house, a conference call was taking place. Kimberly Parker wasn't happy with a foreign supplier and needed to tell them this. The tall woman – Alison Forsyth – was feeling a little uncomfortable. She was translating from English to Chinese, which was one of her best languages. When Alison translated, the same emphasis would be used as the speaker. So, if something was being said in anger in English, Alison would use a matching angry tone to repeat the speech in Chinese.

This was a heated conversation. Kimberly was demanding a faster turnaround of lodges. The build wasn't happening fast enough for her. 'Now, you listen to me,' she said. 'I have paid you lots of money for these lodges to be made. And I have paid you directly, *you* personally, by cash transfer. And *you*. YOU! You promised me you would make delivery happen by the end of April. And now you are telling me end of June?

The end of June is simply not acceptable. I do not care about an outbreak of anything in your workforce, or what's wrong with them. They are meant to be young teenagers, aren't they? They bounce back quickly, do they not? They won't be off for two months. Or were you lying to me? You've taken the money and now you don't care. Perhaps I should accidentally let it slip to your employer that you've taken a payment on the side. But I don't think you would like that, would you?'

Alison felt uncomfortable. She had translated for many businesses over the years. None of them conducted business like this. Her feeling of discomfort had become even greater in recent days. The images sent over by the manufacturer showed the latest pictures of the lodge build. Each lodge came in sections and would be assembled on site after transporting. They slotted together almost Lego-like. The manufacturer had assembled two examples of the finished product. It was clear from the pictures sent they were using child labour in their factory. Alison wished there was no signed agreement preventing her from disclosing any information. Otherwise, these details would have been shared with the relevant authorities. She had also learned, from earlier conversations, about payments to foreign officials to speed the lodges through customs.

Even worse than that, Alison had learned that the deal Kimberly had secured with this company was cheap. There was nothing wrong with the quality of the lodges.

But the materials they used contained illegal chemicals. These were chemicals banned in most countries and forbidden in the UK.

Alison focused on the payment she would receive for her work. That made the whole situation easier for her. Although, she promised herself, there would be no involvement in such matters again. In her head there were often thoughts about a conversation with Kimberly. They started with the sentence, 'I'm sorry, Alison, but you now know too much …' *Surely not?* she thought. *A little less than honest here and there, but it would never end up with me being threatened?* A chill ran right through her body, even so.

The conversation continued, and Alison stuck with her translation. Kimberly was not for moving on the date. The manufacturer would 'do their best' to make the deadline. But another payment to 'ensure the smooth shipment of your order' would need to be made. An official who had previously been 'bought' had been sacked. The new official at the shipping office in China would need to receive a similar payment. Details were exchanged. A final ultimatum was delivered by Kimberly to Mr Zhào, the angry man on the other end of the conference call.

Kimberly relaxed a little, glad she had kept her schedule. Alison relaxed a lot, after having been stressed by being angry on behalf of Kimberly and Mr Zhào at the same time. She was glad that her cat, Rudi, had jumped onto her knee. He helped her relax. He had also heard every word – and memorised important parts of it, clever cat that he was.

Now that the call was over, Kimberly asked Alison if she was OK, in a rare show of compassion. 'I'm fine, thank you. Glad it's all over for now. He was quite an angry man, Mr Zhào, wasn't he?'

The compassion stretched no further than the first enquiry. Kimberly made no further effort to chat to Alison. 'Yes, he was. Angry and incompetent. Now remember, Alison, you have signed a contract of secrecy. Not a word to anyone. No exceptions. I will not hesitate to enforce it.'

And with that, Kimberly left.

Rudi the cat had no idea what a secrecy contract was. Nor did he care. He knew he had to make amends to the forest animals, or he would be chased by them every time he went outside. He was a house cat, but even lazy house cats need to go outdoors now and again.

Alison had gone to make herself a cup of tea, and Rudi ventured out into the garden. Before too long, he spoke with one of the birds and asked if he could speak with Troben the crow or Daley the fox. The bird flew off to relay the message. After about twenty minutes, Troben arrived in the garden. The cat gave her details of what had happened, hoping to make amends.

Troben was pleased to hear the news. She wanted Bonnie to hear this from her, so at once flew to Bonnie's house to wait.

Not long after school had finished for the day, Bonnie was walking along the road towards her house. Troben stood on a fence post and shouted over to her.

'Bonnie … Bonnie.' Anyone else would have heard the crow cawing. But Bonnie understood her. She told her what the cat had heard. She relayed every detail the cat had told her, and the cat had missed nothing. Even the account number and details of the bank used to secretly pay the customs officials in China. He had struggled with the names of the illegal chemicals, but other than that everyone was happy with the detail.

Bonnie was taken aback with what they had learned. She had to take notes in one of her schoolbooks, as she wouldn't have been able to remember all the bank account numbers. She thanked Troben, and asked her to make sure everyone knew that the cat had found this out and passed it on.

There were three people that needed to know this information. First, she would tell her mum. Next, her mum would pass it on to Jack, her dad. He had reported what he had uncovered, and this would help supply proof. Then she would tell William, the news reporter.

'How did you find all this out, Bonnie?' asked Misty.

'There's a woman that translates when Kimberly needs to speak to the people that build her lodges. The woman's cat heard it all in a conversation this afternoon. I'm sure it's right. There's too much detail in there for it not to be. A cat wouldn't just make this up.'

'OK. So, you heard it from a cat.'

'Well, no. The cat told a crow, who told me. The crow is called Troben, and she's very reliable.'

'You know how this sounds, don't you, Bonnie.'

'Mad?'

'Yes, totally mad. Totally, completely and utterly mad. How do I give this information to your dad? I can't tell him you got insider info from a crow, can I?'

'Mum, you need to tell him we found it out, but can't say how. You'll need to tell him as soon as you can.'

And that's what Misty did. She called Jack, who was now back at his home in Boston. It was the missing part of the jigsaw, and he hoped this would now give them cast-iron proof. And, with that, he rang off. He didn't say that he wanted to leave his home in America and come back to Scotland and try again with Misty and Bonnie. But he thought it.

Bonnie had called William to say they had news. He said it would be good to come over for a chat and promised to be there within the hour. True to his word, he arrived less than an hour later. As cups of tea and biscuits were served, Bonnie told him the story. Every detail that had been captured, including bank accounts, names, times and places. There was even a mention of the illegal plastics.

'How did you find all this out?' asked William.

'You'll just have to trust me on this, William. I'm sure it's right. I've told my dad, who has already reported it. I hope you can follow up on the lodges, how they are made, and the child labour used to build them.'

'It's a great story, Bonnie. I've already started to pull it all together, and this is the detail I need to give it some substance. Do you know how long your dad's investigation will take?'

Misty replied to this question. 'Could be days or weeks, is the honest answer. But he was hopeful it would be days. He said that having details like bank account numbers makes tracing funds much easier.'

All in all, it had been a good day. The information they had gathered from the translator's house had been invaluable. Bonnie was delighted and feeling happy with herself. She put her jacket on to give David his last walk of the day. It was dark outside, but a nice clear night. The moon was out, but it was unseasonably warm for the time of year. She took David on his usual walk to the outskirts of the forest. She wouldn't venture in at night, even though it was nice and bright in the moonlight.

Bonnie was waiting on David doing his last bit of business of the day. As was her way, she carried a rubbish bag with her. There were always bits of litter that had been thrown away and needed binned. Bonnie scowled, thinking about these people who didn't care about the forest. She had picked up a couple of bits of waste when she heard an unmistakable voice. 'Hello, Bonnie. Out searching for scraps of food to eat, are you?'

The unmistakable voice of Rachel Parker. With two friends by her side, of course. *Typical bully, always hunts in packs*, Bonnie thought. She didn't want to show it, but she was afraid. A combination of darkness and being outnumbered wouldn't do much for anyone's confidence. A quick look around told her the only choice to escape would be to run into the forest. Getting through the gate would be impossible. Rachel and her two goons blocked that part of the path. But then David arrived by her side, and for that she was grateful.

'Oh, look. The flea-infested dog has arrived. You should get that dog put down, Bonnie. He's a manky, smelly mongrel of a thing.' Rachel's friends laughed at this.

David growled, putting the three girls a little on edge.

'You *know* if that dog even comes near us, we'll report it, and it will get put down. Don't think I won't, Bonnie. 'Cause I guarantee you I will.' Rachel felt a surge of confidence again, as she ignored the voice in her head telling her this wasn't right.

She spoke again, still confident. 'I bet that's all it can do, though, growl and run away. Scared, like its owner.'

David growled again. At least, that's what it sounded like to everyone except Bonnie. Rachel and her friends heard a growl. Bonnie heard him say, 'When I tell you, let the girl know that you are not afraid. And if they want to fight, you'll fight all three of them right now. Trust me, Bonnie.'

And Bonnie did trust David, so she stood her ground and followed his instructions. Rachel was about to open her mouth again for another tirade of insults. Moving forward towards Bonnie, she caught the dog's gaze and stopped in her tracks. He was applying the eyes. All three of the girls stood, transfixed by the dog's stare, unable to speak or move. The signal had been given. And Bonnie played the part brilliantly.

'So, you are here to fight me then, Rachel, is that the plan? But not only you. You and the Spice Girls here. You think, because you are in a gang, you can scare me? Nah. I'm not frightened of you. Never have been. You're a bully, Rachel Parker. You and your pathetic followers. But that's fine. If you want a fight, I'll give you a fight. All three of you. Right now. Or are you afraid? You are, aren't you? You've been confronted. And you're afraid.'

Rachel and her friends stood there, transfixed. They could hear and understand everything that was being said. They even felt the emotional reactions as Bonnie turned the insults on them. But they couldn't do anything other than listen.

Bonnie continued, 'Look at you all. The school's biggest bullies. Always have to be acting tough. But here you are, confronted. And you look like you are going to pee yourselves.'

And that's exactly what happened. David worked his magic, resulting in three unfortunate accidents. The girls realised exactly what Bonnie had said. And they realised exactly what they had done. But they didn't know why. And so, they left. Wet, embarrassed and not uttering another word. Bonnie had settled the score. She hoped all her friends at school would also be saved from the taunts of Rachel and her sidekicks. All credit to David.

As the girl and her dog made their way back home, a black cat sat silently by a bush. He had seen the encounter between the four girls and a dog. It knew that this one particular girl called Rachel needed his help. The cat was aware Rachel came from a long line of witches: some good, some evil. It also knew that the power possessed by Rachel's mother was like that of no witch he had ever met before. He feared the day she learned her true capabilities and knew he must contact Rachel again soon. He was there to protect Rachel and to show her she was on this planet for good, not evil. The cat knew this contact must happen soon, before her mother allowed her evil streak to win through.

Meanwhile, at the entrance to the forest, a late delivery was taking place. Kimberly was so keen to get started, she had paid overtime to get the equipment there as soon as possible. Tree cutters, bulldozers and heavy plant were arriving at the forest. Work would start in the morning.

# Chapter 42

## Arrested

Monday morning, 7:30 am. The police arrived at Kimberly Parker's suite.

Despite terrorising the officers with verbal blasts, Kimberly was arrested and taken to the police station in Glasgow for questioning. And, even worse than that, she had to contact her mother and ask her to look after Rachel. Her mother. Or, as she called her: 'That grumpy mother of mine.' Kimberly didn't get on with her mum. It wasn't because they were alike, far from it. Kimberly took after her father. Brandon Parker had been an old-school businessperson. He had been ruthless in everything he did, back in the day. This was before more tolerant policies for running a business were introduced. If Brandon wanted something, he would do anything to get it.

Kimberly and her father thought only of themselves. Her mother had left her father, due to his selfishness. Now, here we were, many years later and her self-centred daughter needed her. In some ways, Lesley Parker was glad. No-one, including Lesley, wants to hear of their daughter being arrested for dishonesty. Of course not. But she knew the day would come.

Her husband, Brandon, had been too demanding for too long. Years after she separated from him, he'd had a massive heart attack. It was inevitable; no-one can behave like he did for so long, and nothing ever catch up to them. Lesley hoped that she could get to know her granddaughter better. She hoped that Rachel wouldn't show the same character as her mum and grandfather.

The police had a portfolio of evidence against Kimberly. There was documentation of seventeen different transactions. Payments had been made to senior people in the UK and abroad. Anyone who had allowed the shipment of goods had received a payment. There was damning evidence of collaboration between local government and the Devilla Woodland Council. These were serious allegations, and more arrests were expected later that day.

Kimberly could feel her world starting to come crashing down on her. There were so many thoughts running through her head. *My business plan is in ruins. My credibility is in tatters. Will I have to sell my business – or will they take it? What about my other interests? My house? Will I go to jail? And what about Rachel? She'll hate it with her gran.*

She attempted to order things in her head. *First things first*, she thought. *Get a solicitor.* The police were informed nothing would be said until her lawyer arrived. He was due any minute.

There followed a long and drawn-out interview, before Kimberly was charged on seventeen counts of fraudulent activity. The evidence was conclusive. Her solicitor would have a job on his hands to prove otherwise. But that was his job, and Kimberly would instruct him to fight every charge.

Fortunately for her, bail was granted. On her release, the first job was a journey to her mum's house to collect Rachel. Then it would be time to go back home. Or, as was the case, back to her hotel. There was no family home any more.

What Kimberly hadn't bargained on was her mother's mood. Lesley was not normally a woman for confrontation. She preferred peaceful solutions. 'Arguing will achieve nothing other than more arguing,' she would say. But, listening to her granddaughter talk that day, she could hold her feelings in no more. 'Bonnie Banks is awful. They are all liars. I'm going to get that dog put down.' On and on it went, until Lesley could listen to it no more. Her daughter took after her late husband, who was no more than a bully. And it looked like her granddaughter, whom she rarely saw, was the same.

When Kimberly arrived to collect Rachel, it was late in the evening. By this time, Lesley's brooding mood had spilled over, and she was ready to give her daughter some home truths.

Kimberly rang the bell of her mother's house and waited. Moments later, the door opened, and she knew by the look on her mother's face there was trouble ahead. Lesley said nothing, but left the door open allowing her daughter to follow her into her front room. Still no words were exchanged, as she sat on what looked like a new couch. 'Have you recently decorated, Mum? The room looks fresh.'

Lesley spoke. 'Don't come in here with your small talk, lady. What the hell has been going on? Arrested? Kimberly Parker, the super-successful businessperson. Have you been bullying people to get your way again? That was the problem with your father – he had to have everything his own way. And what he couldn't demand, he bought. A selfish, selfish man. And that's exactly your problem, lady. You are exactly like your father. No patience for and no tolerance of other people. And, even worse, you've instilled these behaviours into that lovely young daughter of yours.'

She nodded over to where Rachel was sitting silently and continued. 'She's turning out to be exactly the same. I've heard tales of liars and even heard threats to have a dog destroyed this afternoon. Is that your proud parenting skills Kimberly? Well? Is it?'

This was all Kimberly needed. A dressing-down from her mum. *What does she know anyway? I'm running a successful business worth millions of pounds*, she thought.

Lesley had taken another breath. 'And I know what you're thinking. You're successful and worth millions. Am I right? Well, am I?'

Kimberly said, 'I'm not here to fight, Mum. I'm …'

'No. You're right you are not here to fight. I'm not going to let you. You're here to listen.' Lesley took her volume down a notch or two. Sounding a little calmer, she said: 'Things need to change, Kimberly. I lost your dad from my life because he made me miserable. I'm sad he passed but, to be honest, glad that he's not part of my life any more.

'But I've lost you, too. Because all you want is success and you'll let nothing, or no-one, stand in your way. You can't trample on people to get your way, Kimberly. Or else *this* happens. The police get involved. And what about Rachel? Do you want her to follow in your footsteps? Success at any cost? Is that it? And, I'm sorry, Rachel, but you sound like a spoiled brat and a bully to me. Maybe that's because I don't know you, but you are behaving like your mother and grandfather.'

The dressing-down was relentless. It went on for another ten minutes, and there was nothing Kimberly could do to stop it. She tried to assert herself over the criticism put to her daughter. But Lesley Parker was having none of it.

During the cross-examination by her mother, Kimberly explained she that was staying in a hotel. The half-hearted explanation of the mouse infestation was met by a disgusted look.

Eventually, the telling-off was over. There wasn't even a 'goodbye,' or a 'let me know how you're getting on.' It was simply: 'I think you should go now. And I hope that you take a bit of time to think about your actions, young lady.'

Kimberly hated that. 'Young lady.' For a moment, she thought it was Rachel her mum was speaking to, but no. It was her.

The drive back to the hotel was a quiet one. Kimberly had received a dressing-down from two different women in the past couple of weeks: Misty's mum and her own mum. For once, the fight was out of her. She wanted to go back to her house … sorry – hotel room. There was a bottle of wine with her name on it. Kimberly Parker was feeling sorry for herself that evening.

The following day, Rachel was leaving school and was by herself. Her wish was to be heading back to the house that was once her home. The reality was a journey to a bus stop to catch a bus back to the train station in Wolfscraig. Then, a train would take her to Glasgow, followed by a short walk to a hotel room. All of this left her feeling miserable. She had missed her bus by only a few minutes, so had a thirty-minute wait until the next one came along.

Sitting at the bus stop, Rachel was joined by Grimalkin. He appeared out of the blue and settled himself on the seat next to her. It was time to talk.

'You are going to think you are hearing voices in your head, Rachel. And you may well think you are going crazy. But you aren't. You have called me "Grimalkin" – which means "cat". It's not my name. My name is Dionadair.'

She stared at the cat, unsure what was happening. 'Excuse me, cat, did you just speak to me?'

'I did. And I told you my name is "Dionadair", not "cat". I'm here to protect you.'

'Protect me from what?'

'I'm here to protect you from many things. But first, you must know that you are a good person. You cannot behave the way your mother has taught you. You are here for good, Rachel, not evil.'

Rachel was confused now. *Good? Evil? Am I some kind of witch?* she thought. *Or is something wrong with me, hearing voices in my head?* What surprised her more than anything was hearing an answer to thoughts that had not been spoken aloud.

'The truth of the matter is, yes, Rachel, you are a witch. But you are a *good* witch. Your mother, however, is evil. I must protect you from her. But you need to trust me and trust the voices you hear. The voices come from me. I put them in your head. I know you won't trust them right away – but you are going to start hearing them more often. And, gradually, you will start to believe them.'

Rachel decided to test the cat. She thought: *As soon as that bus comes, I'm going to kick you under the wheel.*

'Now, why would you want to hurt your protector, Rachel?'

Rachel spoke out loud to the cat, as it wasn't as scary as someone, or something, reading your thoughts. 'OK, that was just a test, Dìonadair. So, I'm a witch, but a good one? Do I get a pointed hat or something?'

The cat laughed. 'No, we don't go for that nowadays. For the next few years, I need to protect you from your mother. She will learn her true power soon and we need to make sure you are not harmed.'

'You can't hurt my mum!'

'I'm not here to hurt anyone,' replied Dìonadair. 'Only to protect. But things will start to change in your life over the coming months and years, and you will need me. I will never be far away. If you need me at any time, just think *Dìonadair.* And remember, Rachel, you are here for good. You are not a bully, nor are you evil.'

And, with that, the black cat with the stumpy tail was gone. Rachel was still doubtful about what had just happened, thinking it was in her mind and not reality. But the 'conversation', if that's what you'd call it, was now the only thing on her mind.

# Chapter 43

## Vengeance

Kimberly sat in her hotel room, still feeling sorry for herself. Rachel was already fast asleep. The only thoughts going around her head were: *Arrested – and given a dressing down by my mother!*

Kimberly tried to distract her mind by picking up her phone and trawling through *Facebook*. Her mind moved on to think about Councillor Malcolm and, for some unknown reason, she searched for him. Her findings were surprising. He had placed an update on his personal page to say he was undergoing treatment for a severe nose and ear infection. The comments section revealed more. Cruel people were making fun of his nose and ears – with one even posting up a picture. Kimberly's mind went back to what she said about him. 'I hope your cheap whisky turns your nose a Rudolf shade of red … I hope your ears double in size.' And that's exactly what had happened. And then she thought about that cat: the one at her father's funeral. Kimberly tried to remember what harm she had wished on it. It came back to her. 'I hope your tail falls off.' It was at this point she realised the cat she had been seeing was the same cat.

*What else have I been thinking?* she wondered. Her search moved to Rachel's dad, Alan. She hadn't seen him for years. With a surname of Smith, he wasn't so easy to find. But, find him she did. And Kimberly learned her wish had come true. He would never see his daughter, as he had been registered blind for many years. She recalled her own words, uttered over and over in anger: 'And I hope your father never sees you.'

Kimberly pondered over these three incidents. *Could it be that I can wish these things to happen?* She looked out from her open window, and stared at a group of noisy teenagers in the distance. What was it she had said? 'I hope your tail falls off … I hope your father never sees you.'

Looking at the group of youngsters, she said, 'I hope you all fall over.' Nothing happened. She repeated it, and still nothing.

'I'm imagining things,' she said, aloud, to herself. 'If I could solve everything with a wish, I wouldn't be in this mess. Blasted forest. Full of creatures and vermin. Why did this have to happen?

'Everything was going to plan. And now, here we are. A right mess. A right proper mess.'

And, with every word spoken, Kimberly became more and more angry. She knew there was something in the forest that was fighting against her. There was an energy so strong it seeped into her soul. The energy fed into the only emotion Kimberly knew: anger. As her mood got worse, the teenagers in the street below had become nosier. And closer to the hotel. An already angry Kimberly was becoming even more irritated by their noise. She opened the window fully and screamed, 'Will you just shut up?'

They looked up to the source of the voice and replied with obscenities and impolite gestures. This made her even angrier and she retaliated again. 'You've woken everyone up. I hope you're all soaked in a storm.'

As an angry Kimberly closed the window, she went through her angry routine of repeating her wish. Nine times she spoke it, in three sets of three. It helped to vent her anger and settle her mood. 'I hope you're all soaked in a storm,' she repeated. As the last sentence was spoken, there was an almighty rumble of thunder. A calm, dry night turned into a monsoon as lightening flashed and the heavens opened.

Kimberly was gobsmacked. But now she knew she had some kind of witching power. She could feel an energy glow inside her and, from that energy, there came an ability to cast spells. But they needed to start with 'I hope you …' That was more difficult to work out. Instinctively, she knew her mood had to be angry. And the wish, or spell, had to be repeated nine times to make it work. She was struggling to figure this all out, unclear in her mind how such a thing could be true. And her anger was still present, so she couldn't help but turn her mind to vengeance.

Lying down on her bed, sleep did its best to evade her. There was too much going on in her mind.

Kimberly awoke early from what little sleep she'd had and made an immediate decision to head out to Devilla forest. There was something else at play here, and she would confront it. Kimberly knew a power had been awoken within her. She instinctively knew what to do and set out to have her vengeance.

'Rachel. Rachel. Wake up and get dressed.'

Rachel wiped the sleep from her eyes. 'Mum, it's only just after six thirty. Where are we going?'

'Just get dressed. We're going to the forest. Put something warm on.'

An hour later, they pulled up at the forest. The workers had not yet arrived. Alfie Wright was in his security office and recognised her. He went out to greet the angry woman.

'Give me the keys to the store,' she demanded.

'Erm, good morning to you too!' replied Alfie. 'I can't give you any keys, I'm afraid. Only authorised personnel have access to the store.'

Alfie stood there, holding the handle to the office door.

Kimberly stared at him and felt the anger rising.

Through gritted teeth, she said, 'I hope you're stuck in that spot for the next hour.' Alfie looked at her, a bit bemused, as she repeated this sentence a further eight times.

As Alfie stood there, unable to move, Kimberly walked past him. She picked up the keys to the store and helped herself to a chainsaw.

'What are we doing, Mum?' asked Rachel. 'This doesn't feel right. Why do you want a chainsaw? And why are you always so angry?'

Kimberly ignored her daughter and marched into the forest. Even the weight of the chainsaw didn't seem to bother her. The route into the forest was clear in her mind. Her body sensed the direction as the glow of energy from within her became stronger. There was not a sound in the forest as the angry witch marched through the trees. Kimberly made her way towards the most powerful source of energy in the forest. A tree called Sylvester.

Bonnie awoke with a start. There was a tapping at the window which David had managed to sleep through. It was Iccuat.

'Bonnie! Bonnie! We need you in the forest, now! Bring your mum and David. The angry woman is going after Sylvester with a chainsaw.'

David was now up and charging around the house at top speed, as Bonnie woke up her mum. 'You have to come now, Mum. Something terrible is going to happen.

Kimberly is going to cut down one of the trees. We need to run. I'll explain more on the way.'

Minutes later, mum, daughter and dog headed up the path towards the forest. As they half-jogged, half-ran, two deer appeared. The roe deer said to Bonnie, 'Hop on, I'm faster than you.' And then, out of nowhere a giant stag appeared. Its mighty antlers made it look like the king of forest beasts.

'Tell your mum to jump on and hold on tight, Bonnie.' Which is what Misty did. Where a stag had come from, this wasn't the time to ask. Both Bonnie and Misty held on for their lives as the deer sped their way through the forest towards Sylvester.

The deer slowed. There was silence in the forest, not a breath of wind nor an animal sound. The animals had left the area, all afraid of Kimberly's power. All afraid of the witch's spell. Both deer slowed to a halt and the smaller one spoke to Bonnie. 'You're on your own now. We can't go any further. Please be careful, Bonnie, and please save Sylvester.'

Bonnie and Misty didn't have far to go. A short distance away, they could hear Kimberly cursing everything around her. They knew it was her, but with a gravelly voice sounding more sinister than ever before. They kept moving towards Sylvester. The only animal close by was David – or so they thought.

Rachel was pleading with her mum to stop, but Kimberly wasn't listening. She didn't even look like her mum anymore. The woman that she knew as "Mum" now looked older. She looked evil. Her eyes were black and without affection. They gave off a sense of hatred and even Rachel started to feel afraid of her mother, as tears welled up behind her eyes. Then she heard the voice in her head. The voice of a cat. Dìonadair appeared in front of her.

Bonnie, Misty and David arrived at that moment, stopping to take in what they were seeing.

Sylvester spoke to David, 'You must protect Bonnie. Whatever happens, protect her. She's the most important one here.'

At the same time, Kimberly, now barely recognisable, started the chainsaw. The anger had taken over her thoughts as her body became more and more witch-like. Her upright and assertive posture was now stooped, with her head twisted to one side. But this was no cartoon witch. This was a witch that looked and sounded terrifying. Every living thing nearby could feel her power. It radiated from her and became worse as her anger grew.

Dìonadair spoke to Rachel. 'You must help to stop this. Your mum will be consumed by her own anger. Sylvester cannot die, he is the heart of the forest. Everything will die without him. Even your mum won't survive her own power, if you don't stop her.'

Kimberly screamed. 'I will not be beaten by birds and trees. I will have my vengeance.' Looking at

Sylvester, she continued. 'I can feel the energy from this tree. I know it's behind all this.' She hissed at the tree, 'It's not your forest, it's mine. MINE!'

The chainsaw burst into life as Kimberly made her way towards Sylvester.

'Mum, no!' screamed Rachel. Dìonadair's voice entered her head again. *You must say these words out loud. You must say them exactly as I tell you, and directly at your mother. 'Rashivska shran brosku.' Say it!*

'But what about the others?'

*Misty and Bonnie will be fine. They have the protector's scar. Say the words, Rachel.*

Bonnie could also hear the cat. She held Misty back as she went towards Kimberly. 'Mum, no – only Rachel can stop her.' David sat next to Bonnie, unsure what he was supposed to do.

The chainsaw got louder. Kimberly was now only a metre away from Sylvester. The tree's energy clashed with Kimberly's anger, as she struggled to take the final steps to the tree. But the angrier she became, the closer she got. The blade of the chainsaw was now only inches away.

*Say the spell again, Rachel,* shouted Dìonadair. *And with more anger.*

As the chainsaw touched Sylvester's trunk, it started to cut. Sylvester's energy made it as difficult as possible for the saw to make progress. The noise of the engine became louder as Kimberly fought to control it. She pushed harder to get the saw into the trunk of the tree. Rachel shouted again, this time with volume. And anger.

'Rashivska shran brosku. RASHIVSKA SHRAN BROSKU.' She repeated it. Nine times in total.

Kimberly froze. The chainsaw was touching Sylvester. The witch wrestled with her daughter's spell, trying to break free. There was a job to finish. Kimberly looked at her daughter as she stood there, frozen to the spot. Rachel looked at her mum. But it wasn't her mum looking back. It was something else. Something horrible. Something with deep, red, bloodshot eyes. Someone older and thinner with the blackest of hair. Someone with gnarled fingers and teeth blackened by anger and revenge.

The chainsaw continued to whir.

Kimberly kept fighting the spell. She started to move again. There was a madness about her. Her bad energy was fighting with Sylvester and anything else around her.

*Say it again*, said the cat. Nine times. This time, Rachel walked forward and stood by her mum. Looking into her dark, red eyes. She held her by the arm. Rachel spoke firmly, struggling to be heard over the noise of the chainsaw. 'Mum, we have a power. A witching power. But we can choose how we use it. For good, or for evil. I'm choosing to use it for good, Mum. I want no more part of your greed and destruction. Not any more. It's destroying us. It's destroying *you*. I don't know what's going to happen now, but please know that I love you. I love you dearly, Mum.

'Rashivska shran brosku.

Rashivska shran brosku.

Rashivska shran brosku.

Rashivska shran brosku.

Rashivska shran brosku.

Rashivska shran brosku.

Rashivska shran brosku.

Rashivska shran brosku.

Rashivska shran brosku.'

For a split second, time stood still. Rachel was unsure what was about to happen. Her mother started to look more like the mother she knew and loved again. But only for a split second. Then she vanished into thin air.

The three humans looked at one another. None of them knew what to do. Then, Rachel took to her heels and ran. Ran away from the forest. Ran away from Bonnie and Misty. The chainsaw, engine still running, lay at Sylvester's roots.

David sat, still bewildered and unsure what to do. He said, 'Sylvester tells me he's fine. No lasting damage.'

Then Dìonadair spoke. 'Kimberly will return. And when she does, she will return stronger. She will start to understand how to use her witching power, and her ability to cast powerful spells upon herself. We've not seen a witch with that power for over a thousand years. When she gets to grip with the ability to self-spell, the next encounter will be even more terrifying.'

'What about Rachel?' asked Bonnie.

'Rachel will be guided on how to use her protective spells. I will teach these to her once she comes to terms with what she is. And, of course, you both now know why you have that little scar, the one I gave you. It protects you from spells. You didn't need it today, but you will soon. And if Kimberly doesn't already knows this, she soon will.'

The tension in the air at the forest eased. Misty and Bonnie relaxed a little but were still shaken by the events of the previous few minutes. They walked towards home, with David by their side. They knew they would need to learn more for the times ahead. But the cat would help them. And Bonnie knew that, at some point in the future, she would need to talk to Rachel about what had happened. But not today.

A terrified Dìonadair then sped past them at top speed. David was flat out behind him, giving what he thought was a playful chase.

# Chapter 44

# Saved

At around 8 am, workers started to arrive at the forest. There was a bit of tree clearance work to get underway over the next few weeks. Trees, roots, undergrowth and so on. And there were new routes to be created, to allow heavy plant to access certain areas of the forest. There was some chat between the workers about the strange goings-on in the area. There were some who had heard superstitions of old about fairies and witches in the forest. And, of course, there were others who had no time for such nonsense.

Word hadn't filtered through yet that the contract had been suspended. Police enquiries into bribery and corruption were still underway.

On a fence post next to the manager's Portakabin sat an owl who went by the name of Iccuat. Being out of the forest, he hadn't yet heard about the developments of the past few hours. He sat there, staring at the workers as they went about their business. At that time of the morning, business consisted mainly of coffee and hot rolls.

One of the younger workers was called Kerr. He would handle one of the many chainsaws and was getting ready to start his work for the day. But he was distracted by an owl. It had such beautiful deep eyes. And it didn't appear afraid as he approached it, phone in hand. He was close to it now, livestreaming the video on his *Instagram* story. He was transfixed by the owl's eyes. So much so that he had stopped his live commentary, which was a poor impression of David Attenborough.

Technology is so clever these days, and the quality so good. The definition in the owl's eyes also held the attention of sixty-three people who were watching Kerr's live feed. They, too, were transfixed watching the owl. For the next ten minutes or so, Kerr and the other sixty-three people all exhibited bizarre behaviour.

The antics of those watching the livestream varied. Some were seen, some went unseen. Chicken impressions were popular. For those on their own, this passed away harmlessly. But there were those in public places, shops or at their workplaces. Their antics were a little more embarrassing. One poor lad marched into his work team meeting in full-on chicken mode. He did his best impersonation of a bird laying an egg.

Singing was also popular. If there was music on nearby, it would be mimicked. It was helpful if the singer knew the words, but not necessary. They went full on pop singer, giving their best rendition of the tune they could hear. There was often an accompanying dance routine.

Kev was a friend of Kerr's. Most of those watching his live link were. Kev was training to be a vet and was sitting in the middle of a lecture auditorium at university. He was waiting for the lecture to start. Unfortunately, as it did, he started to perform his favourite party tricks. Not that he did them these days. They were party tricks he had performed as a child to his aunts and uncles at family gatherings, and had earned him a reputation as a bit of a joker.

Now he was older, it wasn't cool to make animal noises. Which was a shame, as he was good at them. The lecturer walked in just as he started to make donkey noises. This didn't go down well.

Then, he moved on to an impressive horse, with actions to impersonate trotting. The dinosaur was his personal favourite from childhood, and he had lost none of his ability. Of course, his university friends didn't try to stop him. They laughed – and videoed him, of course. He came back to his senses after an unfortunate squirrel impersonation. No-one could figure out what it was meant to be.

These antics had delayed the start of the work, but not for long. It would have been impractical for the animals to try and keep this up for hours, or perhaps days on end. But now word had reached the trees that the work would not go ahead. The animals knew quickly thereafter.

The site supervisor was sitting in front of his laptop in his Portakabin office, as an email pinged into his inbox. It delivered the simplest of messages: *All work to be suspended pending a police enquiry. Workers should contact their individual companies for more information.*

There was celebration in the forest. At the last possible moment, work had been stopped. Anyone walking in the trees that day could almost sense the mood. Walking in nature leaves many people with a feeling of joy and relaxation. Today, they would leave feeling elated. The joy and relief were contagious. This was an area full of happy trees and creatures. The forest had been saved.

# Chapter 45

# Cackle

It had been three months since the arrest, and later disappearance, of Kimberly Parker. There had been seven more arrests in the UK since her world came crashing in. More would follow. A date for her trial had been set, with charges of bribery and corruption. But still no-one had seen Kimberly since that day at the forest. Her house had been taken off the market and Rachel was living with her gran. As luck would have it, her gran's house was only a few minutes' walk from Bonnie's house. Not that the pair ever met. Rachel would do anything she could to avoid coming face to face with Bonnie.

Bonnie wasn't sure how to deal with the Rachel situation. The natural response was to despise her because she was a bully and had often made Bonnie's life a misery. But it wasn't in Bonnie's nature to hold a grudge. And, to be fair, it was Rachel that had saved the forest from her witching mother. Bonnie had many conversations in her head. They were all rehearsals of what to say the first time they met face to face. It would all depend on Rachel's attitude, of course. But Bonnie wasn't afraid of her any more. She would not allow herself to become intimidated by Rachel, or anyone else.

Kimberly and Rachel Parker may well have had lots of money. But Bonnie was glad of her own life, and her now much improved relationship with her mum. And she was happy with life. Bonnie now had the strangest circle of friends. Her best friend was still Molly from school, along with Lucy and Jo. There were a few other classmates she classed as friends. They were all people who were kind and supportive towards her – and one another. Misty would say to her, 'Friends are like shoes, Bonnie. You don't need hundreds of them, only a few good ones.'

But Bonnie was also blessed with friends in the forest, as well as her 'people' friends. Iccuat, Troben, Rodger … they would all chat away with her when she took her walks in the forest with David. One of her best forest friends turned out to be a little wood mouse with a deep voice, called 'Burp'. It was odd having a mouse friend, but he was such an intelligent creature. He was always having a rant about being called 'vermin'. He was funny, with his deep voice, when he went on about it. And there was still a murmur of laughter every time anyone said his name.

The other big thing that was happening in Bonnie's life was to do with her dad. Soon, he would be a real part of it again. They had kept in touch since the events of the forest unfolded. Messages were exchanged frequently, with a video call once a week. And Jack Banks had secured a job in Scotland. Over the course of the next few weeks, he would be leaving his home in Boston and settling down in a new home and job in Glasgow. Bonnie had hoped that her mum and dad would become an item again, but she guessed that would be a step too far – at least for now.

Bonnie had talked with her mum, and it was clear the events of all those years ago still hurt Misty. Her feelings ran too deep to allow forgiveness beyond friendship. That, and the fact that her mum had been out a few times with William the journalist. They were getting along well. Bonnie had gone through her life without a father figure, and now she had two. *Settle yourself, Bonnie Banks*, she thought. *It's early days.*

Bonnie's English teacher, Mrs Bell, was helping Bonnie with her book of short stories made up of tales of talking animals. All sorts of creatures, having all sorts of adventures, were involved. Mrs Bell had been impressed with her work and was giving her tips on writing. Bonnie had found this easy to do. She would chat to the animals in the forest and listen to their stories. Then she would write them down, embellish them a bit and the stories were done. They all featured one lead character: a little mouse called 'Burp'. All her recent publicity meant there was an interest in her forthcoming book. There was even a publisher lined up for *Mouse Tales from the Devilla Forest.*

The head teacher had asked Bonnie to do another talk to the school, which was something she had become good at. Bonnie found this gave her confidence a lift. The school was proud of its young eco-warrior and author, Bonnie Banks.

Copsehead is a small community. It was inevitable that, at some point, Bonnie would come face to face with Rachel. This happened on a Friday afternoon, on the way home from school. Both girls were on their own. There was only one footpath, so neither of them could cross the road to avoid the other. Bonnie kept her gaze looking forward. In a show of confidence, she wouldn't lower her head or look away. Not that she was looking for confrontation. It was more a case of never, ever allowing herself to be afraid of anyone again. And she had responses prepared in her head for anything Rachel might say to her. Anything at all. Apart from the one thing she *did* say of course.

'Sorry I was horrible to you, Bonnie.'

This caught Bonnie off-guard. 'Sorry' was not what she had expected. After a moment or two of silence, Bonnie said, 'OK.' There was more silence, then eye contact.

'No, I really *am* sorry Bonnie. I was trying to bully you, and, and … and I don't know why. It's what I do. Or what I *used* to do.'

'You made my life miserable, Rachel. But if you want to forget about it, then that's fine by me. I don't see us as friends any time soon, but if we could walk by one another and say 'hello', that would be a start.'

Both of them avoided talking about that day in the forest.

'I'm fine with that.' Rachel managed the tiniest hint of a smile.

*Or was it a bit more sinister than that?* thought Bonnie.

There were a few moments of silence before Bonnie spoke again. 'Well, I'm heading home now. Guess I'll see you about.'

'Yeah. See you later, Bonnie.'

And that was it. All that planning in her head, and it turned out to be the easiest conversation ever. Rachel was happy to speak to Bonnie and allow the arguments of the past to be buried. Bonnie dismissed the nagging feeling from her thoughts: was there some kind of sinister tone in these words 'See you later'?

All the machinery had been removed from the forest. The Portakabins that had been built as offices were now long gone. Devilla Forest was still managed by the Devilla Woodland Council. But there were now new people in charge, after the investigation. Being a woodland, there was always work underway. And there were managed clearances of the trees. But clearing trees for the survival and well-being of the forest was a good thing. It was essential. Bonnie had been invited along to give talks at forest education evenings. She had even done a couple of readings from her soon-to-be-published book, to anyone wishing to come along and listen.

Bonnie was approaching her thirteenth birthday. It wasn't her style to have a party, but she would have her friends round to mark the occasion. Her dad would also be coming over and that was something worth looking forward to.

Meanwhile, it was the usual routine: school, study, chill and go for walks in the forest. Having been going to the forest for many years now, Bonnie knew her way around. She had only been lost once, and that had changed her life forever.

On this particular day, Bonnie was out for a long walk with David. They headed out towards Grindmill Dam, the largest area of water in the forest. It was a long way. Bonnie had ventured off the main paths again and found herself in one of the denser parts of the forest. It was a lovely day, and the sun filtered through the trees. Bonnie was feeling warm and sat down for a drink, David by her side. He had already topped up with water anywhere he could find it. 'No wonder you need to drink so much, David. You pee on every single tree.' David ignored this but kept on jabbering away to Bonnie as normal.

'Bonnie. Why don't we go to the old cottage? We've not been there for ages.'

'I don't know, David. It gives me the creeps, that place.'

'Come on, Bonnie. It's a brilliant day, and I feel like going exploring.' David was now on all fours, tail wagging at level eight. He was keen, no two ways about it.

'Come on then, David, let's get going. Do you know the way?

David looked at Bonnie. '*Of course* I know the way.'

And off they went, in the direction of the old cottage. Bonnie loved this part of the forest. Grindmill Dam was home to Oilthigh Island. This was a well-known landmark, but Bonnie didn't know how it had got its name. She promised herself she would find that out.

On her way to the cottage, Bonnie passed the nearby 'witch's grave.'

Small and time-worn tombstones marked the spot where three children were said to have been buried, hundreds of years ago. They were the children of a woman who had been convicted of being a witch. Her punishment had been 'death by strangulation at the stake' – as was the way all these years ago. It wasn't recorded how the children had died. Bonnie had visited it once before and had tried to make out the names of the children on the stones. They were so worn it was almost impossible. Only one name had a few letters remaining; the most Bonnie could make out was 'G_ace _a_ _er'.

This spot had always given her the chills, and she vowed never to go back. She didn't like the feel of the place.

Bonnie had also learned a bit more about the history of the forest over the past few months. She knew – as did most people in the area, of course – about the Devilla Witches, and the tales of long ago. There was a time when Bonnie wouldn't have believed in any of that. But now she was wiser. And she became aware of a cold chill on a warm day, from time to time.

After a good walk, Bonnie and David were interrupted by Iccuat. They hadn't spotted him, but he had been following them for about twenty minutes. Deciding now was a good time for a chat, he flew over and perched on a tree branch close by Bonnie and David's side. He was his usual sarcastic self. 'Still scratching fleas from behind your ear, David?'

'Oh, lay off it, snake eyes,' said David.

Iccuat laughed. 'Where you off to today, Bonnie?'

'The cottage. We've not been there for a while. What about you, Iccuat, what are you up to?'

'Sitting on a tree, talking to a girl and her stupid dog.'

'Glad the sarcasm is as strong as ever, Iccuat. Now without being rude – we are asking a polite question. *Apart* from talking to us, what are you doing? Be nice.'

'We owls don't do a great deal other than be sarcastic, you know. Fly. Eat. Sleep. Repeat. There would be little fun without sarcasm. Why are you heading to the cottage?'

'We've not been there for a while. David wants to go for a change.'

'I don't like it there, Bonnie. The cottage never has a good feel to it. We see movement in there at night. Be careful.' And, with that, Iccuat flew off. Bonnie and David didn't see where he went to, but he could see them. Iccuat kept an eye on them both, just in case.

The sun was at its full height when Bonnie and David arrived at the cottage. Bonnie had been to it a couple of times before, but had never ventured inside. There were too many stories about it. It had been abandoned many years ago by the person living there, but no-one knew why. There were a few trees in the garden. Probably planted when they were small, the owner not realising how big they would grow. David made his way over to do his usual thing. 'You'll need more water soon, David,' said Bonnie.

Bonnie stood at the entrance to the garden. It was so overgrown, it looked like the entrance to some kind of wild Amazonian rainforest. She was trying to visualise the lives of the family – or families – who had lived there in the past. She imagined a lovely well-tended garden, full of flowers. She heard the sound of children laughing as they played in the garden and enjoyed the sun. She looked at the cottage, now. It was a stereotypical cottage, with a door in the middle and a window on either side. The roof was grey slate, and there was one chimney on either side of the cottage. It had been built back in the days when the only form of heat was a coal fire. It was such a picturesque cottage, despite now being run-down. The windows were boarded up, plants were growing wild and there were signs of vandalism.

The front door looked closed from a distance. But, as Bonnie walked towards it, she could see that it was slightly open. Of course, she didn't know about the encounter Kimberly Parker had had with the mice. Bonnie walked to the door and gave it a little push, expecting it to make a spooky creak. She felt a little disappointed when it made no noise at all. She walked in and gave a tiny jump as David shot past her.

'David! You nearly gave me a heart attack.'

'What we doing in here, Bonnie? I didn't mean for us to go into the cottage.'

'We're exploring, David.'

'I don't like it in here,' he said, tail wagging at level one.

'Don't be a daft dog. It's nothing more than an abandoned cottage.'

'To you, maybe. But I can sense and smell more than you. I don't like it, Bonnie. Let's go.'

David shot back outside, and stood at the door waiting on Bonnie. It was at that point she realised her body had become cold. *Very* cold. Despite the heat of the summer sun, the temperature in the cottage was freezing. She could see her breath. Bonnie had a sudden urge to get out and to seek warmth, to get away from the cottage.

But something drew her into the old kitchen. She didn't like it in there. It was still freezing cold and had a smell of dampness. And it also had a smell of something else. Was it cooking? David was suddenly at her side again. 'Bonnie. Come on, let's go. I don't like it in here. It smells of rotten rabbits cooking. Let's get out.'

Bonnie turned to leave but noticed a bible lying open on the table. It was as though someone had recently been looking inside it. She noted the handwriting inside the front cover: *To Florence, from Davina.*

Now Bonnie felt even more uncomfortable. David had gone again. Her fingers were frozen, and a shiver ran up her spine. That uneasy feeling of being watched had returned. She turned and walked out of the cottage. Everything in her head said, 'run Bonnie, run,' but her pace remained calm. Bonnie walked out into the sunshine and at once felt better. David was sitting on a small part of the garden path that hadn't yet been claimed by weeds or any other part of nature. 'Let's not go in there again, Bonnie.'

'Scaredy cat,' said Bonnie.

'Call me whatever you want Bonnie, but *not* a cat.'

'Fair enough.'

Bonnie turned away from the cottage. The pair, girl and her dog, walked through the space where there used to be a garden gate. Bonnie was warmer again. There was a difference in temperature between the cottage and outside in the sun. She was glad to be in a bright, warm space, away from the cottage. Her thoughts wandered to Florence and Davina. Who were they? Was a bible an unusual gift to receive? She then gave a little smile as she wondered what Florence had been doing? What had she done such that Davina thought the gift of a bible would be beneficial?

David had shot off at a hundred miles per hour. She heard him shouting 'fresh trees, fresh trees!'

He had discovered an unfamiliar batch of trees that he had never peed on before. *As long as he's happy*, thought Bonnie.

Bonnie was feeling good about herself. Good relationships, and family life improving. She started to think about the future and what her job would be once school was finished. It was still a few years away yet, but she had learned so much in the past few months. Writing stories, the environment, funny videos. All useful stuff. And all things she enjoyed. She walked on, back towards the main path, shouting for David with a smile on her face. But then she stopped and looked over her shoulder, feeling cold again. A shiver. A black cat sat on the windowsill of the abandoned cottage. And what was that sound? It sounded like laughing coming from the cottage. Her mind must be playing tricks on her. No, it was definitely laughter. But not normal laughter. It was more of a cackle.

## Acknowledgements

In late 2020, I embarked on this unexpected author journey as I embraced early retirement. A Facebook advert by the always inspiring Michael Heppell beckoned me to "Write that Book." From this amazing course emerged "Eyes of Devilla," a testament to the power of motivation and encouragement he exudes like no other. Michael, your guidance for this book, and for life's journey, has been invaluable. Thank you. The writing journey is not one to travel alone. The contributions of numerous individuals helped enormously. Stevie and David, your relentless curiosity and insightful suggestions fuelled my progress. Andrew, among the dedicated beta readers, your meticulous feedback shaped the manuscript in invaluable ways. I also extend heartfelt gratitude to Heather, my former boss turned enthusiastic beta reader, who helped way more than she realises. Jenny Williams, with her unparalleled editorial skills, elevated the readability of the entire book, a testament to her amazing talent. To my two cherished sons, your innocence and wonder ignited the spark of inspiration. And I'm sorry about the tearful day when my imagination got carried away and you thought "The Tree People" were about to catch you. As I reflect on the countless hands that have shaped this book, I am humbled by the collective effort and boundless generosity that brought this vision to fruition. To each and every individual who played a role, whether acknowledged here or silently guiding from the sidelines, I offer my deepest gratitude. And finally, to Elizabeth. Your unwavering support and attentive ear have been my biggest source of strength throughout this journey.

Printed in Great Britain
by Amazon